Zahran Alqasmi is an Om
Sultanate of Oman in 1974
published novels, and in 2(
for Arabic Fiction (IPAF) for *The Water Dwiner*.
lished ten poetry collections and a collection of short stories.

Marilyn Booth is professor emerita, Faculty of Asian and Middle Eastern Studies and Magdalen College, Oxford University. She has translated many works of Arabic fiction into English, and her translation of Omani author Jokha Alharthi's *Celestial Bodies* was awarded the International Booker Prize. Her research publications focus on Arabophone women's writing and the ideology of gender debates in the nineteenth century, most recently *The Career and Communities of Zaynab Fawwaz: Feminist Thinking in Fin-de-siècle Egypt*.

Honey Hunger

Zahran Alqasmi

Translated by
Marilyn Booth

The author and translator are very grateful for the support of the Oman Cultural Club, without which this translation could not have happened.

First published in 2025 by
Hoopoe
113 Sharia Kasr el Aini, Cairo, Egypt
420 Lexington Avenue, Suite 1644, New York, NY 10170
www.hoopoefiction.com

Hoopoe is an imprint of The American University in Cairo Press
www.aucpress.com

Copyright © 2017 by Zahran Alqasmi
Published in Arabic in 2017 as *Jaw' al-'asal* by Mas'a li-l-Nashr wa al-Tawzi'
Protected under the Berne Convention

English translation copyright © 2024 by Marilyn Booth

All rights reserved. No part of this publication may be reproduced, stored in a retrieval system, or transmitted in any form or by any means, electronic, mechanical, photocopying, recording, or otherwise, without the prior written permission of the publisher.

ISBN 978 1 649 03390 1

Library of Congress Cataloging-in-Publication Data

Names: Qāsimī, Zahrān, author. | Booth, Marilyn, translator.
Title: Honey hunger / by Zahran Alqasmi ; translated by Marilyn Booth.
Other titles: Jū' al-'asal. English
Description: [New York] : Hoopoe Fiction, an Imprint of AUC Press, 2025.
Identifiers: LCCN 2024019814 | ISBN 9781649033918 (hardback) | ISBN 9781649033901 (trade paperback) | ISBN 9781649033925 (epub) | ISBN 9781649033932 (adobe pdf)
Subjects: LCGFT: Novels.
Classification: LCC PJ7958.A86 J813 2025 | DDC 892.7/37--dc23/eng/20240716
LC record available at https://lccn.loc.gov/2024019814

1 2 3 4 5   29 28 27 26 25

Designed by Adam el-Sehemy

Dedicated to Husain Al-Mahroos

Chapter One

Herdswoman, sing …
your herd finds pasture in the heart
in the pupil of the heart's eye you dwell

HERE, IN THIS SOLITARY HOLLOW, he performed what looked like a prayer ritual in perfect tranquility. The silence was uninterrupted save for the trilling of nightingales nearby. In a region so unfamiliar to him, he had come upon and chosen this roomy patch of land sitting amongst groves of gum acacia. When he arrived, the leaves on those samur trees were already falling, stripping bare the branches to herald the coming season of new buds. For the ample streams of water were flowing across the land from the pebbly soil surface of the towering White Mountain range all the way to the foot of the black granite Hajar mountain range.

From a nearby plateau, at a higher elevation, a pair of eyes shifted towards him and lingered, and then looked towards the herd of goats grazing on the nearby mountain face. Everywhere one looked, the land had sprouted green. Not far away from the watching figure crouched a Saluki, eyes half-hooded in drowsy boredom.

He showed no interest in the grazing forms around him, letting the animals wander as they pleased. Or perhaps he was simply waiting for the slightest of hand gestures from his herdswoman, as her voice rose in a sad, lilting taawibeh on that early morning.

On parallel metal tracks sat rows of wooden boxes, carefully arranged. Moving amongst them and bending over them, he seemed oblivious to his surroundings. And then the silence was broken momentarily by the growl of a vehicle on the dirt track as it headed northwards, leaving a thick train of dust that erupted from beneath the wheels only to drift downward once again, slowly, reluctantly, as though it would have preferred to continue floating on the streams of air.

He paid no attention. Anyone coming through here would continue on their way, disappearing in mere seconds as they followed the route into the mountains. What occupied his thoughts instead was the time of year: the bees ought to be increasing in number now, some of the worker bees flying off to graze on the nectar in the flower buds that had begun to open already on the branches of the scrubby trees and bushes native to these parts. Every week now, he must examine these hives closely, one by one. Or possibly twice a week, in search of the queen bee cell that the worker bees would have begun to construct.

A melodious taawibeh hovered above his ears as he drew out a frame, having just noticed a queen bee cell here in this hive that was now packed with bees from one end to the other. He set the frame down carefully, sliding it into a small, empty wooden box just to the side of the hives. He began looking for the queen bee herself, the mother bee, examining each frame carefully.

He was humming to himself, something cheerful. Or perhaps he was trying to echo the rhythm of the faint mountain song that the breezes carried to him; he could hear the tune more clearly now. He was too far away to make out the words. Yet, even the hint of mellow warmth in that feminine voice stirred him, leaving a slight sense of euphoria—especially since he had just located the queen bee, huddling in a corner of one frame and encircled by a throng of her subjects.

He worked on, turning to a final hive that had remained unusually tranquil. As he carefully raised the lid, a great mass of bees poured out to circle around him, buzzing loudly as they all tried to invade the mesh veil protecting his head. Acting particularly irritated, one insistent bee came closer; when she could not pierce his mask, she began releasing venom into the air, hovering close enough to him that the smell of the pheromone would reach his nostrils.

He had learned long ago to remain calm and to avoid sudden movements. He knew what the bees wanted him to do; and he knew that any jumpiness on his part would allow them to get in where they wanted to be. Sensing the slightest stink of fear seeping into the air around them, they would hunt for the tiniest fissure—any crack where they could sneak in and aim their stinger. But this man simply continued inspecting the frames, one after another, despite the fierce, unremitting attack that now began to target his gloved fingers, too.

He was reaching deep into the hive, all the way to the center of it, when he felt the sting beneath the fabric that closely encircled his wrist. Swiftly he returned all of the frames to their places and did his best to close up the hive, postponing any further examination until another day when there might be less commotion greeting him. But now, even as he closed it, here was a bee funneling its way inside his loose white izar. He could feel it bobbing about under the garment, between his calves. It didn't give him time to jiggle it loose from beneath his robe; there was the sharp jab and then the numbness which he felt just below his left knee.

He put his hand to the spot but another bee had gotten inside now too, animated by the odor of the poison and able to figure out the secret pathway inside, the route to his body. This one stung him on the foot. Now they knew: now the way was free and clear to mount an attack. This man must be expelled from their territory.

He tried to shake out his izar and he pressed his legs together to prevent the bees from getting in there between them again. But there was really not much point to it now. He clamped the lid onto the hive quickly and hurried away from the colony, trying as best he could to avoid any further stings.

The herdswoman stood at a slight distance, facing him. He supposed that she must have something to say to him. He raised his hand in greeting and she raised hers and smiled. He was in pain from the assault just now mounted on him. The bee venom was already numbing his leg muscles and the burning sensation was spreading, as if tiny arrows were embedding themselves everywhere along his legs and feet. He had come out of this battle as the loser, confronting these creatures whom he loved—even if they did flare up like this now and again, and despite the pain running through his veins. Even with these aches, he felt such sadness whenever one of these little beings of whom he was so fond perished. He knew very well that a single stab of the bee's stinger into his body meant her death. For as the stinger left the bee's quiver, it took with it a chunk of her body. The bee could not survive the wound.

How many stings had he gotten this time? He didn't know; perhaps seven or eight in different places across his body. But that wasn't uppermost in his mind as he stood silently facing this woman. She hadn't moved, hadn't attempted to come any nearer. He tried to steady himself, to regain his composure. He turned more fully towards her, stepping a bit closer to learn what she wanted. But he warned her with a gesture not to come any closer herself, fearing that she might be taking a chance if she did so and that the outcome might not be a pleasant one.

Her face was burnished by the many suns that had beat against it. This face sketched the image of a woman he had heard spoken of in villagers' stories as they sat together conversing in the evenings. Those stories described a woman's face that was as shiny, limpid, and smooth as a well-worn stone. A few soft strands of hair danced across her brow. Beneath, he saw a small, thin nose set in a narrow face. Her eyes seemed to blaze and the light of them set his insides on fire. Although several meters separated them, he could read her features perfectly. Now he spoke, greeting her and apologizing for any harms or pains that his beehives' presence in this place might cause her.

She shook her head. The land belongs to God, she said.

Scattered across the front of her bright-colored tob was a field of flowers, as though she were submerged to her neck in a riotous, blossoming meadow. Her head was wrapped in a vivid yellow cloth. The mistress of colors and the fields, he thought to himself.

Had he ever seen her before this day? He didn't know. But the image of her, or her shadow . . . yes, he thought, he had caught sight of it on a lane, or down a path, here or there. His eyes, well-practiced at absorbing the infinitesimal details of places, held a memory of seeing something of this figure one day in Wadi Alka. Or perhaps he had glimpsed it moving beneath the shade of the ghaf and sidra trees in Wadi al-Raak. It might have been her, or perhaps it wasn't; but now, he suddenly felt spring coming, peeling the blanket off a meadowland of mountain shrubs. The coming season would be a generous one. He would harvest a lot of honey.

Have you got any honey?

Too early—it's not the season yet.

I want some of it. Of yours. Don't forget me. They say your honey is good. Zeen! they say—very good.

Where will I find you, then?

Everywhere. When the time comes.

She smiled. Like an ancient goddess who inhabited these heights, coming from a time human beings no longer remember. Like a goddess who had come down to meet him on this morning. She waved goodbye and left him there, standing as perfectly still as an ancient tree deep rooted in the land. He didn't even know, now, whether he had fled in this direction in his attempt to escape the bee-stings, and had come upon her; or whether it was she who had come to him. Suddenly, there she had been—an apparition from the unknown, coming to give him something to live for. As he had caught sight of her so suddenly, now she disappeared just as abruptly, just as completely, leaving an absence he could feel inside himself. What had she done to him? What had this apparition planted in his heart, and now what had she taken away with her as she climbed toward the summit and vanished into the great rock crevices?

He walked over to his pick-up and took out some heavier protective clothing. It was still early, too early to leave the hives for the night. But because of what had happened earlier and because of how well he knew these bees, he had to proceed very cautiously. He armored himself with this extra layer of body covering and went back to peering again into the two parallel rows of hives, completing his examination, his search in each hive for the queen bee's chamber.

This year, winter had settled harshly onto these hives. The unusually severe cold lost him many of his bees. Whole populations died; some of the hives plummeted in number until they all but vanished. Had it not been for God's grace, his losses would have crushed him—he who tried as hard as he could to make a success with what he had in his hands, no more, and with whatever lessons experience had taught him.

After having dropped out of contact for months—work pressures, he explained—Azzan's friend Mahmud bin Abdallah had phoned him. Mahmud was a beekeeper who lived over in Mudaybi Town. Azzan chided him for disappearing like this, and asked after his health. The next subject of conversation, naturally, was their bees, and how the two of them had fared with their colonies through this most stressful winter. Azzan found himself unable to say anything, really, beyond confessing how powerless he had felt, and how he hadn't known what to do to preserve a colony of bees on the edge of annihilation.

I've got a place in mind for you to go to—good grazing for those bees there, said Mahmud.

Azzan had never moved his bees any distance from where he lived—no further than thirty kilometers or so, that is. But Mahmud was insistent. And so had begun a new story. On his friend's advice, Azzan made the decision to move his bees from the White Mountain region to Juba, easily 250 kilometers south, further into the interior of the country.

Mahmud assured him that the pasturage there was lush and vast. Many beekeepers had taken their hives to the plains of Juba, he said. Once there, his own colony—its vitality lost over the winter—had filled their frames with new eggs. In fact, after a mere two weeks all of those empty frames he had removed were now back in place. He had reinserted them in the hive boxes because the bees were thriving, their numbers were abundant now, and the beeswax they produced was dripping from the top slats of the frames. In fact, he had had to replace them with new frames.

Two days after their conversation, Azzan bin Said loaded everything he would need into his pick-up, ready to set out on this desert caravan. In their boxes, the beehives would fill the small truck. Mahmud loaded the metal bases on which the boxes would sit into his vehicle. At sundown, and once the last bees had returned from their rounds in search of pasturage, they shut the hives and set off.

It was a very long trip—for him and for the bees. At one point he wondered how he would even manage to get through the rest of this all-night drive to reach the place Mahmud had proposed. And could it really be worth it? Yet, all the while he felt gladdened and comforted by his friend's words. He was so grateful for this magnanimity; he knew that nothing was expected in return. It didn't come as a surprise. Anyone who lived on the generosity of bees, Azzan knew, would learn charity from them. Any beekeeper would come to know how to give without anticipating any return favors.

It took hours to get there, going at the moderate speed of eighty kilometers an hour. But finally they were there: a wide, flat expanse stretching as far as one could see, bordered by soft rippling sand to the north and reaching all the way to the edges of the enormous Lake Mahout to the east, a vast space unbroken by even a single mountain. Mahmud had already positioned a water basin there for the bees, a pipe draining into it from a small tank. He had chosen the location with care—a lowland sunk between two ridges that acted as windbreaks. It would not be much exposed to the daytime winds; for the gusts coming across this plain were capable of driving bees off course and scattering them widely enough that they would not know their way home.

Still, worry gnawed at Azzan. How could he leave his beehives here on their own, in these wide-open lands? But Mahmud convinced him that it would be less painful to lose his bees here because of something happening that he wouldn't be able to predict or see, than it would be to lose them there, at home, dying in front of him when he could do nothing to keep them safe and well. Nothing but mourn them. Their destruction would be an ever-present grievous reminder of how disastrous everything had been for him. Out here, as long as nothing happened to interfere, the hives would grow strong and active and he would be spared the ruin which had seemed, he thought, decreed for him.

It was nearly three am by the time they finished arranging the boxes along the metal tracks and opening the hives to the outside. Once they were satisfied that all the hives were open, they unrolled their sleeping mats in a space to one side. Exhausted, they fell asleep immediately and neither of them woke up until nine-thirty. The sun had been up for a while but even so, there was no sting to it yet. Going over to his hives Azzan bin Said could see that the bees were spreading out, moving in all directions. Some bees were already returning to the hives with beads of pollen clinging to their tiny legs. He could feel himself relaxing. He felt happy, and he thanked his friend again.

Just before noon the wind began to come up. They could see blowing sand, little whirlwinds here and there, but none of it reached them in this sunken spot sheltered by its low elevation. Azzan noticed how steady the bees sailing in and out of the hives seemed to be, how little agitation or discomfort they were showing. Yet the open breadth of this land steeped a sense of fear in him. He didn't like being so aware that he was easily visible here—and from every direction, and as far as the distant horizon even if that was marked by a thick banner of dust. The scene in front of him tugged at his heart. How could he leave his beehives here alone with no one watching over them? What if they were stolen or destroyed by some force, some power, that he could not predict or stop? He had a sense of heavy foreboding yet at the same time, he did have confidence in this friend who knew the terrain, knew the people here, and had had enough experience to sense where the surroundings were best for bees. And so he remained silent, mentioning nothing about the anxieties that filled his heart.

Mahmud took him on a tour, wanting him to see for himself the lay of the land surrounding his newly re-established bee colony. They went a great distance among the groves of stubby alqaa bushes with their tiny, pearl-like white flowers. He saw bees clustering there, taking sustenance from the flowers. In the distance, on the edges of this expanse, white rue petals were opening too, such an expanse of them that an onlooker couldn't help thinking they must be standing at the center of a vast field, one of many, all sown with care and deliberation. The severity of the desert seemed to lift, its harshness no longer so intimidating. Awed by the sight, Azzan felt the tightness in his chest loosen up. But for the rest of the afternoon the friends remained close to the hives, having decided to spend another night here. Early the next morning they would leave for home.

Coming from the direction of the sands to the north of them, the winds had grown in strength. Now, as far as they could see, the air was filled with sand borne along on the fiercely whirling gusts of wind. But as the sun sank gradually toward the horizon, the winds calmed little by little too, leaving this spot they had chosen wonderfully still and silent. The temperature had dropped slightly. And then a gentle evening breeze came up, partnering with the night to announce its usual hospitality to any travelers who might yet be making their way across this vastness—exactly as caravans of Bedouin and merchants had once crisscrossed it, north to south, and back again. The day's reward was a restful sleep. Azzan woke up only once, to change position.

The next morning they drove away.

Soon Azzan was pondering how the village space that was his childhood home had come to seem so vacant to him. He couldn't escape this thought; it revealed to him how attached he had become to these tiny beings who captured almost all of his time and attention. All he needed in life, all he wanted from life, was to sit amongst them every morning, or in the evening, listening to the sounds they made—that range of humming and buzzing their bodies produced. How would he spend his time now, here in the village, when no bee circled close above his head warningly, or delighted his ears with its steady hum? Without them, where would he go now on a winter day? The mountains nearby would not welcome him: they were submerged in frosty isolation. Nor would human beings, engrossed as they were in their own lives. He couldn't help but see it: his life was entirely empty without this little world he had made and in which he dwelt.

Each morning he had awoken with the energy and focus of one who is eager to head for a familiar and absorbing workplace. But then he would freeze as he suddenly remembered that there was nothing there waiting for him, nothing but a terminal loneliness and the implacable cold that he had got used to resisting as he went outside on these winter mornings. He had been fueling himself on hope: the sight of his bees gathering pollen seemed to inoculate him against his worries. But then there had come the extreme cold of this particular winter, so harsh on his little bees who could not withstand the unremitting iciness. It had pained his heart to watch them: before sunrise, bees returning from pasture, their tiny legs gripping the nourishment they had found only to drop in exhaustion, dying on the roof of the beehive to which they had been returning. Examining the hives had left him in a state of utter dejection as he saw before him the destruction of whole phalanxes of bees. Cleaning the empty frames of dust and debris, as he removed them to store inside the house until a time came when he might need them again, he was numbed by this enormous and painful loss. He had feared that before the winter ended, all of his bees would be dead.

Depressed as he was, he would return to the hives in the evening just to be close to the bees who remained. The next moment he would be making a vow to himself to leave them alone, to stay away for an entire week. But no sooner would he have prayed the late-afternoon prayer than he would jump into his pick-up. He was addicted. He no longer even spent any time caring for his date palms. He left them entirely to the Bengali worker who helped him tend the palm grove. But now, the bees' absence left him aimless.

Five days after their return, he decided to go back to Juba. He phoned Mahmud to tell him. Here in the village he felt suspended, lifeless, held motionless beneath a huge column of emptiness, and he could hardly bear it. He was getting pains in his shoulders which he interpreted as the result of having too little work to do. He was afraid that if he stayed here and got accustomed to doing nothing, he would fall apart and lose his ability to do anything at all. Whatever fire still smoldered inside of him would die. Suddenly, the idea of going to Juba popped into his head. Immediately, he rummaged for a pen and began to make a list of everything he would need in order to stay there for a longer stretch of time.

A cooking ring and a gas canister, a few clothes that would fit into a small suitcase, a mattress and a pillow, a mat to sit on and a stool, a tent to give him shade, his radio, some cooking pots and implements, a medium-sized water tank, spices, flour, rice, some vegetables and fruits, eggs, cheese, a few canned goods, and a lamp. And a few additional odds and ends, whatever occurred to him right then.

He arrived very late in the afternoon, just before sunset. There was still some time before darkness fell to settle on a camping location that would be free of hazards. It had to be protected from the winds sufficiently that he could put up his tent without disruption, and could cook his meals without any trouble. He found a spot to his liking and arranged all of his belongings. After an hour or so of work, the place was organized. It even had a settled look, now that it was furnished with all of the things he had thought to bring.

All there was here to fill this vast flat empty space was the humming of his bees and the swoosh of the soft breezes skimming along the rises of sand. The sun was depositing the last of its golden rays in slanting lines across the endless swells of sand. Against the horizon stretched ropy, elastic clouds which converged into larger masses or faded away only to reappear. And now he was part of this picture, here with his two rows of boxes, painted white and starkly visible, performing the rituals he loved. His face settled into a more hopeful expression with every hive he examined. He found a good store of pollen already stowed inside the bees' hexagonal wax cells.

In particular, he found five hives that seemed to be waiting for him to show up. They were ready for him to notice the heavy accumulation of beeswax and to replace the frames. He had to pull out some empty frames from other hives to be able to put a new one in each of the hives that needed it. His sense of well-being was returning. Just before sundown, he stopped working and sat down in front of his tent to type into his phone the tasks he still had before him, and all of the things he must ready, as early as possible in the morning. A hundred more frames, he estimated, and five packs of wax foundation comb; ten fifty-kilogram sacks of sugar and a large basin to hold the sugar solution; pieces of cork for the bees to perch on so that they wouldn't drown while drinking; medicinal strips to protect his bees against Varroa mites and other parasites that would prevent them growing and multiplying rapidly.

That night he slept outside his tent. Lying on his back, he gazed at a sky luminous with millions of stars. His eyes roamed to the far edges of Aries, the great ram, and across the Milky Way, Darb al-Tabbana as they called it in the village. He slept deeply, not waking up even once during the night. He opened his eyes just before dawn. The silence surrounding him seemed itself to flower and grow green leaves, yielding only a few flies whose zzzz cut through the predawn calm.

By eleven o'clock, he was setting up the basin that would supply the bees with added energy. He opened a sack of sugar and measured a few cups into the bucket he used only for this purpose, one cup of sugar for every two cups of water, until the bucket was full. With his hand, he swirled the solution around until the sugar had dissolved completely. It was ready for the bees. He poured the solution into the basin and set enough pieces of cork floating on top that he could see bobbing cork covering the entire surface. He settled nearby to watch.

A few bees began circling over the basin. One landed, tasted, and sailed back to the hive. Others alighted on pieces of cork, jerkily, apprehensive at first, and then seemed sure enough to drink. More bees began to reconnoiter, flying back and forth over the basin, landing here and there until the basin was covered in them. Now whole squadrons of bees were coming out of their boxes to nourish themselves. They were stirring up what looked like a miniature storm, and their humming filled the place. Reassured, he moved away from the bee settlement to prepare his own meal. He had set up a tiny kitchen in a corner of the tent. After eating, with the afternoon wearing on, he let himself doze off. After a short nap he went out for a walk, following the contours of the sands. He wanted to discover this place on foot.

He followed the contoured veins of sand upward to get a more panoramic view. Did anyone at all live nearby? Did people ever come this way, beyond the occasional passing jeep? The sand plied its curves like a sea, waves birthing new waves into the distance, on and on. He began scrambling up a higher hill, his feet plunging deeper into the sand as it became softer. He found it a challenge to make his way to the top; he was already panting hard. He understood now how much more difficult it was to climb a sand dune than it was to clamber up the rocky hills near home. Once he reached the top he watched little whirlwinds cavorting across the sands, on and on into the distance. Up here, though, he felt only a light breeze, just moist enough to soften the atmosphere and gentle all of existence.

In the distance he could see a tail of dust rising. A vehicle was heading across the desert, having turned off the paved road towards the sea of sand. He watched it disappear into a dense patch of ghaf trees. He waited, expecting to see it emerge on the other side of the thicket. But as the dust that had flown up in a wild dance behind it settled, he gazed on a scene that was once again entirely still and silent. There must be a house over there. It could not be very far away. He must pay a visit to his neighbors, then.

He came down quickly, climbed into his pick-up, and headed toward the ghaf grove. He estimated the distance to be about ten kilometers but it turned out to be considerably more. As he arrived at the patch of mesquite, the odometer registered sixteen kilometers. The flatness here gave the impression that the small clutch of scrubby trees was closer than it actually was.

Reaching the grove he could not see any signs of life. But he went on, following the dirt track, which led him to some more sandy hillocks. At the first sharp bend in the track suddenly there he was. This was a Bedouin dwelling, a circle of tents and trellises enclosed by a length of coarse brown woven material. Nearby was a pen holding nearly thirty head of camel, fenced in with heavy rope-like wire.

He was approaching the encampment when a woman came outside. She seemed to be in her thirties. She was of medium height. As she emerged, she was tugging a burqa over her face. He braked his truck and got out. They exchanged greetings. She asked why he had come. What did he need? He responded as succinctly as he could, trying to explain who he was. He could tell that she wasn't taking in much of what he said, because his speech differed so much from the way people spoke around here. She opened a flap in the enclosure and invited him to come in for coffee while he waited for the head of the household to return home. He did not object. He wanted to learn what he could about the Bedouin—what they were like—for he had heard so much about them.

The woman was hospitality itself. She set down a tray of dates and coffee within his easy reach and seated herself further away, on the edge of the mat. She asked where he was from. How had he come here? Where and how had he learned of this place? What was he doing here, alone, in this place where there were no companions, no entertaining company to pass the time? He answered her questions and he talked about how necessary it had been to remove his bees to another site in search of good pasturage—exactly as Bedouin did with their animals, he said, moving from one area to the next in search of new life, fertile herbage amongst the desert scrabble.

It wasn't long before Azzan heard a vehicle driving up, but then the rising sound got fainter. It must be heading directly to the camel enclosure. He could hear a man shouting and then he heard the braying of camels getting louder. This Bedouin man was feeding them grass and dates and they were jostling to get nearer to him, keen to capture their evening meal. Shouting at them, his voice accelerated. Azzan thought he could hear loud oaths mixed into his speech, flung here and there, but he couldn't really understand most of the man's words. Entering his home, the man hastened to welcome his guest, this person whom he had never seen. As Bedouin do, he put nose to nose with an affectionate sniff. A warm greeting. They sat down for another round of coffee.

He could not detach himself from the Bedouin's grasp before a sumptuous dinner was laid. This platter of rice and meat was the best kabsa he had tasted in years. The Bedouin declared that he must visit them again, and as often as he could. If he needed anything at all, he must ask; the Bedouin swore not to spare any effort. Finally, he learned the names of his hosts: Hamud bin Ghabish and Salama bint al-Saab. Their children were still small—under five years of age. He could see already that these were two generous, self-reliant young people who were living their lives at a distance from the society of others in this stretch of sandy pasturage called Shuggat al-Manakh.

For some time now, Hamud bin Ghabish told Azzan, he had been training racing camels. He was commissioned regularly by a goodly number of eminent people including some of the governorate's most senior men. He mentioned names. In these circles he had become known as an expert handler, a trainer of rare talent. He had visitors coming here every week and they came from all over, even from beyond Oman. They came bearing offerings, gift upon gift, yearning to spend a night or two as close as they could to his encampment shaded by ghaf trees. Their presence filled the surrounding area with the fragrance of grilled meat, enhanced by the variety of fruit and other delicacies they brought with them.

Hamud bin Ghabish told his guest the story of how it had all happened. The very first camel he trained had come first in a major Gulf racing event. The owner gave him a share of the prize money, amounting to tens of thousands of riyals. From that moment on, many Gulf shaykhs had tried to secure Hamud's involvement in training their camels. Every year, one or another camel that he had had a hand in training placed highly in such competitions. Now he had hundreds of thousands of riyals in the bank and he owned properties in various places, raking in prodigious rents. When Azzan asked him what his intentions were—and when would he change this life he had now for city life?—Hamud exclaimed immediately, *This* is my life! I can't change it and I wouldn't replace it for anything.

On the way back to his beehives, steering around the endless dunes, Azzan lost his way in the darkness. He drove further west than he should have gone. At some point, he did realize that he had been going across the sands for longer than made sense. He stopped. He climbed a nearby rise to survey the area but it was too dark and he couldn't make out anything clearly. He recalled the stars he had studied the evening before and he tried to work out their positions in terms of where he stood now. He could see his error and he retraced his path, following the marks that his wheels had made, hoping to get all the way back to where he should have been before the shifting sand erased them. He turned to the right and continued on straight ahead, until he could tell that he had nearly reached the paved road. He drove parallel to it, north, and finally he recognized his surroundings and knew where he should turn off—onto the dirt track that would deliver him to his campsite.

As on the night before, he unrolled his mattress beneath the stars. It was a quarter past midnight. Getting lost—and it could have been the end of him—meant his return had taken hours.

In the morning new visitors showed up. Hearing a shout somewhere close by, he climbed up the nearest rise to find out what was going on. He saw a vehicle pulling what looked like a small metallic hut behind it, with a train of camels strutting behind the trailer. They were all coming toward him.

Two men climbed out and strode over to where he stood. They greeted him but they didn't wait for a response. What brought you here? one of them asked.

He told them he had a bee colony and that he had been looking for good pasturage in these parts. One of the men raised his hand and swept it across the horizon.

No, no! These are our lands, this is where we live, and we're stopping and staying here.

The land belongs to God. It's big enough for everyone. Please—you're very welcome to find a good place to put up your tents. We'll be neighbors.

The man shouted closely into his face. We don't want anyone anywhere near us here. These bees of yours are harming our children and our women.

Azzan bin Said closed his eyes, as he did whenever he knew he had to restrain himself. He needed a pause. He had to relieve the tension, the anger that swelled and roiled inside of him.

After a moment he was able to speak. If you want to camp here, ahlan wa-sahlan. If you want to go on, may the road be green and prosperous in front of you. This desert is enormous and there's plenty of room for everyone here.

The other man was frowning as he broke in for the first time. Are these your final words?

Azzan gazed down at the sand around his feet before answering. I don't have anything else to say.

He watched as the caravan of men and camels moved off, heading across the desert. Now, he realized, he would have to anticipate some sort of fight with these men, and he might well be the loser. But he also knew that it wasn't over yet. He sat there until mid-morning watching for any new movements on the horizon.

Precisely at half past three in the afternoon, just after he had awoken from a short and pleasant nap after his lunch, he got a phone call from his friend. Mahmud informed him that an official at the Bureau of Agriculture had contacted him to ask about the bees that were in Shuggat al-Manakh. Did Mahmud know their owner? He had told the official that the owner was a beekeeper from Wadi al-Taiyyin and that his name was Azzan bin Said. The bureaucrat was very irritated. How could this man have moved his bees without getting permission or a license from the Bureau? The people who lived over there, he said, had made a complaint about his bees. They said the bees were stinging their children and their animals. He must remove his bee colony and go back to his own district. Otherwise he would be faced with the regulation fine for an infraction of this sort.

Azzan heard his friend out before saying anything. But you told me no one lived here.

Mahmud's voice over the phone sounded anxious. There's some kinds of meddling going on—by some folks we have no power over—

So, tell him this, Mahmud: My friend asks for a few days before he has to move everything out. Inshallah it will all work out fine.

After that phone call, he sat there for a while, trying to think about what he ought to do now. How could he resolve this problem which had suddenly burst upon him from the silent interior of these endless sands? How had this great expanse—this wide stretch of flat land—come to be too small for those who lived here? How could it be too small, when his own village, despite all its tensions and conflicts and incongruities, was big enough to hold everyone and everything, and no one grumbled about living so closely with others?

He jumped into his pick-up and headed once again towards the ghaf trees. Salama bint al-Saab welcomed him. Billahi hayk ya Azzan! I guess you must like the taste of our coffee.

He told her that he wanted to speak to her husband about a personal matter.

You're wanting to marry—you're ready to find a wife here, a woman from among us.

Azzan laughed and protested her words, though he quickly amended his energetic denial. You are people of such nobility and generosity—this would be an enormous honor for anyone, to marry into your people. But that's not what I've come about.

She made space for him to sit down where he could wait for Hamud bin Ghabish's return. But today Hamud was very late coming home. The sun had gone down and it was completely dark by the time Azzan was apologizing to Salama and getting up to leave. She tried to convince him to stay for the evening meal, but he refused. Then, she assured him that Bin Ghabish would come and see him in the morning. As he got into his truck, she said, I'd like a gharsha of honey from you—a jarful of the purest kind.

Azzan smiled and promised, and went off into the darkness.

The next morning, it was still early when he heard the sound of a motor—a vehicle approaching his beehive settlement. He got to his feet hurriedly as Bin Ghabish stopped his pick-up and climbed out. As he did so, he was already teasing Azzan, and in a very loud voice. Wallahi! he said. You're a good Bedouin already, all you need is a little plot of land with a few head of camel, and then you have got to marry a good Badawi woman of local stock, a woman from the folk who live in these sands. You'll forget all about those town people of yours.

Done! said Azzan, laughing. He told Bin Ghabish what had happened—the men coming here and then lodging a complaint against him with the Bureau of Agriculture.

Wallahi! By God, you're not moving an inch from where you've settled as long as I'm Hamud bin Ghabish!

For a few seconds the visitor scrolled through his contact list. He found what he wanted. The phone rang and rang. Bin Ghabish was clearly losing his patience when finally a languid voice answered. As the person on the other end of the line realized who it was who had phoned him, his voice changed. He greeted the caller with a warmth that had been noticeably absent when he picked up the call. Bin Ghabish went right to the point.

Azzan bin Said and his bees and his family and anyone he wants, he can bring them over here. I'm his neighbor and this is my territory. Do you hear me, or don't you?

But this man didn't get permission to move there.

So, give him permission. Starting today.

There's a complaint against him.

Don't worry yourself about any of it. Consider the complaint dissolved. By me. Anyone who comes back to you on it, tell him he's got to talk to Bin Ghabish. You got it?

The fellow on the other end had no choice but to submit to this Bedouin. How could he do otherwise? He was speaking to the district's most famous man, the guy to whom everyone came about anything.

After a round of coffee, Bin Ghabish got up to leave. Azzan asked him to wait. Going into his tent, he came out with a jar in his hands.

This is for Salama.

The Bedouin took the jar of honey and drove off, disappearing into the sands, in the same direction as the caravan had gone the afternoon before.

Chapter Two

Sweet bloom on this hard mountain
the pot is brewed and steaming
your morning coffee, from my heart and hand

ON HIS WAY BACK TO the site where he had settled his bee colony in the Najd, in the high plain between the White Mountain range and the Hajar Mountains, he saw her again. She was standing on the edge of the wadi, her animals clustered tightly around her. At her feet sat her dog, facing the path expectantly, his tongue lolling.

Alone. She was alone there. He didn't understand from where, or how, she could have suddenly emerged or where she could be going. She'd appeared to him all at once like some guardian angel, one of those beings who stand watch over particular sites. She seemed singular in this time when so many mountain herders had flocked to the cities, abandoning their herds and leaving the mountains where they had always roamed, their voices swelling across the mountain faces as they sang their plaintive taawibehs.

Her apparition floated from daytime into one of his nights. It was early enough that he hadn't yet gone to sleep. He saw her face, polished by the sun and the wind, its sunrise glow lighting up the space around her and releasing a perfume he caught in his imagination, that of a mountain wildflower. He could almost touch, almost cling to, her eyebrows, the arcs that nearly met across her brow like the dark, thin wings of an eagle ever circling in the high winds far above. His night was scented with her delicate, elusive smell as her sorrowful tune wafted across the high mountain sweeps, carried by her mountain voice which was sweet, gentle and hoarse all at the same time. He didn't know exactly what it was in the image of her that he wanted to hold, or what had drawn him to feel so close to her. Ever since their one encounter he had felt something like a twinge of discomfort; traces of irritation, unease, even anger; but that wasn't exactly it, either.

As soon as he reached his apiary here, though, his work absorbed him so fully that he lost all sense of time passing. He nearly lost a hive as it was about to swarm. He could hear a queen bee's voice, making a sound designed to send the packed throng of worker bees rising out of the hive. He understood instinctively that amongst his hives was one that he had not examined carefully enough. He listened closely for that voice, amidst the accelerating *tintintin* of bees bursting from the hives to head for the pastures and fields. Her voice, coming from the perimeter of the bee colony. He came closer to her hive and the voice he had picked up became more distinct. He did not want the queen bee to make an escape. He hurried over to a trunk he had positioned at one edge of the colony, which held some of the things he might need in such a moment. He took out a plastic sheet covered in fine netting and laid it over the hive opening to block it. The bees could still get through the net as they headed for pasture, and it allowed worker bees that had been out foraging to come back in; but the mesh was fine enough to prevent the queen bee from leaving the hive. He used it to keep the queens confined when the hive was bursting, and also when he was harvesting honey.

All right. Now – he was saying to himself as he opened the cover to the hive. With the experience he had built up through these years, he listened intently to her voice which came up from amongst the frames. He pulled up each frame in turn, gently and slowly, looking for her and attending closely to the mass of moving bees around her. He pulled out the first frame, and then the next, until finally he came upon her. The worker bees encircled her as she emitted that sound meant to encourage her bees to leave and to take her along, ready to form a new colony. He drew out the frame carefully—it had so many tiny bodies clinging to it—and set it inside a small crate which he closed tightly. He came back to the hive, inspecting the remaining frames and searching for his new queen who would have just been hatched.

Just as, finally, he spotted the new young queen on one rim of the final frame he inspected, he heard her voice, coming from far away. Or at least that was how it seemed to him. He raised his head sharply and studied the heights surrounding him, hoping to hear goats bleating or the bark of a dog. And then suddenly the voice went silent. Had the voice come from inside of him? Maybe he had imagined the sound, the strains of her taawibeh. Or had he really heard her?

Working since early morning, he had been able to form twelve new hives. He would take them over to the nearby site he had already selected. Separating these bees from the others meant he was expanding his colony. He had placed several hives in that new location and now he could deposit the new groups in them.

Because he needed to be sure that he was not depriving the old hive of its vigor, he would take out a small number of bees along with their queen, their mother bee, leaving the rest around the new queen. If she was laying eggs, then he would know that his hive was strong, that it had a young and energetic population, that it would fill up with newly hatched bees who would contribute their share when the gum acacias flowered, for then he would be able to see masses of lively bees bringing back nectar and pollen, inundating the hive with honey.

Once he was certain that the new hive was launched, a few days later, he would provision the old queen bee's hive with new, closed frames that would be filled with their own eggs about to hatch. That would guarantee its viability through the approaching season.

He worked for three solid hours and then stopped to brew coffee. He drank several small glasses of it. He must finish this task and deliver the new companies of bees to the other site.

A cup of coffee, ahh?

This unexpected query startled him. He had been so deeply inside of his own thoughts and plans. She didn't give him time even to stand up before she sat down opposite him.

The honey has stolen you! she said, her voice teasing him. All your time and attention … She picked up a date and rubbed it between two fingers to soften it before popping it into her mouth. As he poured the coffee he was stealing glances at her face. He tried to bring back the feeling that had haunted his mind following his first encounter with her. And he sought a way to break the heavy silence between them.

Where do you live? he asked.

She stared upward into the mountains. Everywhere, she said. A person like me doesn't need a house. My home—it's the high plains and the wadis.

She told him that she had been in these parts for several months. That the pasturage here was rich and provided good grazing for her animals, and so she was partial to this region. It was why she would settle here for long stretches of time, moving from one locale to another amongst its hillocks and higher elevations, always looking for new pastures and searching for watercourses where she and her herd could drink. For a time, she had camped beneath a particular gum acacia that grew on the edge of nearby Wadi al-Ghaf because the wadi provided such an abundance of water. She'd left all her belongings there beneath the samur tree; early each morning, she took her goats to pasture, returning only in the hot midday or even not until the late afternoon as the sun was beginning to dip in the sky.

A woman alone with her herd and a dog; these animals were her only companions. How was she able to live by herself, so completely cut off from the world? His mind was asking him that question before his voice asked her about her family. She swallowed her coffee and gave him a sharply condensed version of her long story. She was an only child and her parents had died some time ago; and then her husband followed them to the grave. She and he had not had a child. She had no family in this earthly life apart from these goats, no home other than these wilderness lands.

Something in his spirit seemed to grow lighter as he gazed at her face. A tiny seedling was breaking through the dark soil of his days, opening its minute leaves to fresh air and sunlight. The arcs of her eyebrows sloped lightly to each side of her brow. Her eyes were large and clear and he thought he could see the legendary magic of the ancients reflected in the soft whiteness around the pupils, shaded by long lashes which tracings of kohl had made even lovelier. Her nose was small and delicate over small lips. The smooth, flat surface of her chin was interrupted only by a slight, pointed swell outward.

Like a thirsty creature yearning for a sweet gush of water to engulf him, he wished she would go on speaking. He wanted to keep on drinking in her words. The hoarse tone infusing her mellow voice did not startle or grate on him—this low melodious voice that seemed to have been formed inside the herders' songs, and yet was one with the open spaces that gave rise to their taawibehs .... This voice made his blood quicken. He felt the heat of it in his fingers: a voice, a timbre, he had never heard before, or perhaps he had but he didn't know where.

After her fourth cup she got to her feet, thanking him and in the same breath teasing him again. Town folk, she remarked, are so miserly! They don't invite their neighbors over. He apologized, giving the excuse that he hadn't been aware of her presence here until she had been there asking her question. She laughed and the sound of it seemed to split open the stony interior that had been his heart as long as he could remember, opening a space from which imaginary birds burst forth to circle overhead.

His eyes were speaking to her. Sit down, stay here, I have not had enough of you. He was already sensing that a mystery, a secret, had begun to reign over his nights and days, a sweet agony whenever he thought of her. As she began to walk away he stopped her. He wanted to know her name.

My name's Thamna.

He had never heard this name before. Another surprise. He took a step toward her.

Thamna—your eyes are beautiful.

She smiled shyly and ducked her head. She tugged forward the shawl wrapping her head to conceal that bashful smile and her eyes which seemed to glisten. He sensed that he had embarrassed her and he pulled himself back. He spoke in a lighter tone, hoping to undo the confusion he had caused.

I promised a gharsha of honey. It'll be here—don't forget, now!

She answered with a little laugh as she walked away. Yes, I want one from the new season.

And so Thamna walked away while he stayed where he was, unable to move. He followed her path with his eyes as she vanished behind the sumar trees. Moments later he could see her come out of the gum acacia grove, climbing, driving her animals before her as her dog darted right and left, attempting to corral stray goats and bring them back to the group.

This secret. It did not lie simply in the features of that face sculpted and singed by the sun, nor in the particular timbre of her voice with its touch of mellow hoarseness, nor in her small mouth. No—it was concealed beneath all of that, in that space where now his spirit ran and, he thought, must always have floated. His spirit swept on, sailing deep into a bottomless crevice that was all beauty and sweetness. The sparkling sweet secret, the painful tormenting mystery, that enigma he had seen in the pupils of her eyes—those brown eyes that had etched a little green bird inside his chest .... His spirit began to beat its wings, trying to rise out of its cage to soar into the lands behind those mountain peaks and the dips and gorges that separated them. If he had not suddenly remembered the new and still sparse swarms of bees he was trying to establish here, he might have stayed on exactly in this spot, as incapable of moving as were the very mountains themselves.

When Hamud bin Ghabish departed, he left Azzan feeling hopeful that his problem with the nearby Bedouin was resolved. For several days he expected his new friend to pay him another visit. Finally Hamud appeared, accompanied this time by the two men who had demanded that Azzan move his bee colony away from this territory. After a round of coffee Bin Ghabish informed Azzan that his neighbors—he gestured to the men—were to host a banquet for a large gathering at the end of the week. They had come with him now to request Azzan's presence there. To deflect any excuses he might try to make, one of the men declared that if he did not show up there would never be another such occasion to attend.

Just as the winds expunge the traces of all things in these sandy reaches, what had taken place between him and the two men was now erased. He promised them that he would be there at the hour they named. He considered it an honor, he said, and far beyond anything he might deserve.

This particular location that his friend Mahmud had chosen for him was not immediately within the band of thick pasturage. But these men were well aware of the distances bees could cover in their daily search for sustenance. A worker bee could travel as far as ten kilometers, they knew; and so here in this spot there was ample grazing within his bees' range. He hadn't needed to settle his colony in the lushest area; the bees knew instinctively how to find what they needed.

Even if this region in which he found himself was remote, isolated from other parts of the country and very sparsely populated—indeed, much of it was not populated at all by humans—he could sense that it had a very different temper to the mountain villages that had formed him. He didn't miss that village atmosphere, though. And here, he wasn't plagued by any sense of the days passing slowly, or of nights too heavy with solitude. In fact, what he felt was that this wide-open space had truly released him from the constricted sphere within which he had always moved, from his fields to the homes of his companions in the village and back again. Here, instead, he felt free to climb to higher land—and comfortable on the heights—but equally happy clambering through the low sand dunes. He got into the habit of taking along his coffee pot and radio and mounting up a sand hillock where he could recline happily, his feet plunging comfortably into the sand and his back against a mound of sand that he had patted into place himself. Staring into the horizon he would notice how the sky took on many colors in the blaze of hard light that flared shortly before sundown. Not once did he begin to feel that this was a place he must leave. With every day that passed he felt more a part of it, and more as though he were one of the creatures of these deserts—a wolf or a gazelle, a rabbit or a viper, or one of the camels that passed through. And then, there were the many sand insects he was discovering in these excursions of his. Perhaps he would grow to be more like one of the Bedouin whom he saw passing by now and then.

As part of his morning routine, out on training runs with his camels, Hamud bin Ghabish got into the habit of coming by to see the beekeeper Azzan bin Said. He timed his visits for the hour Azzan considered his well-deserved battlefield break, ready to relax with a few cups of coffee and listen to the stories Bin Ghabish spun so dexterously. He regaled Azzan with tales of the Bedouin and the desert, the shaykhly leaders of the tribes, the big capitalists he had gotten to know, and then, always, his explanations and anecdotes about the camels he worked with. This one—he would say—is owned by

Shaykh So-and-So from the Emirates, and her name is Ghaliya. The Precious. The shaykh had paid a hundred thousand for her, and then another shaykh, one from Qatar, offered him two hundred and fifty thousand for the animal but he wouldn't agree to it.

Over the coming days the man's fondness for Azzan became abundantly and generously clear. Sometimes Bin Ghabish showed up with breakfast. Bint al-Saab swore I wasn't going anywhere today, he declared, unless I brought you food.

Azzan could feel the spirit of this Bedouin in his pulse. Partly it was his sense of awe: how could this one man so ably arrange all the matters he was obligated to handle? How did he manage his lands and train his camels; and attend banquets all over this desert region—indeed, he travelled to far locations in order to show up at some of them. Azzan wished that half this energy could be channeled towards him, so that he would be capable of a similar attentiveness to the obligations he still faced in the village—back home. But instead … well, what was it that afflicted him so badly? Whenever he thought about all the things he wished he could exert himself to work out, he felt nothing but helpless.

His own spirit had grown cold long ago, and no live ember could warm it into life now. Were it not for this bee colony in which he had immersed himself day upon day and night after night, he did not know what force could have kept him amongst the living.

When he had held that very first beehive in his own hands, carrying it from a mountainside near his village to a box hive belonging to his friend Abdallah bin Hamad, he had felt himself to be undergoing some kind of change. And then there really were the new beginnings, as he lived the experiment of tending to that hive and later of buying his own first five hives from a beekeeper who had come to the outskirts of their village. Azzan sought him out and grilled him about everything having to do with beekeeping. And then he had come home from that meeting with five hives. From that moment Azzan had devoted all of his attention to raising these bees and learning what he could about their needs.

Years had passed. He lived in an isolation and a stasis he had chosen for himself. He did not marry nor did he look for any regular, waged job. He existed on the anxious edge of poverty; sometimes, he did not know where he would find the nourishment he needed to get him through the day. Still, the date palms he owned and the fruit he could sell each year did keep him going. They allowed him to buy the basic necessities, more or less. That was before he had come to have a thriving bee colony. This had opened a door for him on to a good livelihood. From the proceeds he was able to buy a pick-up. His living conditions were improving now, with every day that passed.

Where had all of these people come from, to make such a crowd here? The whole surrounding area was a sea of motor vehicles and camels. What kind of evening was he about to have among these Bedouin? As it turned out, he saw things he would have never expected to see. He had assumed that he was simply attending a meal, if a lavish one. But there was a lot more than that going on. He watched them dance. He listened to the constant buzz of talk and the louder reverberations of ululating voices. From time to time during the evening, Salama bint al-Saab came over to him. At one point she was waving at a young woman who stood on the opposite side of the dance space. The woman wore an embroidered yellow gown; a Bedouin-style burqa covered part of her face.

You see that lovely girl? I'm going to call her over here and introduce you.

He chuckled at Bint al-Saab's words. She strode towards the knot of women who stood nearby, observing the dancing, and went straight to the young woman she had pointed out to Azzan. She seemed to be whispering something into the woman's ear as she gestured rather obviously towards Azzan. The young woman smiled and gave Bint al-Saab a little shove with her wrist, playing along with this caper. Then she glanced in his direction. Then she fixed her gaze on him.

How handsome the Bedouins were! he thought to himself, almost saying it out loud. And a very long time ago they had liberated themselves from the noose of village life—from the sorts of obligations that had little day-to-day meaning and yet could hobble a person forever. And here they were dancing together, men and women, and singing and shooting bullets into the air out of sheer whooping joy. Shaking hands, embracing and rubbing noses in greeting, men with women and women with men without any artificiality or hesitation. He wished he were a Bedouin. If he were, he could roam through the sandy stretches of these deserts, from

Lake Mahout as far as the gravelly outskirts of the Wahiba Sands. Perhaps, if he had grown up as a Bedouin, he would have been able to choose a life different to the one he was living now, this frigid life to which no embers in his soul had been strong enough to impart any real warmth.

He lost himself in watching—feeling—their dancing. At the center of the space made for dancing, a woman who looked to be in her forties, her substantial figure commanding attention from the onlookers, was dancing with a man. The drummer furnished them a strong and regular rhythm while everyone who was gathered around the space clapped their hands to the drumbeats. There were hoots here and there, and ecstatic yells coming from somewhere in the crowd. From the dance floor a loud raucous laugh rose, before the woman clapped her hand over her mouth and muted it.

Suddenly the fragrance of henna seemed to be everywhere, around him and inside of him too. The soft hand that had produced the aroma tugged him onto the dance floor, and into the center of the dancing. The fullness of her form: as if her long green tob were packed with some kind of stuffing. Beneath her head covering he could see her hair floating onto her shoulders. She wore a light rose-colored litham across her mouth.

He took two steps and stopped. He didn't have a clue as to what had just happened. Where had this woman come from, singling him out for this dance? His reluctance was obvious enough to bring words from the edge of the dance floor. He heard a man's voice. Dance with the beauty, dance with her! And then a feminine voice commanding the same. Dance with the gazelle! whoever it was called out.

The woman gripped his hand as her body moved and shook in time to the music of the dance. When one of the Bedouin men nearby gave him a strong shove, he found himself at the absolute center of the dancing. He stood there a bit woodenly, looking from side to side and feeling embarrassed. The sounds of clapping rose and the drumbeat picked up. Again he looked around, and he noticed Salama bint al-Saab. She was watching him and smiling, even laughing. Her clapping encouraged him. She was gesturing at him as she shook her body in time to the beat, telling him to follow her example. What could he do but throw off the robe of embarrassment that immobilized him? He began to follow his dance partner's steps. He was trying to enter into the dance, to keep to the regular beat of the drum with his movements so that he would not appear ungainly and hopelessly at odds with the rhythm.

Facing him closely she rocked as fiercely as a dangerously swaying tree that has so few roots in the soil that even the ground beneath it shakes. Her full chest reminded him of a pair of mangoes ripe enough to fall off the tree, swaying and dropping to the beat of the drum, pulsing and stirring up the entire tree until it trembles as if in a storm. Her buttocks swayed close to his body, touched him briefly, moved away. She gave her waist to his arm and he submitted his to her hand. He fused with this tree, danced with it, steps forward, steps back, following the movement of her torso, of the tree trunk, his shoulder nearly touching the ripe, hanging mangoes.

Now another woman pulled a man onto the dance space and the two of them twined into the dancers already there. Somehow the dancers became pairs facing each other, stepping apart and then drawing closer together and meeting in the middle. The number of dancers grew gradually until there were two rows of six dancers each, three men and three women. The clapping grew louder and fiercer, the beat grew faster, and shouted urgings from every direction ordered the group to go on dancing and not to stop.

After the banquet, for which the hosts had slaughtered camels, the place was readied so that guests could go to sleep. Azzan wanted to make his excuses and leave but he was told that the festivities had not yet ended; there would be something unexpected awaiting him in the morning. So, instead of leaving, Azzan stayed there, and he stayed up very late talking with Bin Ghabish and his friends as the charcoal on the cooking fire still glowed. The conversation moved from topic to topic until he felt his head was about to drop off from exhaustion. He crept over to the spot that had been prepared for him and fell asleep immediately.

That night his dreams were all confusion and loud voices. In fact he wasn't certain whether he had really slept or whether all of the commotion around him had simply carried him somewhere far away. Because all of this was happening to him for the first time—and all at once—he couldn't help but feel like a character in one of those ancient tales that you could never really believe because they were so full of wondrous doings. In the morning he awakened to the sound of the muezzin.

Everyone was getting up and he did so as well, to perform the first prayers of the day.

He had heard about certain Bedouin customs, of course, but he had never experienced them in his daily life. And now here he was; and in a single night he had discovered the vast difference that existed within a not-very-vast space. There was the life of his village, where every day was a succession of complications and complexes and one had to conform for as long as one remained on this earth. Meanwhile, only a few hundred kilometers away, another set of human beings were living out their lives far removed from the array of complications which those village people in their built-up societies considered to be the fundamental necessities and duties of social life.

With the prayers over everyone gathered for the finale of this festive overnight. A veritable racecourse had been prepared out here. The camel drivers came leading their animals and waiting for the starting signal. Soon, they would give their beasts free rein and the camels would gallop off down the course to loud shouts that created an ongoing chorus rippling all the way down the line to the very last moment of the race, over where the judges were waiting. But now they were poised to start. Atop the camels sat boys younger than ten years old, each one fastened securely to his camel with a strong rope so that he wouldn't slip off during this furious gallop. A few minutes later the reins restraining the camels were relaxed and they plunged forward. The dust rose from beneath their hooves, marking the racecourse all the way to the finish line.

Some people tried to race alongside the coursing animals, steering their vehicles to follow as closely as they could and trying to guess who would be the winner. Who had the honors waiting for them? Which camel's owner would receive the coveted purse for having so well trained and readied their animal?

The gathering broke up, everyone said their goodbyes, and Azzan returned to his bees. He squatted in front of his tent, slowly regaining his accustomed state of absolute quiet. His ears picked up no sounds apart from the low and steady hum of the bees and the faint chirping of a few birds. He gave in to the drowsiness that had settled heavily onto his head like a thick fog swooping in. His head dropped, and he slept.

There it was. The sounds of a taawibeh echoing amongst the mountain crags, the voice of a woman moaning her songs far up in the heights, the strains of it piercing veils and crossing barriers to reach him as she sang of great loss. Whenever he heard a song of loss he could not but think it must be for him. Her voice was carried by the winds coming down from the passes up there in the White Mountains. Or so it seemed to him when it arrived here in his camp, fragmented and faint from its journey but telling his spirit that she was there. But then it would come back at him with a different message. No one is there. And he would tell himself: This voice was inside of me, only inside of me, that's all. The silence around him, the apprehensions and premonitions that he seemed to hear nevertheless, disturbed him: an illusion hiding in her voice. Perhaps she has gone far away by now, he thought. He did not know this place, Wadi al-Ghaf, which she had mentioned. Maybe, exactly at this moment, she was returning there with her herd and getting ready to sleep. Making her bed as the mountain slopes protected her; singing her sad songs of parting, of distance and absence and death.

He took himself to the spot where he had set down the small hive of bees that he had separated from their original homes. He wanted to reassure himself that these bees were active. That they were still there and settled into their new homes, these infant hives he had placed carefully on the ground next to each other without having raised them onto the special flatbeds that could protect them from attacking ants. It was early in the season for ants but when they did come, they could file directly into a hive and would not leave until they had stripped it bare, expelling the bees who lived there in order to occupy their frames, devouring the honey and larvae they found there.

But here in the deserts of Juba his bees were removed from the danger posed by ants as they nestled in the soft sands where the heat stung by day and the night was thick with cold. There was nothing here for ants to eat. But he had brought the platforms with him anyway, so that his hives would not sit directly on the ground. Even if there weren't any ants in sight, they could be vulnerable to drifting sands getting inside the hives through the tiny apertures.

Here in Juba's desert, where he had found his own Bedouin spirit, he also found himself feeling more intimately attuned to the life of the Bedouin freed as it was from so many of the social obstacles familiar to him from his life there in the village where he had grown up. Here, everything seemed so deeply entwined with nature and detached from human artifice. He mulled over how, one morning not long ago, he had gone to the Bedouin household of Bin Ghabish and had not found him there. But Salama bint al-Saab had welcomed him saying, God has brought you here—if you hadn't shown up this morning, I was going to come by to see you.

She told him she was about to go to Mahout Town because she wanted to buy some supplies. Since her husband had gone into the interior for his work and would stay away for some days, it fell to her to shop for whatever their household and the camels needed. She asked if he would go with her so that she wouldn't have to go into the souq by herself.

When he had made those first, earlier visits to her home, Salama bint al-Saab had dropped a litham over her face as he appeared. After some time had passed, she began to leave it aside and now he could see her entire face. He knew that Bedouin women always wore lithams when they were in the presence of an outsider but no face veil when they were with their own folk. Now, it seemed, he had become like a member of the household; he was there so often, stopping in on different occasions. And here was Bint al-Saab asking him to accompany her to the market.

She insisted that they take her pick-up. She sat next to him and talked the whole way there. She spoke about many things and he thought she was trying to break the barrier of distance and unfamiliarity that still held sway inside both of them. In the souq, he helped her carry the fodder and the other goods she needed. They packed everything carefully into the back of the vehicle. On the return journey, she drove.

More than once she asked him what he thought of these desert girls—weren't they pretty? On his wanderings around the area, had he run into any of them? Sometimes as she asked these questions she gave him a suggestive little wink. From the way she repeated and emphasized her words, he thought he understood what she was getting at. He shook his head while she studied him thoughtfully but said nothing more.

Still, he was a bit confused, or a bit suspicious perhaps. Sometimes he felt unsure of what she meant when she talked about mazyuuns, 'the gorgeous ones'. Or she would mention gazelles or birds. Has a little bird come by to see you? she would ask him. Are you telling me you haven't seen a single gazelle since the day you arrived? she might exclaim. He just shook his head and laughed. But sometimes, he tried to find something to say in response. Whatever words he could find always seemed to show him up as a bit slow and dull. No, he hadn't seen any gazelles; the desert around here was really empty, wasn't it—there was nothing to see but sand. There were no gazelles here, no birds … Where would the gazelles be coming from? he asked her. In his head, he was trying to understand what she really meant by all of this talk. He wasn't certain whether she was trying to sound him out, to get him to reveal something. Perhaps she thought he would let spill a secret, like divulging that one of those gazelles had visited him furtively without anyone being the wiser.

A few days after their trip to the market, one evening he heard footsteps close by. He went to investigate: perhaps it was a desert animal coming a little too close to the bee colony. He saw her standing there. She was wearing a red gown sprinkled with bright blue and yellow flowers. A woman of medium height and build. She shook his hand and put her nose close to his in what was by now a greeting familiar to him. As astonished as he was at this unexpected visit, he invited her to have coffee.

From behind her litham, the woman's voice was delicate, a slight raspy tone modulating its sweetness. She told him she wanted some honey. He went into his tent to fetch a jar. He was astonished when she followed him inside. He stood there bewildered as he saw her slip off her litham. She put her arms around him.

Sometime in the middle of the night she went away, leaving her aroma in his tent. She walked away and he followed her shadow in the darkness until she vanished. He heard the sound of her car motor; she had parked behind the sand dune. He could hear the motor for a few moments as it faded away.

Two days later Bint al-Saab came by to take him with her to the souq. As they were on their way, she asked him, Any news of the mazyuun who came to see you?

Her question startled him. How had she known about the woman's visit? When she saw the unmistakable look of mingled surprise and discomfort on his face, she laughed.

I redeem you with all my heart, my dear!

He dipped his head, not wanting her to see his face. He was embarrassed but at least now he understood the little conspiracy that Bint al-Saab had organized. He felt enormously grateful for this honor she had done him, and very contented. He could never have anticipated it.

Chapter Three

the sugarcane stalk …
herdswoman, your voice
awakens the whitened bones of those long dead

IT WAS LIKE A JET of water erupting suddenly from a dry crevice on what appeared to be a uniformly rock-faced and barren mountainside, and running with fierce energy to join the larger watercourse down in the wadi. Sweet water that refreshed the pulse as it ran in one's veins and greened the spirit but then all of a sudden stopped or went dry … yet the traces of it remained etched along the ground for all to see. When someone passed along this way they would see signs of it and say to themselves: Once there was water here.

This was precisely what had happened to him. He had drawn some kind of sustenance from those brown eyes and this had given him a sense of new light; it had birthed the idea of being with her, spending time … but then she had vanished without any sense on his part of what had happened while she was here, or of where she had gone.

He searched in all of the likely places within reach of his bee colony but he found no signs of her. He watched and watched, hoping she would suddenly appear at a moment when he was—as usual—bent over, a supplicant's form at prayer, as he tended his tiny beings. He was calling on their sympathy—calling her through them. Might they possibly tell him the path she had taken? He listened hard to every sound he could catch coming from afar, hoping to discern the tones of her taawibeh or the barking of her dog, or the bleating of her animals. This vast space with its rich forests of sumar trees now seemed empty, arid and even parched.

He had waited so intently for her ever since that last day on which he had seen her when he told her that her eyes were beautiful. He had waited in hopes of seeing her sun-polished face, those eyes that sang to him of all the honey in the world. But she didn't appear again. He sought whatever information he could get about Wadi al-Ghaf from whoever he encountered traveling through these parts. But he put his questions to them as though none of these encounters with her had ever happened. Until finally he stumbled on what he had been looking for, under a gum acacia clinging to the rim of a wadi, near running water coming down a rocky slope and along the smooth rocks on the river bottom. He found a lighter, some coffee grounds scattered across the hard ground, and a few date pits tossed here and there.

In her roamings Thamna had gone to more distant wadis. She had left these parts suddenly without any particular plans to do so. She had gone to sleep that night and the next morning she set out on a new route that would not pass through the high terrain of the White Mountain region. She loaded her provisions and her few belongings onto her donkey and gave her small feet free rein.

Thamna had always lived with her mother. Amongst her earliest memories she recalled the two of them moving frequently from the wadis into the heights and back in search of pastureland that could satisfy the needs of their animals. Hearing talk of rainfall in a particular area, her mother would decide to head there.

Her father had died when she was a very small child. Her mother had remained on her own, raising her daughter and taking no interest in the men who came seeking her hand. For the rest of her life she lived with this young girl, never leaving her for an instant.

Sawwaada bint Khalaf had long been known near and far amongst the settled village populations because she came among them often to purchase what she needed and to sell the fiber she had spun from her own animals as well as the bounty that the mountains granted her at times: fine honey, wild thyme, mountain figs and the dark berries of the buut trees. Piling her own purchases from the village souqs onto the back of her donkey she would return to wherever the little family had made their home—which they only inhabited for a short time before moving on to another.

And then Sawwaada bint Khalaf lost her husband, Ali bin Hamdan. They were living in Raddat al-Rawgh on Wadi Qaabat. On that awful day it had begun to rain very hard. Ali was worried about one of the goats because it had not returned from pasture. The sky had gone dark as the fog sank over the land. It was already nearly sunset but he scaled the mountain anyway, refusing to worry about the rain or the possibility of a sudden onrush of water down the mountainside. When he entered Wadi al-Raqqas, Sawwaada could still hear his voice, a singsong that always calmed their animals down. Soon the strains of song died out, swallowed up by the thunder and the roar of the winds.

She stayed where she was, huddled over her little girl and trying to protect the two of them from the rain with nothing more than a blanket. As the night closed in and Ali did not return, she carried her child to a cave halfway up the mountainside. Next she moved all of their belongings into the cave. Its shelter kept them safe from the slashing rain and the heavy cold winds that she could feel piercing her body to the bones. She removed the child's clothing and wrapped her in dry things and changed her own clothes. She lit a tiny fire on a little pile of wood that she had found inside the cave. And then she sat in front of it waiting for her husband to come back. She was accustomed enough to his absences, his comings and goings.

But he did not come back. When the rain lessened and the clouds broke up Sawwaada bint Khalaf ventured outside the cave to inspect the surrounding terrain. From here she could see that the wadi bottoms were completely flooded. The loud tumult of rushing waters resounded from one mountain to another, fast streams of water surging in from more distant wadis and sweeping along everything in their path: trees, dead branches, animal corpses, rocks. Her goats were safe beneath the big sidra tree which the waters had not reached. This was high ground, a stretch of level plateau. She saw the donkey standing there stolidly, bare and wet, the rain having washed over him again and again ever since the downpour had started many, many hours before.

Day after day she waited for Ali to appear. But there was no sign of him. She ventured out from their shelter and tried to follow the path he would have taken through Wadi al-Raqqas. She found no traces of him there either. She called out his name repeatedly, shouting it across the mountaintops. Maybe he had taken a fall somewhere and broken something; and now he was not strong enough to move. She listened hard, hoping against hope that he would answer. She searched the slopes and plateaus and ducked into all of the caves she knew. She moved from one wadi to the next, peering into every one of the water-filled basins and crevices. But she did not find him.

Finally, she walked to the cluster of villages nearby and asked there. She told the village folk what had happened and everyone went looking. Surely one of them would come across him. But after searching for hours they called it off. They told her to put herself in God's care; she must accept God's will and reckon that he had been lost forever. The village headman told her that legally she must wait four years. If he did not reappear in that period he would be considered deceased and then she could begin the four-month waiting period that was obligatory before she might remarry.

She didn't wait four years for him; she waited the rest of her life. Day and night she looked out for him. Perhaps, one night, he would be here, coming to slumber in her embrace. Or perhaps he would suddenly appear one morning, his face lighting up all the space around them. She would spring up from the gray ashes in which she lived and abandon her grief at this absence which had stretched on and on.

The little girl grew into an adolescent whose loveliness filled the emptiness wherever they might be. A young woman at the start of her life: a handsome face, and a soft, slightly gravelly voice. Every man who caught sight of her wished for her to become his lot in life. For her it would be a choice made by the heart. And then she saw the man. He plucked her heart from its cave and placed it in a locked cage.

Salman bin Abdallah had come to seek her hand. He had come from distant territory, his own birthplace. He had come alone and he followed her tracks through the wadis. He asked people for information on her whereabouts until finally he found her. She was not at home when he appeared. She had gone out to gather firewood and as she was returning she heard his voice speaking to her mother. When he greeted her, her heart skipped a beat but she hadn't a clue why. He opened the subject with her mother. Sawwaada responded as people in these parts typically did: she would give him an answer sometime later. When he had gone away she recounted their conversation to her daughter. Thamna was silent. But there was something she could feel in her chest, rising and falling, a something that seemed to be like joy and sadness all at once. The next morning she informed her mother that she would accept him.

As her lawful husband Salman moved in to live with Thamna and her mother. He had not organized a large wedding. He invited some relatives and friends from surrounding villages and he laid on a simple wedding repast for them. He settled into this nomadic life, spending his hours searching for pasturage like most of the herdspeople: the shaawis, as people called them, who were natives of the mountain ranges.

Only months after they were wed, Thamna's mother fell ill. And then it turned out that she was very ill. With her condition worsening rapidly they took her to the nearest hospital. She was in a fever for three days and on the fourth night, nearly at dawn, her soul welled up and departed, sailing away to hug the peaks wherever it might alight.

Thamna took the loss of her mother very hard. This trial was so severe, so painful, the grief so heavy, that she lost the baby she was carrying. The next months were dark ones. She could barely feel or sense anything. Her husband assumed all the responsibilities: he was the goatherd, the cook, the sole support to her on this earth. She did not get pregnant again. It was three years before she emerged from her debilitating grief and began to return to herself, bringing life back to the household with the sound of her laughter and the taawibehs that echoed across the plateaus. Happiness returned to Salman bin Abdallah. The world could not contain him for joy now that Thamna had been able to wrench herself from that dark canyon—the black void of loss.

But the fates were lying in wait for her as if they had no creature in the universe but her to plague. As if no one else deserved the woes and miseries of separation and repeated farewells. Once again she faced the worst blow of all, when she had to look upon the corpse of her husband lying beneath the samra tree on Jabal al-Manazil.

It happened in summertime. Wild bee hives had been particularly abundant that year. Salman was one of many who went in search of them. His first finds gave him strong hopes: surely he would net a good amount of honey this year. The honey produced by wild bees was especially desirable and people sought it out. This honey commanded a good price because even in a good year like this one, it was rare. Salman seized the opportunity: here he was in this fertile pastureland of Jabal al-Manazil, this chain of high peaks pockmarked with caves and covered in luqum trees and the large isbaqs, hydrangea bushes where wild bees liked best to construct their homes.

One day while trying to track a beehive that he thought must be nearby, Salman bin Abdallah spotted some bees at a water source tucked into one of the crevices that riddled these heights. He began to climb and finally he came upon the hive hanging from a large boulder. He would have to cut through the outer layer of the wild hive in order to get at the honey. As he was trying to do so he slid on the sloping ground, his foot slipped, and his body plunged into a gorge.

It was already very late in the day; he should have been home long ago. She went out to look for him. Her dog scampered ahead, sniffing for his scent and led on by it. His nose told him that he was getting close and he ran faster. He came to a stop at a small rise and let out a series of barks and howls. Her heart seemed to detach itself from her body; she ran toward the dog and toward a body that was visible below. She found him curled up like a fetus around the vessel of honey he had managed to grasp in the moment before he fell.

These places had been her refuge, her sources of safety and repose. Now they seemed hostile and savage terrains, spaces of loneliness where a silent gloom gathered thickly over everything. Close to her small herd she slept in the embrace of this impermeable terror and grief: she who had seen death, a beast of prey poised to ambush her loved ones, one after another, leaving her alone to walk these lands side-by-side with her memories. In her head she carried fragments of their lives, preserving their stillness along with their quick liveliness, their pains and joys, their voices which now and again exploded suddenly against the walls of her skull. Sometimes she heard them so clearly and closely that she could not help but whip round—wherever she happened to be—as though to pinpoint where those voices were coming from, at this very moment. And she cried. Crying was the only way she had of working to extract herself from the swathes of pain that wrapped her so tightly she could barely move, that kept her losses there looming before her. Then the tears froze and her eye sockets went dry, her face arid. She tried to summon back her tears but it was no use. She was truly alone now, she knew, except for the memories of those lost beloved people. These memories that kept watch over her and prevented her from dissolving into nothingness as she trekked through the wadis and forded the watercourses on the heights, singing her sad taawibehs, mourning those who had gone away. Life swept ahead of her like a solitary spring welling up in the midst of uninhabitable stretches of desert.

Azzan bin Said must have known instinctively that the folk of his village could not repress her story forever. Like all villages, his village gleaned and processed every bit of information that anyone might possibly hear—though sometimes the news was sparse. He was spending the evening with his friend Nasir bin Salim al-Hatati. Did you ever happen to see those eyes I've heard tell of? Soft eyes the color of honey? he asked his older friend.

No, I haven't seen those eyes. But I heard something about a herdswoman, people say she has the eyes of a real beauty.

Named Thamna?

Al-Hatati's grin was so wide that Azzan could see something of his molars. He spit out the tobacco that clung to his gums. He had some recollections; the story of Thamna tumbled out. This was the history that had made the rounds of the villages around here. Every time he opened up a chapter in this story, Azzan's heart opened up a wider expanse for her to inhabit.

In his imagination he would suddenly see her eyes sparkle. And then he would pause whatever he was doing. If he was driving he would stop his vehicle on the side of the road and stare ahead into a space where he could see nothing at all. Or nothing save her honey-colored eyes. If he was examining one of his hives, gripping a frame and pulling it out slowly and gently, he would see her there standing in front of him. He would close his eyes and stand still, hand still on the frame but unable to move, suddenly absent from the vitality around him as the bees jostled and buzzed in a cluster against the frame and some fled back inside the hive he had opened.

He would hold her memory there, close inside of him, as his usual bedtime approached—and then he would find himself unable to sleep. She came to him when he was praying and he couldn't keep track of how many repetitions of the ritual prayer he had completed. In the mornings her voice guided him along the paths. In the evenings her taawibehs bent over him, sentinels of his solitude.

This was a memorable year: the bees were especially numerous. They filled the hives, jostling closely together and ultimately leaving the boxes overfull. He began working on those hives where the bees had occupied ten frames. He had an open box ready, sitting on the raised platform he had built. He would set this new box on top of the existing hive and move five frames up there from the lower box to distribute the bees as evenly as he could across a hive now composed of two levels. This way he would avoid overcrowding and the inevitable swarm that would result in a much smaller hive. He monitored these bursting hives continuously, watching them closely and always ready to insert additional frames. He placed new wax base in them. In a day or two, he knew, the worker bees would begin to stretch and draw them out. After that the queen would lay more eggs, in the new frame this time, so that the hive would be ready to take advantage of the robust pasturage that would come with springtime.

He bought a goodly number of cartons of wax base and set them near the hives, inside a metal chest which also held ample empty frames that were ready for use. Moving the colony to Juba would be especially beneficial this year because he had managed to preserve the bees in good health through the winter and they would begin the new season's work with an abundance of energy.

Once they were there and he had settled into his accustomed spot, he devoted himself to treating his bees as was necessary to protect them against all the diseases that might possibly hound them. First he put the strips in place that would guard against the Varroa mite: one strip per hive, placed exactly at the center near the hatching area. In the days to come he would inspect the hives to check on how well the treatment was progressing. Hanging from the highest frames, the strips gave off a poisonous substance that killed whatever parasites had massed in the hexagonal cells to feed on the tiny larvae. The deadly poisonous fumes from the strips caused them to detach and fall to the base of the hive box. Azzan had to clear the hive floor of these pests so destructive to the bees. He swept them out onto the ground nearby. He left the strips in place for four weeks and until he could make certain that the new generations of bees were free of parasites. The Varroa were amongst the bees' mortal enemies, nourishing themselves first on the blood of the larvae and then seeking to consume the wings of the tiniest bees, those just hatched. If they lost their wings, naturally these baby bees were unable to fly. All they could do was to crawl along the floor of the hive and eventually they would die.

Each time he had applied this twice-yearly treatment, the Varroa's destructive energies were already evident and he could see the tiny mites multiplying in the hexagonal cells of beeswax and honey. They were about the size of lice and they travelled to the hives by clinging to the backs of worker bees returning from pasture. Once inside, they embedded themselves in cell after cell and began to multiply. But only recently had he started to use this treatment. Before that, he had witnessed the lively crowds in his hives decreasing day after day even though he could also see that larvae were hatching—enough larvae, in fact, to fill two whole new frames. Sad and feeling helpless, he had attributed the sudden decrease to a spell of extreme heat—or perhaps it was due to an earlier period of fierce cold. Meanwhile the Varroa parasites were destroying the entire younger generation.

And so he had lost many, many bees. Some hives had died off entirely. In other cases, when the epidemic strafed a hive the bees themselves knew they could not survive in their boxes and so they flew away, somewhere far into the mountains. After his belated discovery of this scourge he began treating the remaining bees immediately. He was astounded at the number of Varroa carcasses that piled up on the floors of the hives. The bees began to recover, to slowly regain their vigor. He put several afflicted hives together into one box, hoping not to lose them completely.

There hadn't even been any Varroa mites until recently. It was like many of the maladies that were assaulting bees in these times. The parasites had entered the country in shipments of imported bees. Most of the beekeepers he knew had experienced the agony of these diseases and had been forced to begin following more stringent procedures to keep their bees safe and healthy. Every week now he made alterations to his bees' treatments. Sometimes he would put a spoonful of garlic paste at the top of the frames. The next week he would immerse cotton balls in concentrated alcohol solutions. He switched between these two strategies, hoping for the best. His accumulating experience with beekeeping had taught him the usefulness of garlic: it inoculated the cells from many kinds of germs and pests and helped to restrict the population of Varroa. The fragrance of garlic enhanced the queen bee's egg-laying vitality, while the alcohol concentrate seemed to invigorate the bees in general.

All of this got him into the habit of cleaning the insides of the hives more regularly, ridding them of the awesome debris that this battle for the bees' lives deposited.

He also inspected the box bases closely and cleaned them rigorously. The wax moths liked to lay their eggs concealed in the little corners and crannies of the box. Even in that remote spot in Juba he found moths invading some of his hives. The weaker a hive was, the more ferocious were the moths, filling empty hexagon-cells with their eggs and spoiling whole frames completely. The moment he discovered moth caterpillars in a frame he had to take them out and burn them in a spot well removed from where the bees lived.

Whenever he gave some thought to these diseases harassing his bees he would recall the words of al-Shayib Salim bin Ali. Every time the old man had discovered new diseases on the nearby trees or in animals, he would ask whoever was with him: What is coming to us from over there? All the disasters, they're coming from there, and all we seem to do is to fling open our country's doors to all the evil that comes in—and it's bigger than any good that comes in.

Azzan stayed in Juba for a month and a half, leaving his campsite only to buy what he needed and returning to home base as quickly as he could. Sometimes Bint al-Saab or her husband came by for a visit. In the evenings he waited to see what company the desert's bounty would grant him. He would hear the rumble of the Bedouin woman's vehicle. Occasionally, she showed up to spend a few hours with him. She would have rubbed scented oils into her long jet-black hair. The fragrance washed his lungs clear of the dust of days gone by that had piled up inside of him. The muted tinkle of the bangles on her wrists was as soft and low as her whispery voice, which he could barely hear. Her body undulated as though it were floating on the sea. As he lay somewhere between sleep and wakefulness she would go away, tiptoeing out, thinking he was asleep as he listened to her steps and then the gradually fading squeal of her car.

His friend Nasir bin Salim al-Hatati got in touch to ask him how he was keeping, and probably to reassure himself that Azzan was all right. They exchanged news. Azzan had never been away from the village for such a long period as this. Azzan told him exactly where he was located. On the spot, al-Hatati decided to come and see him. He would bring along their friend Abdallah bin Hamad.

A few days later al-Hatati phoned again. They were on their way, and in fact they were almost there. Azzan came outside and walked to the main road to welcome them. When he had guided them back to his tent, al-Hatati showed some amazement as he saw how his young friend was living. He began asking all sorts of questions about the conditions here. Azzan gave him detailed answers, and both of his friends were shaking their heads in wonder at his ability to stay in a place such as this for as long as he had.

That same evening Hamud bin Ghabish phoned Azzan to say that he would be coming by around half past eight to pass the time. Azzan hadn't told him about his friends' planned visit and he didn't say anything now. He left it as a surprise—nor did he tell these old friends of his what he and Bin Ghabish had agreed on.

He prepared a fine meal of fried meat and roast chicken. He brought out a jar of baram honey for the occasion—the finest Omani honey, produced from the blooms of the sumar trees. Everything was ready minus the final touches. At a quarter past eight he heard the sound of the Bedouin's vehicle stopping near the sand hill and then his voice calling out as he approached.

The Bedouin was astonished to see these two friends sitting there with Azzan. He rebuked Azzan for not alerting him: he would have wanted to be ready to do his duty as a host. He invited them to come to the compound the next morning for an early meal. He wouldn't listen to anything about anything until he had secured their promise to come.

As the evening darkened they swapped story after story, each one casting the tales he had to tell across the sands where they sat. At some point they heard the sound of a motor. It came closer and stopped at the foot of the rise. Moments later the motor started up again and the sound of it grew gradually fainter as the mysterious vehicle dissolved into the darkness.

Abdallah bin Hamad could hardly keep himself from jumping into his own little truck and following the mystery motor to find out who had stopped but not stayed. The Bedouin gestured at him firmly to sit down again. Your friend's guests—they don't like to find a crowd, Bin Ghabish said, as he gave Azzan a wink. Azzan showed no sign of the agitation he was feeling, neither displeasure nor pleasure. For as long as these friends had known him this had been Azzan's way. You could never tell from the expression on his face whether something was right and true or whether it was utterly misplaced.

On the morning his friends left to return to the village, Azzan accompanied them as far as the main road. He promised he would be with them again soon. He had to get through some remaining work on the bee colony and then he would take some sort of break for a few days, away from the bees.

He stacked new supers atop the hives of his colony—now twenty hives, each of them holding two layers of frames. He could tell that it was time to begin dividing them, forming new hives. He placed an order with Gunter Honey, Inc. and he secured one hundred new young queen bees. He kept as many of them as he thought he would need and then announced by SMS that he was selling the extra queens, setting the price at three riyals per queen. He got so many responses that within two days he had sold the last of the lot. He got more messages still, urging him to come up with more queens, which spurred him to repeat the experiment, working to produce more queens.

He hears barking. It's coming from the edge of the plains but the sumar trees cloak the sound. A muffled barking; it must be reaching him from a long way away. He stands still, listening intently, hoping he can make out exactly where it is coming from, and that this will tell him how to get there. The barking goes silent and then starts up again, the sound repeated time after time but at more distant intervals. He goes on listening, hoping to hear the bleating of animals, or singing, but there's nothing to hear beyond the barking of a dog somewhere in the distance.

He jumps into his vehicle and drives in the direction of the barking. He is certain now that the sound must be originating no more than two minutes' drive away. He makes his way through the grove of trees, following tracks that someone has already made, though at certain points he shortens the distance by breaking a new path. He stops and shuts off the motor so that he can listen for the barking. He wills it to return, to come to his ears once again.

There it is, a white dog with black spots covering its body, standing on a large rock and barking. This is not the herdswoman's dog. So it wasn't her. It must be one of the other goatherds, moving their animals from Wadi Haam to Wadi Mansah. Passing along here he gave himself some moments of rest beneath the slab of rock. A few dates, two tiny cups of coffee to help him go on. He might have a long path ahead of him before reaching his destination.

This is real madness, Azzan tells himself, amidst his inchoate thoughts. That I still cling to the idea of hearing her voice, or expecting to see her form coming towards me from that clump of trees. What has happened to make my heart tremble like this? I don't even know her—not at all. The only thing I know is her story because I heard it from al-Hatati. That's all—but here I am, ready to follow her without a care for anything I might have in this world. She disappeared all of a sudden and she took something of me away with her. She left me incomplete. And I think she must have planted something else, something entirely new, in me—something I haven't ever known that leaves me feeling I am somehow becoming whole even if I don't know how it's happening. Some of the fog I always sense inside of me has lifted and it has brought all of me out here, from within that blur. It must have been her, then, who carried me out of my long drunken oblivion—but if only she had not! Ahh, this land, it is this very place that has driven me to her—but where in this land will I find her? And then, if I do find her, what will I say to her when I know very well that she doesn't like to get close to anyone? This mountain jinni-woman—she is like the witches whose voices lure young men into the deep wadis where they are gone forever. These witches whom the youths follow, stumbling on until they fall into the deepest crevice possible—out of love, as victims to the jinn's enchanting melodies.

On the first days of April, the sumar trees' buds began to open and the whole area around him was perfumed with the distinctive aroma of those pearl-like flowers. It was only a few days before he could smell the same scent in the hives themselves whenever he lifted the lid off one of them. The new scent told him that in preparation for the new season, he must clear the hives of old honey and leave them ready to fill with the new honey which would be infused with the scent of the gum-acacia blossoms.

The honey he removed he poured into a container with a strong and tightly fitting lid. It would be of use as spring turned into summer and the heat intensified. Flowering plants would wilt and die and there would be little left for the bees to graze on. He would have to replenish his hives with this preserved honey. He would knead into it the natural pollen that he bought periodically from the store that sold beekeeping equipment and supplies. This was one of the difficult stretches of time for beekeepers. Every year some of his beekeeping friends tried taking their colonies south, all the way to the Dhofar region, since precisely at that time of year it would be entering the monsoon season which would last for three months. Grasses and shrubs would sprout and shoot up, the buds would open, and the land would become a mass of green as far as you could see. By the time the fog lifted and cleared, the grasslands and mountains would have been transformed into colorful carpets woven out of the flowers these species produced. The bees found plenty of fertile grazing there and they would grow and multiply.

At one point he had wished he could find an opportunity that would take him to Dhofar. At that time, he had not yet moved his colony, until he moved it to Juba. The summer season had been an endless stretch of exhausting work that brought him to the brink of collapse; and whatever portion of his bees he managed to rescue from the heavy heat might well be decimated by the red wasps that were inevitably thick in the air at that time of year. They fed off the dates on the palm-tree tops—those wasps with no occupation whatsoever other than hunting bees. The wasps would lie in wait for them like snipers as they exited the hives heading for pasture, and then would pick them off.

It had tired him out, trying to stay one step ahead of these perils, trying out whatever stratagems he could think of when in fact he never knew what to do or how to manage it all successfully. Around the colony he would lay trap after trap for the wasps, feeding them on leftover scraps of fish since its odor was particularly attractive to these sorts of insects. Hundreds of them went straight into the traps every day and perished; and yet there were always many more to replace them, hovering constantly around the colony.

He searched out their nests in the mountains nearby, following them as they headed home after emerging to find sources of water. He found their nests and destroyed them; he smeared poison around the doorways into their tiny homes; he ended their lives. But big swarms of wasps could come from further afield. He could not mount surveillance over all of this vast area in an attempt to rid these sites completely of wasps' nests. He wished he could find a spot near home that was wasp-free but the creatures seemed to be everywhere in the vicinity of these mountain reaches and the appetizing date-palm groves. He must consider moving his colony to Juba or else he must take them south.

His apprehensions about going to the very south of the country—along with his wariness about the likelihood of losing his bees if he stayed at home—outweighed any arguments that might keep him from going to Juba. Although what he had heard about the stunningly lush pasturage of Dhofar was attractive, the monsoon rains there could be very heavy, sometimes continuing for days on end. Such storms could lead to hunger so extensive that bee colonies might turn on each other, he knew, attacking competitors because they were not capable of flying far enough to locate the sustenance they needed. Scores of bees would die. One year the rains had pelted down incessantly for more than a fortnight, and many beekeepers in the area had lost their colonies. The hives were inundated. They filled with standing water and rotted, and the bees sheltering inside died. Instead of returning home with active healthy hives, the beekeepers came back with empty boxes which were themselves eaten away by water and rot.

Every year, the Ministry of Agriculture generated new regulations that put more of a stranglehold on beekeepers who wanted to relocate their hives temporarily to other parts of the country. The regulations obstructed free movement and Azzan knew all about the risks his friends had faced when, despite these new rules, they travelled to other parts of the country because they did not want to lose the resources they had worked so hard to build up and maintain. These circumstances, what he knew of them, blunted his own will to do whatever he could to nurture his bees. After all, by nature he was the sort of person who didn't like having to move around any more than necessary. Hearing the stories of what had happened to other beekeepers left him feeling anxious and hopeless. He had thought there was simply nothing that could be done. He had heard that one beekeeper's whole colony had been set on fire because he didn't have the proper permissions to transfer his hives to another location. Or maybe the story was that he had placed his colony in a site that had been ruled off-limits to beekeepers.

Now, and here, successive waves of bees began to emerge from their hives and to fly off in the direction of the thickly flowering patches in this area. Since early morning he had been watching the activity going on in the hives as the bees came back and flew into the openings that allowed them to leave and return to the hive. He saw armies of bees bearing tiny globules of pollen. Day by day the frames filled with the honey these worker bees had been making. Within a fortnight the bees were beginning to secrete wax around the frames—it was their way of announcing that the honeycomb was complete. It meant that the worker bees had masticated the honey over and over, and had removed any excess moisture. It was still early in the season. This glorious abundance meant he could remove and clarify the honey produced in these hives more than once this year, yielding the greatest possible harvest by the season's end.

He had brought his honey separator with him. Al-Hatati and Abdallah bin Hamad and a Bengali worker they knew came to help him. The four of them began before sunrise, working in pairs. Azzan and the hired worker pulled the honey frames carefully from the hives and set them into empty boxes. When the back of the truck was full of boxes they drove the load over to where Abdallah bin Hamad and al-Hatati were waiting, ready to remove the honey.

The season was a bounteous one. They worked two long days to remove all of the honey. His harvest was nearly 1200 kilograms. They filled all of the honey barrels they had—those enormous stainless steel containers. The honey would rest there long enough to allow the moisture to evaporate and then they could transfer it into purpose-made glass jars.

The honey season was over for the year. Summer arrived with its anticipated flaming heat. Azzan bin Said meant to move his colony to a secure spot, a well-shaded one still within his farm. But he and his friends were also set on making an excursion into the mountains. Abdallah bin Hamad in particular wanted to go in search of wild honey. So they postponed moving the hives until after their return from the heights near the village that was home.

Chapter Four

From sumar tree to sumar tree
my longings sent me wandering
a live coal in my depths

AT THAT EARLY HOUR ON a summer morning the sun's rays fell at a slant across the mountain plateaus of Aqabat al-Nakhla. It was still early summer, before the heat would become truly overwhelming, which would likely be in the last ten days of June. Water welled up amongst the pebbles and trickled into a small shallow basin interrupting the dry ground. The fresh gurgling sound of it punctuated the profound silence here, as the water filled the basin with the cold sweetness of a night strafed by the rising summer winds known around here as al-Kous. Overflowing the basin, water poured over soft sands that were still pliant with the night's dampness, and dropped into a stony expanse that covered the valley bottom. Were it not for this solitary and tiny spot where the water gushed from its underground source, there would be no trace of moisture anywhere nearby. It was such a dry area, and over the past winter the rain had been especially scarce.

In the yielding sand just a few steps below the rocky basin, tiny bees bobbed up and down in a joyous dance incited by the sweet water source's very existence. Growing still, they stuck their tiny tongues into the wet sand and drank. The minute bodies rose into the air and hovered and then flew towards the peak of the eastern mountain range which formed the border where Wadi Waala ended and Aqabat al-Nakhla began. They followed a path so straight that they appeared to be attached to their destination by threads spun from the glinting morning rays. Their little wings sparkled and glistened. From a distance, they looked like pearly winking stars piercing through the motes of dust suspended in the atmosphere at this high elevation.

Dancing across the sand and flying alone or in groups as they raced each other to the water, the wild bees drank as much as they could hold and carried their prize to the hive they would have built in a concealed spot near the summit. They had to complete this race before the heat grew any heavier. Just before noon the bees would grow quiet and placid, ceasing their energetic to-and-fro.

The blue sky was slightly dust-hazy but the air was clear. On the wadi's bank and above the spring stood two gaunt palm trees; in the middle squatted a broad lathab tree whose generous shade spread across the interval between the palms. Yellow stalks of mountain grass surrounded it as if to protect this site and hide it from any intruder who might come this way. And in fact, within that expanse of yellow there was hiding a man who looked to be in his forties. He was wearing a cotton tunic in a shade of yellow that blended into the flora. A dark msarr wrapped his head. He swayed slightly back and forth, his movements blending into those of the tall grasses around him. He made no sharp movements: quiet and still, he sat and stared into the soft sand, relishing the sight of these tiny creatures as they came and went and trying to map in his head their route to the hive that was their home.

With his companions he had arrived the evening before. They deposited their belongings at the base of the tree trunk; this spot seemed a good stopping place. But before the sun went down they climbed further, ascending the rise on the west side of the mountain. They decided to set up camp there in a spot open to the al-Kous winds. Despite the mosquitoes circling round and attempting to mount attacks to secure their meal of blood, the men slept deeply, uninterrupted by anything that could assail them here.

He woke up twice, changing position and checking the time on his watch. He sank back into his sea of sleep, comfortable in that deep silence there in the stony black Hajar range, twenty kilometers south of the village.

Now that it was morning, an alert readiness clothed his body. He sat erect, leaning forward slightly with his elbows on his knees and lifting his right hand to shade his eyes from the sunlight. He had crept into this spot early enough that the bees had not yet come down to the flowers they would surely seek. He was hidden well enough, he thought, that he could easily inspect everything in sight without the bees figuring out that he was there. He and his mates had come especially to search for that one hive—now that so many others had grown tired of looking for it across the surrounding mountains. Those who had gone in search of it had been looking in the wrong places. He was certain of it. What he had to do, before looking for it in this terrain, was to trace the route followed by these tiny creatures. Where were these bees coming from, and where were they going?

Sultan bin Hassan, now concealed on the mountainside, had discovered this particular bees' watering place as early as last April. Suddenly one morning, it had appeared to him. He had arrived here at about ten am when the sunlight was already beating down onto the entire area. He could not follow the bees' path at that hour of the day because the strong light concealed them as they flew. You could not know in what direction they were going simply by seeing them rise and hover in the air.

Sultan bin Hassan set the supplies he was carrying down under the lathab tree, lit a fire and made his coffee. Before praying the noontime prayers he had already cooked his midday meal. He would stay right here, he had decided, until the sun dropped westward. Around three o'clock in the afternoon he crept up to the basin but his eyes could not capture the flight path of any bee. The bees must have sensed his presence and changed their route. Some were heading west, dissolving into the white glare of the sky while others seemed to be flying almost vertically upward or perhaps were concealing themselves among the clumps of tall grass and then taking a spiraling route into the sky. It was impossible to keep them under close surveillance without the help of the early light which would reflect their wings. They were so tiny, and they flew so fast.

Sultan spent his fourth night in this spot searching for the beehive on the high plateaus of the nearby jabal. But every time he came close to a water source and thought that finally he was discovering a new path the bees were taking—a route different to the first one he had watched them trace—the bees would stop coming there to drink. He waited for a long time, but in vain.

He returned to the village. He told his brothers what he had seen. A few days later they all set off in search of the honey that he was so certain was there. They stayed out in the mountains for four days and looked everywhere. When they gave up, fatigued with the search, they told others where they had seen the water source and what it looked like and how they had truly tired themselves out on this attempt. There was not a single spot that they had not searched closely, they insisted—the caves, the trees, the rocks. They had turned the area upside down but they had not come across anything.

Abdallah bin Hamad heard about the water source but he didn't pay much attention at the time. Nor did he hurry to the location the brothers had described—as others did do. He waited until things had calmed down and people were no longer so interested. Until the beekeepers and bee-searchers had all gone home.

Wait.

That was all he said to his companions, who were urging him on. Everyone had been searching for this elusive pot of honey since the beginning of April, clambering eagerly through the wadis and across the mountains, scouring the rocky expanses and the crevices, always on the lookout for any bee they could detect in the air. But all of this commotion subsided as the heat got worse and summer overtook the mountains. No footsteps resounded on the desert paths now and there were no more campfires lit in the far-flung wadis. Stillness prevailed everywhere, a deep silence broken only by the cries and grunts of the few skittish creatures who inhabited these wilds.

Abdallah bin Hamad was well aware of this bee story. Whenever anyone recounted it (yet again), he would ask just how the bees had behaved in flight. He was assessing the situation at a distance; in any case he would not go until he knew that the time was exactly right. It was his unshakeable belief that people's livelihoods—the bounty a person had on this earth—had been parceled out an eternity ago, long before any human beings existed, before Creation. And here before his eyes was the evidence for it: every last man who had gone in search of that wild honey had returned empty-handed when he, Abdallah, was quite certain that it would be a simple task to find it.

On one of those late-June days when the heat had picked up, Abdallah packed his food and drink into his rucksack and turned his back to the village. He had accepted a quiet, self-imposed challenge: to find the honey and to not come back without it. He arranged the excursion with Nasir bin Salim al-Hatati, the oldest of his companions, and with Azzan bin Said. The three of them agreed to meet at Aqabat al-Ayn. Al-Hatati was late enough arriving that his friends had begun to worry about the older man. Azzan was on the point of urging his companion to go on ahead. But when he turned toward Abdallah and was about to speak, he saw al-Hatati below them, leaning on his case for a moment's rest and scanning the heights with his eyes.

A few minutes later al-Hatati reached them, panting. He had an excuse ready for his friends: he had been napping at home and he had slept a bit longer than he'd meant to do. Abdallah bin Hamad was adjusting the strap on his bag and his head was bent. He glanced over quickly at Azzan whose lower lip was twitching in a playful little smile. But with that swift glance from Abdallah bin Hamad's narrowed eyes, his smile vanished. No one said anything.

The three of them had left the village, each on his own, soon after the afternoon prayers. Now they continued together to Wadi Qaabat and turned toward Wadi Maqdisi, and then climbed the long mountain road and took the pass into Jabal al-Tayi until they had ascended high enough that they could look out over Aqabat al-Nakhla below them.

The sun was above the horizon, but only by about the height of an average person; soon it would sink. They sat down, breathing hard, tired and thirsty. Azzan fished some dates out of his bag and a bottle of water and they shared the sustenance around. The evening breeze was gusting up the slopes, still carrying the heat of the scorching day that was coming to a close.

From here one could survey the range of distant wadis and see the huge lathab tree over in Shaghaf Habib, tousled by the wind. They could see the sidra tree that sat at the opening into Wadi al-Malil; they observed the sidra's pale greyish-green color, its leaves drooping in the heat. They craned their heads and peered over into the wadi bottom. That was where they were headed. They studied the dipping disk of the sun: they knew they must descend quickly if they were to reach the site before it got too dark to see their way.

It was in the dawn gloom the next morning that Abdallah bin Hamad made his way into the thickets of yellow grass and hid himself. He sat waiting, patiently, watching the morning open little by little like a mountain wildflower displaying its petals. The peaks were still smothered in darkness; they looked like enormous, blue-grey wild beasts mounting watch over the wadi. And the luqum trees on the distant slopes had assumed the shapes of legendary animals observing him from their perches. From one of the peaks came the sound of the little mountain masmim bird, delicate and sweet like a long-forgotten song intoned by a herdswoman as she leaves her spot in search of new pasture. Swarms of mosquitoes rose in flight to dive into the darker thickets, escaping the light that alarmed them. He heard the buzzing as a large swarm of them passed close by. He sat as still as a stone. A few of the mosquitoes circled round his body and head and buzzed close to his ears before settling down to their daytime slumber. They knew that the heaviest, fiercest midday hours would soon arrive.

He had asked his companions to stay away from this spot and to avoid making any noise or commotion. His request was to al-Hatati's benefit. It meant he could prolong his dozing through the short interval between the predawn light and sunrise.

The only sound to be heard here was the trickle of water between the stones as it descended into the rocky basin below. It was still very early, too early for the bees to leave home. So he kept to his position, submitting himself to the light rustle of the grass stalks as the morning breeze played with them. It was a sound gentler, fainter, than the voice in his memory of a long-ago woman calling out to him.

Gradually the morning was emerging into sharp clarity as the threads of sunlight extended ever further, arcing downward from the eastern heights. A bevy of mountain doves alighted not far from the basin while another few, smaller and more agitated, hopped onto the little stones around the water. Five grey long-necked doves there were, feathers glinting with color. He found the sight of these mountain doves so pleasurable; their closeness gave him a sense of comfort and well-being. He studied their every movement as they came right up to the water and bent their necks to drink. They flapped their wings, suddenly uneasy at his proximity as if the smell of him had just reached them but they could not make out quite where the danger was concealing itself. They drank quickly and flew away in an agitated flapping of wings, following the line of the wadi and finally disappearing into the gaps between the rocky precipices.

By now, the light had arced across the mountaintops and was creeping downwards into the spaces between. He turned his gaze toward the summit above Wadi Habib. The light gave it more definition and sparkle, like the head of a helmeted soldier giving off flashes of brightness. The sunlight spread slowly and the shadows shrank, besieged and cowed, fleeing into the depths— those secure impermeable keeps where the light could not reach them. More moments passed and as the sun rose still higher, it sent its light further down into the wadi bottom.

Inside the thicket, in the tall grass stalks, a pair of eyes glitters. Eyes fixed on the water. The sharp glow of light hits the crystals of soft sand and is reflected back as a sudden flare of little stars glinting through drops of water. In seconds, he hears the drone of a single bee arriving to occupy this scene, hovering and circling above the pool of water, and then moving to the cache of large pebbles where the water spills out and trickles over the rock. The bee begins to hum loudly as if it is discovering this site for the first time and wants to test how safe it is and where bee enemies might be lurking. The bee goes on circling and humming for a few moments before alighting and poking its proboscis into the soft sand, sucking in the fresh water it finds there.

Abdallah bin Hamad senses that the bee is taking an unusually long time to drink—what seems an eternity, and his mind begins whispering to him that the bee itself has already gone away, and its tiny body is no longer actually perched there.

Had he not been able to see for himself the intermittent glint of its little wings in the flashes of light reflected on the sand, he would have believed this quiet little voice and its insistent, tempting whisperings and he would have ended his watch. But he did see it. He had even stopped blinking, so afraid was he of losing sight of it. He could feel a light burning in his right eye but he didn't pay it any attention. He couldn't ignore the tension he felt, like a physical pain squeezing his chest.

Tedium is a creature that at any moment can bring out its antennae, especially in a place as utterly silent and still as this spot, he told himself.

This is no bee—it's just a big water tank!

He was pleasantly surprised by this description his mind had come up with unbidden. He could feel his face relax. He saw the tiny shape shift position in the sand. He raised his eyebrows, but then knitted them in a frown. He could sense that it was about to take off. He narrowed his eyelids, the lashes held tense, to be able to see even more sharply. The bee flew away, taking a straight path. Far. He shaded his eyes with his hand and followed it as it circled higher and higher. For now, the reflection of the sunlight glinting on its wings kept it in his line of sight. The bee sailed over the first mountain rise, descended towards the wadi, and rose again, though not as high, in order to cross the second line of peaks and the breadth of the wadi from its eastern side until finally it scaled the heights on the far side of Wadi Waala. It was almost out of his sight when suddenly it entered a dark patch in the lighter blue of the sky. At the last moment he was able to keep his eyes on it, still following as it flew toward the far peak on the other side of Wadi al-Nimarat. There, finally, it vanished from sight.

He stayed where he was and kept perfectly still. He was waiting for more visitors to arrive. He knew now where he would head in search of the beehive, but he still wanted more evidence anyway. He got his binoculars out of their case and set them down on the ground. He would need them to survey that enormous distance the bee had just crossed. He took his hand off the binoculars very slowly and steadily, and then grasped them without taking his eyes off the water source. He brought them up to his eyes. He stared through the lens until the fuzziness of the image grew clearer. He pointed the glasses at the mountaintop, threads of light filtering through, where he had seen the bee make her way across a qafas tree growing on the edge of a crevice. Above it was an outcrop of white rocks, making the shape of a bow. He lowered the binoculars and once again focused his eyes on the nearby water.

Only a few moments after the solitary bee's flight three more bees arrived. They flitted and danced above the surface of the water, half-hidden in the thicket. They stopped moving and began to drink. One after another they flew off on their long path upward to the distant peak as if they were following a straight, taut thread through the sky.

He lifted his binoculars again and studied the bees as they circled above him. The magnified view made them appear so close that he could cup his hands around one of them. He fiddled with the focus until one tiny creature was as clearly outlined as could be, there just in front of his eyes. The bee pursued its path toward the heights as he refocused repeatedly to bring it closer, hoping to keep it in sight. He was humming a jaunty little song. He was very pleased with these binoculars that gave him such a clear view and so easily magnified these far-off spaces.

He had bought the glasses over in Dubai. He had another pair, slightly bulkier; with time, the lenses had grown cloudy. He thought of those binoculars as if they were an elderly person whose sight had grown weak over the years. Old age conquered everything—that much seemed sure—from living creatures to the gadgets we use. He had gone to Dubai with Hilal bin Aziz—or, as he was called in the village, Computer Hilal. That was because the fellow had a shop where he sold computers and such. He bought most of his merchandise in the wholesale market in Dubai.

Computer Hilal went to Dubai every week and sometimes more often. The distance from their village to Dubai was about 450 kilometers. Hilal had to leave early, before dawn in fact, in order to be there by ten-thirty or eleven am depending on how many stops he made on the way and how heavy the traffic was.

Abdallah bin Hamad had gone to the shop to ask Computer Hilal if he knew where binoculars were sold in Dubai. Yes, he knew more than one place, Hilal responded. If they went together he would take Abdallah to the shop with the widest selection. What persuaded Abdallah to come with him was his assurance: With what I can find for you, it will be possible to see a dust mote even if it's moving away over there across Jabal al-Dharwa.

It was wintertime. They left the village at four in the morning and stopped on the road when it was time for the dawn prayers. They didn't stop again until they reached Shannaas where Computer Hilal was in the habit of having breakfast at a particular restaurant. They went on without any further stops, crossing the border into the Emirates and then on to the outskirts of Dubai. In the city they disappeared into the computer souq and stayed until nearly one thirty in the afternoon.

It was nearly evening by the time Hilal could affirm that he had bought everything he needed. They went to the souqs in the older Dayra neighborhood. In the hunters' shop there Abdallah bin Hamad had bought the set of binoculars he was holding now, after having tried out many of those on display. Bringing one set up to his eyes, he had commented to Hilal: So many durbeens, so many telescopes, it could make you cross-eyed! Finally he had settled on this pair and he had had no reason since then to regret it. Every time he saw Computer Hilal, he thanked him again and praised the binoculars, as if this was the first time the two men had seen each other since that trip to Dubai.

He was convinced by now that the locations the would-be honey-gatherers had targeted in their search for the legendary honey were completely off the mark. He knew the way easily and now all he had to do was to get himself ready to scale those heights and search over there. Every detail of that terrain was already mapped out in his mind.

Abdallah's companions called him the Man for Tough Missions. His wiry build and physical capacities meant he was especially good at climbing these heights and moving through this hard terrain. He could scramble up the most forbidding slopes as though he were a mountain goat. All a man had to do was to draw him a map for the search, and then give over the truly rough, most inaccessible parts to him—this man whose friends had never ever heard him complain of fatigue.

Meanwhile, Azzan bin Said was occupying himself with gathering up pebbles he had scrabbled from the dust and piling them nearby, while letting his mind roam far away from their camp. He was waiting for his turn as he glanced at the empty water container that had to be filled. The drops of water rolling down the outside of the vessel glimmered and somehow became Thamna's eyes. He was longing to set out, to climb the peaks shadowing these wadis in search of her. Stretched out nearby, al-Hatati snored lightly, his dreams surely coated with honey. Azzan heard a voice—Abdallah bin Hamad's, as he emerged from his thicket hiding place to remind them sternly that it was high time they made the trio's morning coffee.

Azzan picked up one of the pebbles he had collected and tossed it lightly at al-Hatati's foot. The older man sat up suddenly and immediately stared at his watch. Looking around for Abdallah, he squinted into the sunlight. His eyes were red from sleep, like a pair of live embers. That's how his friends always described al-Hatati's eyes. Whenever he napped, even if for only a few minutes, once awake his eyes glowed red. You could not see the whites at all, but only the blood-red stains. Whoever saw him awake, or waking up, assessed their owner as a supremely anxious and jumpy man, always on edge. But in fact, no one could have steadier—steelier—nerves. His friends were always trying to rile al-Hatati but they always failed to stir up a reaction. When the tables were turned, though, al-Hatati could rouse the demons of anger inside their breasts and bring those devils out one after another.

But whatever he might say to their faces, al-Hatati had no feelings of resentment against his companions and they never felt any rancor towards him. They understood those waves of emotion in a man that would come and go, but which in any case deposited only affection in the heart as they receded. And after all, *they* were the ones who always provoked him first. And so, these friends had patience with him in equal measure to the harassment they visited on him. It was their heart muscles that seized up when his normally peaceful, even meek, state suddenly turned into its opposite—*the viper state*, Abdallah had labelled it.

Among this tight little circle of friends, the one who reacted the most strongly to things and turned the angriest was undoubtedly Abdallah. But he also had the biggest reserves of laughter and told the most stories—and the funniest. Abdallah's most wondrous feature was his unerring ability to choose his words so carefully. He came up with expressions and phrases that would never have entered their heads. Somehow he knew the perfect phrase for every occasion. He was as quick-witted a person as you would ever see, such a glib and engaging speaker that one couldn't help thinking he must be getting these phrases and sentences straight out of some book or other. In fact, his friends thought this was a rather weak point in his character but it wasn't one they could change. It accompanied him on every excursion they made together. But it didn't deter them.

Al-Hatati straightened up, in the spot where he had dropped off to sleep. Azzan was sitting in a relaxed cross-legged pose. The older man yanked Azzan's feet apart. Get up! he barked. We're not sitting around any longer. This rebuke all but released Azzan's demons into the air. Al-Hatati's snoring had already interrupted his own reveries. But he sent his demons packing and went along with Abdallah bin Hamad, who had asked him to follow behind.

Abdallah neared the water source. A bee appeared and began to buzz loudly, showing it was aware of this alien presence. After buzzing about some more it flew off. Abdallah couldn't see where it had headed. The bees had halted their flights here; for long moments, there was nothing. Azzan caught up with Abdallah and stood nearby. Abdallah told Azzan which direction he had seen the bees going and explained how agitated they would become as soon as they sensed a human in the vicinity. Bees are very intelligent and perceptive, he said; the more honey they have got to protect the more careful they are not to let anyone know where they live. Azzan raised his binoculars to survey the area and especially to study the direction his friend had indicated. He could make out the details of the distant jabal and its plants; they would need to inspect the whole area closely. By now the aroma of coffee was heavy in the air and Abdallah felt a twinge in his stomach. Of course—they had not yet had their breakfast. He crossed to the other side of the thicket where al-Hatati was making coffee. Azzan followed a few seconds later, after squinting at the sands for a few more moments—waiting, hoping, for the arriving bees to alight there.

Anyone on the hunt for mountain bees will need to find a few dry branches nearby—offshoots of an oleander or a qafas tree—and some dry sakhbar, the rushes light and thin, to provide kindling enough to light a fire and then to keep it burning hotly for the time it takes to make the proper mountain coffee that relieves thirst and improves a person's mood. They drank their coffee with a handful of dates and sat listening to Abdallah bin Hamad as he described in great detail the path the bees had taken and the way they had behaved, the particular drone they made when they were just above the surface of the water, their manner of flying and then their abrupt cessation of visits to this particular water source. These were all signs that the hive was surely very close by; but also, that it would be that much more difficult to find because the bees were so careful, so protective. They were defending their fortress against any living creature who might come into this area.

Bees did not generally stray far from the source of water they had found or stay away from it for long. That was especially so in these mountains, the Hajar. Bees would build their hive on the summit closest to the water. If they were to venture beyond that summit and its environs, they were not likely to cross beyond the next summit. But the extreme aridity of the wadis this year appeared almost impossibly forbidding even for bees. They might have to go a great distance in search of a source of water.

Abdallah bin Hamad knew all of this very well. He had experienced years of drought like this one and worse, and he knew how difficult it was in any case to mount a search across the mountain heights that Aqabat al-Nakhla joined. He remembered searching for honey in this area with his brothers, Sayf and Zayid. They had looked for three days. On the fourth day they had been on the point of leaving Aqabat al-Nakhla but that was the moment when they found the hive—very near to the spot where they had made camp. It was hanging on a branch of the lathab tree there. Yet, his brother Sayf always had one thing to say about Aqabat al-Nakhla: The honey there is monstrous. You have to exhaust yourself and you go through endless pain and trouble—and after that you may not even find it.

The brothers had located the watering spot where the bees drank on the edge of the thickets of tough hilf grass. Abdallah had been young and energetic then. From his brothers he learned the ways of the honeybee hunter, the methods to use, and the paths to take. On that trip they had not been aiming to stay in Aqabat al-Nakhla but when they came upon this watering place they couldn't leave. They had been planning to go to Manzilat Bint Saad and from there into Wadi al-Malil, and then they would ascend along the side of Wadi al-Kharif. But they had come in search of honey, after all. They couldn't let pass a source they happened to come upon. Honey in the hand was better than honey in the mind.

The bees, he remembered, had flown sharply upward on a nearly vertical path until they melted into the whitish sky, some of them veering off westward as they continued to fly upward. Sayf bin Hamad was watching the bees' movements closely; he was certain that the honey was sitting somewhere on the western peak. They divided the area amongst themselves. Abdallah took the descending slope from Aqabat al-Nakhla, and Zayid decided to go and have a look halfway along the pass. Sayf climbed to the higher elevation, parallel to Shaghaf Habib.

It was almost eight o'clock in the morning when they began their search. Abdallah would recall later how there was not a stone he did not turn over, nor a single qafas tree whose branches he did not inspect one by one, nor an isbaq whose stems and spikes he did not scrutinize, nor a crevice or boulder he did not peer into. But his inspections were all in vain. He made good use of his binoculars from time to time, making out the distant spots, but still he didn't find anything.

They had all come down around ten o'clock. The sun had eaten away their energy. They were exhausted and very thirsty. Sayf was first to arrive and he began making coffee. His brothers went back to the watering place and followed the bees' path with their eyes as the tiny forms flew upward and away.

We've got to search from the peak down, said Sayf, his mouth working a date. But they delayed until the hard sunlight would begin to dissipate. As the light slanted across the mountain range in the early evening, no longer beating down on them directly, the brothers observed the bees' path again as the creatures headed westward or took a more vertical route. What they saw convinced them that they were searching in the right place.

After three days of going up the western jabal as far as Aqabat al-Nakhla, searching in the early mornings and again in the evenings, still they had found no trace of this honey. The more Abdallah observed the bees the more he noticed a few of them going straight into the hilf thickets. When he came down to their meeting spot on the fourth day, exhausted from his search and knowing that his two brothers were still clambering along the slopes, he decided to search inside these thickets themselves and around the lathab tree, and also amongst the date-palm fronds on the banks of the water source where the bees had seemed to be heading. He was extremely careful. He knew to be wary of snakes and the pesky insects that infested these thickly grown patches. He reached the point where the palm tree cast its green fronds over the lathab tree. Together, the two species of tree formed a very dark shadow. In that dark shade, lifting and pulling away the fronds with great care, he found the hive.

He gave out a whoop. He called as loud as he could to tell his brothers where the bees' home was. Scrambling down from Shaghaf Habib, his tone betraying his exhaustion and irritation, all his brother Sayf could say was, Burn it ... burn it.

Sayf had known what he was talking about when he said the honey at Aqabat al-Nakhla was a nigh-impossible mission. There it was: only a few meters away from their camp. But before they stumbled over it, their discovery had to humiliate them, bringing them to a low point physically and mentally. Years later, here it was all over again—once more exhausting and disdaining those who had been here before them. They had returned to their villages after having expended all of their energy with nothing to show for it.

In the same location where he and his brothers had searched so long ago, Abdallah was attempting now to invent new routes. Perhaps, just perhaps, a new path would allow him to understand the ways of these mountain bees. But would he simply fall into the same crafty trap anew? With these two companions of his, was he simply wasting whole days and nights floundering in the wadis of Aqabat al-Nakhla and al-Nimarat?

This desiccated and forbidding place frowned eternally on life—on the barest notion of security one might try to hold onto. The fertile region below, on the other hand, beckoned to them in all its lush presence, offering pleasure and sustenance. Up here, this time of year was particularly harsh. There was no water running through the wadi, no green trees on the slopes. The sakhbar scrubs were dry and dead and the leaves of the mountain zufra shrub—its little purple flowers now dead and gone—had yellowed and scattered with the wind. The corncockles had withered and folded into themselves; the thorns on the branches jutted out like a wary hedgehog anticipating its enemies. On the western end of the wadi at the boundary separating Sumut Muhammad from Wadi al-Nimarat the last traces of bees had vanished. But since this was where they had suddenly receded from his view, the three of them must start their search from this point.

It did not come as any revelation that the bees had covered such an enormous distance to find a drinking place. There was no water to be found in the wadis but for that small spring in Aqabat al-Nakhla. And bees were very light and very swift: they could cross the entire distance in a matter of minutes.

These many years of experience had taught him that bees heading home took the most direct route, flying in a straight line. All he had to do was to sketch that long imaginary line in his mind and then mount his search by following it. But this would be no easy search, of course. How long now had he been hunting beehives in the wild? How much energy and fatigue had gone into it all? And then, often he had returned from the mountains empty-handed, as his brother had predicted. Anyone who knew these parts well knew how dangerous it was to go searching through these severe crevices. It took great patience: he must be as tenacious as any other creature who inhabited the jabal. In a single day he must make many ascents and descents, and he must be constantly watchful about every footfall, always alert to everything around him in these treacherous highlands.

He remembered searching for honey in Shaghaf Barakim, closer to their village. He had watched the bees as they drank water. And then with his brother Muhammad he began looking. He came upon the hive in a little cave that suddenly opened up virtually beneath his feet. He had crossed the narrow opening a number of times without even seeing it and his brother had searched the same area too. Neither of them had noticed the tiny aperture. Before they began their descent towards home, having given up the search, in one of those moments which seem the dividing line between hope and despair, Muhammad sensed something. He felt as though tiny insects were crawling beneath his feet. He descended one meter and there he saw the hive.

Now, on this excursion, the three of them ascended together and parted so that each man could cover a single area. At the summit stood a great isbaq whose stems and spikes spread across a wide area. Around it were dotted small isbaq saplings. Azzan had come this way before and he knew the path here very well. If his memory didn't deceive him, somewhere in the mountain crevices that he knew were all around here, he had seen traces of an old hive. Someone had taken the honey but left some of the wax behind.

He remembered whispering to himself: Sometimes bees return to their old homes.

He climbed on until he was standing at the giant isbaq and gazing into it. He parted some branches and peered further inside. Maybe he would see some sign that bees had been coming here. But all was utterly still and silent. He inspected the baby isbaqs around the huge tree but he didn't find anything. He mounted further, until coming to a crevice that split the mountain wall but he didn't see anything there, either. He searched the whole area until he was convinced that there was no honey anywhere in this particular part of the jabal.

Coming from distant summits, the wind picked up. Borne on the air, he thought he heard the faint strains of a taawibeh. The commotion and noise of the gusts of wind enveloped him and seemed to pick him up and carry him, as they buffeted the branches of the nearby shawaa tree. He listened hard, trying to make out from which direction that voice was coming across these expanses. He studied the surrounding terrain hoping he would catch a glimpse of her looking down from somewhere on the heights as she watched over her charges. Maybe—even—some of her goats were somewhere close by. Maybe, they could lead him to her. But had the wind really carried her voice to him, or was it just his imagination working too hard again? He felt a throbbing in his chest and a tiny quiet sigh moved through him like a little sliver of pure joy.

There on the summit he stood as still as he could, on the border between the Great Wadi and Wadi al-Nimarat, staring down at the lowest point where the two valleys bisected. There was a large qafas tree down there and its branches were dancing with the breeze across the little tributary feeding into the wadi, as the whorls of wind scooped and swirled the brownish pebbles there. He stood, his face turned now toward the watering place below. He could see the glinting light reflecting off the water's surface edged by the thick tall grass. He drew an imaginary straight line coming up towards him from that spot and then descending on to the qafas tree. He guessed that if the bees were still coming up here the honey must be in the area facing the mountainside at Wadi al-Nimarat. Their descent would take them in the direction of that tree. But he must really be certain before mounting a search. He headed down towards it, on his way inspecting closely everything he passed.

Likewise, every tree big or small that Nasir bin Salim al-Hatati encountered he examined top to bottom. Every stone or little crevice he stopped to inspect, sometimes using his binoculars so he could see features of the further landscape clearly. He stopped near a cactus and gave it a thorough examination but there was no hive there either. How beautiful this place was, he said to himself, a perfect site for honey! A person thinks about many things, and hopes for many more, and yet they do not come along. But there glowed in his mind a memory that lay nearby, enfolded in the village lanes.

Chapter Five

Your winding mountain paths call
a figure moving gracefully
glowing like a flower in bloom

ABDALLAH BIN HAMAD—WILDBEE EXPERT of the mountains who grew to manhood amongst these rocky heights—never hesitated to join any excursion his friends might suggest, even when these ventures were to last several days and involved trekking deep into the mountains. In fact, propositions like this simply intensified his gusto and resolve. It was almost as though he were returning to his childhood, sailing merrily back into the headwinds of his imagination at the mere suggestion of such a journey, ready to discover this world anew and with as much wonder as ever.

The perfumed aromas of the flowering plants on the mountains intoxicated him. They left him floating along in a kind of euphoria inside the magical kingdom formed by the mountain springs and the blooms on the wild trees brushing against his body. These slender branches, touching him, released scents that tumbled him into a state of ecstasy. All it took was seeing a germander-bush shoot close by. He would stop and breathe in the sharp scent as deeply as he could. He felt, more than he smelled, that perfume as it ran along the crevices of his skull and reached the very summit of his head. This jaada plant had given him his very earliest memory: going to Jabal al-Hadma, shimmying up the boulders that had looked so huge to a small boy transfixed by the precise, sharp outlines of the great White Mountain peaks. Up and up he went and all the while he was studying the many creatures around him. A bevy of sand grouse rose abruptly next to where he stood. They were so close that he started at the sudden flapping of wings as the birds fled to another locale. He could hear the trills of the shannaa bird at the top of Hadma, echoing now and again. He asked his older brother what that sound was and his brother described the bird's shape and the beauty of its eyes. Then he dreamed of capturing one of them, holding it in his hands, as he had caught a corn crake, wings flapping, in a trap he had set on their father's farm.

The safrad, with its downy feathers, the color so like that of the mountain rocks, brown speckled with black; this corn crake resembled the sand grouse in shape but made a different sound, a warble he found particularly pleasant to his ear. That safrad bird he had trapped remained in the house for days, since he had plucked out its feathers until it could no longer fly. And he had bound its legs together with a cord the way you would tie up a new hen somewhere until she had gotten accustomed to staying where you wanted her to stay.

But the safrad would never grow used to a human dwelling or be content there. He kept on bringing it grains and water, and for days on end he watched it. He could see the hens strutting over to where it sat and snapping up the grains from beneath its feet. And then he thought the safrad had finally gotten used to him and felt at home here with him. He sat beside it and observed its every movement. He loved the beauty of its eyes. Day after day he fed that safrad with whatever crumbs and grains and seeds he could gather.

Some days later he undid the knot that bound the safrad's legs. The bird walked like a human toddler taking its first steps. It walked slowly, stolidly, and nibbled at the ground. It approached the hens who tried to peck at it—to alert it that it was not a hen, it was not one of them, even though he had heard his mother call the safrad the hen of the mountains. His safrad walked slowly away from the hens, making lines in the dirt with his feet, testing the ground, discovering the place, now and then seeming to stare at the tops of the palm trees and at the tree branches lower down. The boy felt sure that his safrad was tame now and he left its side. He joined his friends at play, eager to tell them that his project to tame the safrad had worked. He stayed on with them for a while because he liked the game they were playing. When he came back at noon bringing four friends with him, the safrad was gone.

They looked for it everywhere—in the nearby tributary, among the date palms. They examined all of the trees closely. He tried to imitate its voice; maybe the safrad would hear him and respond. But it relied on its camouflage, blending into the brownish grey of the mountain, and it vanished. The memory of the safrad had always come back to him. Since that time he had hunted many safrads but he still felt the loss of that first one—how he had failed in his attempt to possess that bird.

Back then, he remembered how a piercing smell that seemed to be coming from a nearby bush had assailed his nose and startled him. The perfume of it was so strong that it brought him to a sudden stop. He had stepped on some branches and as they broke they released the aroma. He asked his brother what it was: a jaada plant, he was told. He picked up some stalks from the ground—they were still green—and sniffed at them. He was transported. All of a sudden it seemed that there he was in the sky, careening through it just as the small mountain hawks did. He loved to watch the hawks, the way they flew. Sometimes he had the thought, and sometimes he even said it to others, that in the deepest part of himself, he was like this bird. Both he and this hawk loved the summits and the new vistas opened up along the mountain slopes. He admired the hawk's lightness, how rapidly it could take off in flight and its skill at cornering its prey in mere minutes.

The hawk's eyes even looked like his! Surely, their souls had mingled. Whenever he caught sight of one he stopped whatever he was doing to stare at it. He studied its flight for as long as he could, following its movements as it soared into the distance.

The hawk did not come out of hiding unless it had spotted a likely prey nearby. Like the hawk, too, he searched here for prey. His eyes did not have quite the sharp eyesight of a hawk but he tried hard to be as familiar as possible with the terrain where prey tried to hide in fear of the dangerous presences hovering nearby. The game would go on, all the stages of it: each party knew its role well and played it perfectly. The hawk's role was to circle overhead and around the prey, waiting for the moment when its desired target would shift position and reveal itself. The prey's role was to remain absolutely still and silent in its chosen hiding place which in fact was perfectly visible if you knew where to look. The prey was always poised to slip away in the instant when there was no other choice left to make. His role was to search everywhere in this scenario for the hiding place—or the place of the hidden. To become another hawk, waiting, spying out the precise location, before homing in for the attack.

The hawk screeches and the slopes carry its piercing sound far. He smiles, squatting on the slope-edge of the jabal as if he too is ready to take off in flight, to chase after the bird that he will corner. The hawk soars upward and suddenly vanishes into the blue. This is the moment when the bird will swoop and pounce. The prey understands it all perfectly; wings trembling, it beats against the shawaa tree branches, a few feathers falling through the air from the trauma of colliding into the tree. This time, it was one of the sand grouse he had been following with his gaze as he awaited the return of the soaring celestial figure whose sharp claws would close around the sand grouse's body.

The sand grouse had all but disappeared behind the nearest slope when he saw the hawk come down like a bullet-shot oblivious to matters of mercy. With almost unbearable lightness and swiftness it landed on the sand grouse and dug its claws in. The bird fluttered and jerked trying to break away. Its soft feathers scattered, gusts of breeze carrying them here and there on the jabal, announcing to any creatures living nearby that the game of chase was over.

Ever since childhood he had watched these hawks circle overhead, or sometimes hover near to where he and his family lived. The hens were the warning sirens; they put the entire place into a terrific flurry. No sooner did a hawk so much as pass their line of vision than the hens began their ruckus, enveloping the dwelling and indeed the whole area around it in their loud and continuous squawks as though they were calling out to each other, passing the warning from one to the next to beware of the mortal danger overhead. The women would run out of their homes, screaming as well, swinging their arms overhead and waving their hands around in hopes of alarming the hawk enough to send it away. They had to maintain their vigilance at such moments, keeping watch in every direction lest the hawk try to descend suddenly and snatch its hoped-for prey.

Much of the time the women's hue and cry was successful, but at other times the hawk persisted and struck with no warning. There was no predicting its comings or goings, when it might carry off a hen in its claws and not stop until it reached a distant peak where all the women's shouting and the hens' squawks would make no difference whatsoever.

Once, as he made his way through the palm grove he came upon Asmaa bint Nawfal, wife of Nasir al-Hatati, as she plunged forward, moaning and shrieking, having come out of their enclosure on the jabal side of the village. She was trying to rescue her hen, assaulted by a hawk. This particular hen was so fat and heavy that the small mountain hawk could not lift it and carry it away. But he got his claws into the hen as it kicked and scrabbled at the air under his feet. Every time the hawk tried to take off, clutching the hen, the bird got a little higher and a little further, but then it fell back to the ground.

Asmaa bint Nawfal didn't give the hawk any time to work on escaping with her hen. She ran straight over to it, her shrieks filling the air. She charged at it like a bull who has just managed to break out of its pen. The hawk did not budge, did not give in to this show. She came closer, a long stick in her hand, and when she whacked the bird, it finally let go and shot into the air and beyond her reach. Asmaa bint Nawfal picked up her hen, bleeding from the wounds left by the hawk's claws. Her face went dark red as she cursed the hawk, calling him the worst names imaginable. The blood ran hot from the hen's body and Asmaa's tears ran with the blood as she stood there weeping and howling.

The germander produced a mood that Abdallah bin Hamad had experienced only in the mountains. He had only drunk tea flavored with jaada on a wild-honey excursion. Reaching the spot where he intended to make camp he would immediately search the surrounding area in hopes of finding green jaada branches. He would cut down only a few. This would suffice for several days since germander tastes bitter if one uses too much. Half a stalk in the teapot was just right: clear red tea with no milk, giving off the scent of jaada. His jaada tea was the best; he sipped it slowly, keeping the pot on the embers to stay warm until he had poured and swallowed the last drops.

Jaada was not only about states of mind, though. He understood well its medical importance, described by the ancient herbalists in their pharmaceutical manuals. It was often prescribed for stomach pains and bloating around the intestines. He knew it had proved useful in cases of snakebite and scorpion poisoning: he himself had used it for that purpose. He boiled the stalks and gave the victim the broth to drink, placing the softened stalks directly on the sting. They lessened the pain and encouraged the wound to heal.

Experience is the ultimate proof, as they say, and in this case he had had the experience. He and his eldest brother Sayf and their uncle Abdallah had been heading for Wadi al-Ays at the time, nearly fifteen years ago now. They stayed overnight in the wadi and a scorpion stung his brother on the hand. It was a big yellow scorpion; whenever the memory of that accident came back to him, he would say to his listeners: The scorpion was bigger than the palm of Wad Marzuq's hand! A big yellow scorpion and its poison seemed to spurt from the color yellow itself. Sayf, lying down at the time, screamed and jumped up and danced about in frenzied pain. It was just before dawn. The scorpion had buried itself in his sheet, which he had immersed in water hoping to cool the breeze which blew so hotly in June. The coolness attracted the scorpion and it sheltered itself in this little oasis away from the heat, burrowing into the folds of the wet fabric that was wrapped around the boy. The yellow scorpion snuggled in further and further and stayed there. No one knew how long it had been there. When Sayf turned over in his sleep it sensed the movement and pounced.

Sayf was shivering hard from the force of the sting. The yellow scorpion's poison is one of the strongest these mountain reaches held. Although it was rare—a subspecies that humans did not often encounter—on that night the fates hurled it there in a bid to silence Sayf bin Hamad's light snoring. At least that was what his uncle said, teasing him once the pain had dropped considerably. Hearing him scream they had started from their sleep in fright. As soon as their uncle understood the source of it he said to Abdallah, You watch him, I'm going out to find some jaada. They had all been in these parts before and they knew what grew here. Very soon their uncle was back with some green germander branches. As his nephew writhed in pain Uncle Abdallah lay the branches on a flat stone, picked up another stone, and pounded them into a pulp which he scooped up and rubbed into the wound. In a few moments the pain began to lessen and Sayf's trembling grew quieter.

Abdallah was shaking out the sheet in which his brother had cocooned himself. The big scorpion fell out and began to scurry away. Training their torch on it, Abdallah chased the scorpion and finally killed it. His brother was still gripping his bitten hand tightly in his other hand but now he was well enough that Abdallah could joke with him. If you were to spend a whole year searching for a yellow scorpion like that one, he said, you probably wouldn't find it—but this one came right to you, right into your bed!

By the time the dawn light was shimmering around the lower peaks the pain had receded almost completely. It was an excursion that Abdallah would never forget. That was the same trip in which they found more honey than their containers would hold—despite the disturbance caused by the sting of the yellow mountain scorpion.

There were people who had died from the strong poison emitted by those scorpions. He had heard this in the tales told by other honey-gatherers, and by hunters and people who collected wood on the mountainsides. The unfortunate victims had not been savvy enough to know how to quell the terrible pain or that it was necessary to treat these stings immediately. But Abdallah bin Hamad also believed that it had to do with a body's ability to withstand such an attack as this. Some people recovered and others did not. And not every scorpion poison or every sting was like every other one. Not all of them were fatal. Some of them were barely even painful.

And—there did exist those human beings who had some in-born resistance and simply did not react to scorpion toxins. Al-Shayib Salim bin Ali—Greybeard was how he always referred to himself, when telling stories about his own experiences—did not feel anything when a scorpion bit him and it had had no effect on him. He was frequently exposed to these stings but all he felt was a pinprick. Afterwards he might discover that indeed it had been a scorpion.

When old Salim bin Ali was still a suckling babe—as he always told them—his mother would go looking for scorpions, kicking at rocks and pebbles and turning over heaps of dried palm leaf in the search.

When she found one, she would pick up a date-palm leaf and use its bristly surface to puncture the scorpion's back, pushing the needles all the way through until she had pinned the scorpion to the ground. The critter was wriggling fiercely but it could not shake off the palm needles. His mother opened her tob and squeezed her breasts until drops of milk appeared on the nipples. She squatted over the scorpion so that the milk fell onto the scorpion's back and eventually the scorpion turned white, in a deluge of mother's milk. She left the scorpion wriggling there for some time. When the milk had dried up she picked up the whole thing, along with the palm leaf bristles, and held it underwater until the insect was dead.

If my mama hadn't done that I would have come back a corpse just from one single yellow scorpion bite, declared old Salim. This was the inevitable finale to his story; he was absolutely convinced that his mother's ritual had preserved him from scorpion bites throughout his life. After all, he had lived all of these years without ever knowing any of the pain that these dangerous stings caused. He had never had to dread the sight of a deathly yellow scorpion.

Perhaps it was also the luck of children who are born in the summer when there are lots of insects about. Children born in wintertime, on the other hand, would always have to endure the pain or at least they must be on guard throughout the summer months, year after year, carefully searching their clothes and closely inspecting everything around them to make certain that no scorpion was huddled in any folds or crannies.

Later on, Abdallah learned about a small scruffy shrub called the Scorpion Tree. But it was rare to find one even in the mountain ranges where it grew. The stalks were thin and sticky; it had large round leaves which blanketed the ground when autumn came, and it gave off no discernible odor. He did know that this great plant was miraculous when it came to treating scorpion bite victims. It was so effective, so quickly, that the victim was left wondering whether the pain had even been real. That plant—you chewed it to a pulp and applied as a salve to the wound—surely held some great mysterious secret!

Even if it was rare Abdallah knew this shrub well. He knew its characteristic shape and how tall it grew. He had learned about it first from his brother. Walking along the wadi, they came to a dense green patch. The ground was soft here—it was damp enough to be muddy—and so there was a lush thicket of reedy khasht growing. The stalks with the rounded white grain-like ears at their tips grew high. Within that woody thicket of khasht, the Scorpion Tree grew, the small, white hairs on its leaves clinging to the khasht stalks.

Sayf had stopped and peered into the thicket, examining the leaves. Yes, he told Abdallah, this was certainly the Scorpion Tree. Abdallah had heard of this species but he had never seen one. Since it was rare, Sayf cut a few branches off and stuffed them into his rucksack. Later, he would pound the branches into a soft, gluey substance to keep on hand for a time of need.

Then Abdallah bin Hamad heard of a spot near the village where the Scorpion Tree grew. He went and found it. He memorized its exact location. Now and then he would go and check to see whether it was still there. He went at different times of the year and always he found it thriving. A day will come when we'll need this, he would tell himself.

And he did need it on one particular day. That was the day a black scorpion stung his daughter Mayya. She was ten years old, this Mayya whom he loved to pamper and tease, calling her Mayyooo. When it happened he was coming home from the wadi. He had a favorite spot there, where he performed the afternoon prayers, and then he would sit down for a game of halusa with Miallim Khamees bin Suud, the Quran teacher.

Even from there, as they were moving the pebbles around the game, he heard her screaming. At first he thought it was just one of her usual wails—her brothers, who were older than her, must be ribbing her again. But this time her cries were longer and deeper. He realized that something must have happened and it sounded like she was in pain. When he got home she had her hand pressed to the spot on her leg where she had been stung. His wife told him it was a scorpion and it had happened just minutes before. Abdallah tried to calm his daughter down but it was no use. The pain must be very intense. He picked up some straw and rolled it over the sting, back and forth, reciting the healing incantation for sting victims and then the Fatiha. He repeated the opening verses of the Quran three times and followed that with the Chapter of the Elephant. When he got to the last line, describing the elephants' destruction in battle, *fa-ja'ala-hum ka-'asaf ma'kul*, he changed the words a bit. 'He left them like chewed-up straw' became 'He left them like cool water,' *fa-ja'alahum ka-zulal barid.* He repeated the phrase ten times and pressed the straw on the wound. He told his daughter to sit still and to stay where she was until he came back.

He found the bush there, its branches so long and heavy that they bent all the way to the ground. He cut off a few branches and hurried back. His daughter's loudest sobbing had subsided but she was groaning in pain. He put the branch tips in his mouth and worked them until they were mashed and tenderized by his saliva. When he put the wet mass on the wound, his daughter's moaning stopped almost immediately. The pain subsided and then went away completely. Mayya stood up and pranced around the place happily as if the sting had never been.

He also remembered, as a very little boy—and ever since—seeing the pot of honey in his mother's room. Mostly it was kept inside an old mandus studded with brass nails. When he really longed for that taste he would open the chest and take a little of the honey, scooping it out of the jar and savoring it slowly in his mouth. He was transported by the taste and the aroma of mountain flowers that scented it.

Now, whenever he happened to catch sight of a young mhadhidi plant on his route, with its small yellow flowers already open, he would close his fingers around one of the flower-laden stems and bring it to his nose. The fragrance broke over him: the smell of all the time that had passed since then, the smell of the past, of his mother's room, the aroma of the mandus's old wood, the concentrated oud oil she kept in there along with the fragrant pounded petals of the myrtle tree, protected in a cloth sack, the tin of shurana with its saffron-like blossoms, the perfume of his mother's clothing, which she also kept in the mandus. And then the smell of the aged honey they called asal hawli. It sat there year after year, thick and sticky, its color turning as black as pitch.

Every bloom on a mountain plant had its unique savor. His insides knew each distinct nectar from which the bees made their honey. He knew all of the trees and shrubs and grasses and exactly how they bloomed as intimately as the herbalist knows all the substances and fragrances in the shop. As a child—and then forever after—he scooped up handfuls of flower petals and crushed them to his nose, breathing in with his whole body, intent on inhaling the particular scent of whatever flower it was. He kept the bouquet imprisoned in his lungs as long as he could, storing as much of it as possible in the spaces of his body and his mind. This was his practice with every variety of flower, every species of plant, repeatedly until he could be completely confident that the fragrance would stay with him. It would sit in his nose forever; it would never leave him.

He usually singled out a particular flower for attention. There was the time he was standing next to a riyyih plant. The white, pearl-like flowers had just opened; seeing it, he didn't think he had been aware of this flower before. The stems were like the mountain shikkaa plants except that they didn't seem to have any thorns growing on them. They had mhadhidi-like leaves but these leaves were a bit stubbier. He patted the plant, rubbed and tousled it gently as though it were a sweet little creature that he wanted to tame and lure. He took a handful of these flowers in his usual way and sniffed them. The smell went straight to his brain, a pure and unfamiliar perfume. Different to the jaada. He was confused by this one, and startled; he had never stumbled across a basil bush. How could that be? It was only later that he learned its name: riyyih. After that, whenever he tasted mountain honey he could sense whether it was present—the particular zest of that little white flower in his gullet.

The winter rains brought him especially close to the flowers and fragrances that these myriad growing beings gave off. For him, a year in which the winter rains were heavy and constant was a gift: it meant going again and again to the places he knew and basking in these natural perfumes. In this season of the year, over the damp mountain crevices hung vapors that cradled the aromas of these savory plants. From early morning, the heady smells hung richly, densely, in the air. His only desire was to find an empty space big enough that he could lie down full length; and there he would stay, in harmony with the morning—one with the morning—observing the crawling insects and the tiny flies as they darted about, coming and going, made as dizzy as he was with the scent as they perched on the edge of one flower and then hopped over to another. There were so many of these tiny creatures: bees, and various kinds of other flying creatures, some of whom looked very much like bees. But they were larger and fuller-bodied and the droning sounds they made were different. Every species of flying or crawling creature had its own particular buzz or hum or chirp, its own pitch: grasshoppers, dung beetles, the little maqabir locusts so much smaller than the desert variety, tiny flies with multi-colored wings. Here he was one with the light and the smells; closing his eyes, he floated in the glorious festival that yesterday's rains had yielded.

He remembered watching his mother engrossed in preparing a little cup of honey into which she mixed in some shaynuz—black caraway seeds. She made this concoction for his father, who was very fond of these added ingredients. He believed they boosted the honey's medical properties. He had read it in an ancient book of herbal lore, *The Fruits of the Wayfarer*, a treasure chest of herbal and spice concoctions to treat every ailment. He kept the volume in a corner of the majlis where he and his friends gathered to converse and drink coffee, along with a selection of books on jurisprudence and poetry anthologies. From time to time he tried making one herbal remedy or another according to how their preparation and mixture was explained in the book.

Honey with shaynuz wasn't like any other taste on this earth. The aroma of the shaynuz wafted from his mother's frying pan as she toasted the caraway seeds before pounding them and putting them into an empty aluminum container for later use.

Chapter Six

In my face, you closed your doors
and deprived me
of your sweet tenderness

IN THE VILLAGE, HE HAD become known as Azzan Hilliya because he had become addicted to alcohol and especially to cologne. This was the same boy, the same Azzan bin Said as the man who now had a bee colony so substantial that people referred to him as Azzan the Beekeeper. But from time to time he teased his mates. Whenever he knocked on the door of one of those friends and a child came out to see who it was, he would instruct them to say to their father: Tell him Hilliya's here.

Remembering the state he had been in and all he had gone through did not appear to trouble him much now. He had gotten beyond it, after all. He had come to terms with his past and with the name by which some still called him—poking fun at him or worse, although usually only in a whisper or when no one much was around. Even some of the children—the most annoying boys of the lot—might sing it out as he passed by. Hilliya, ooh Hillhil! Azzan didn't pay much attention to these things he heard in passing. In fact, he would give the boys a little smile. It gave him a certain contentment to hear someone saying something that took him back to those ancient days at Zayid bin Marzuq's farm.

Just to the south of the village there was a plot of farmland ringed by barbed wire, surrounding a two-roomed structure. A verandah ran along the entire front of the house and overlooked the falaj below. Large quartz blocks had been set into the ground to form steps that led down to that irrigation canal. The site was called al-Quwayra. It was a fair distance away from the village lanes, perched alone and apart next to that mountain tributary and connected to the world of human beings only by means of the falaj. There was some greenery here but the plot was unsuited to agriculture because the steady rush of water had replaced the soil with sand.

Here in al-Quwayra Zayid bin Marzuq spent most of his time. He pruned the date-palms and the mango trees and quince bushes with their sweet orangey fruits. They all flourished; to an onlooker, his farm looked like a dense forest of towering trees. He had built a majlis outside the house where men could gather. It sat on the north-eastern corner of the property facing the jabal. As evening approached he would begin his preparations for the festivities to come. The essential ingredients were his oud, a bottle of whiskey, and some meat sliced into chunks that he stuck onto wooden skewers. He set the place up for the evening, unrolling a red carpet and placing cushions embroidered in red and black around its border. When everything was ready he would pour himself a glass to start the evening as he waited for his guests. They would show up one by one.

Years ago Zayid had retired from his job as a guard in the British Petroleum Company. He had spent the years of his young manhood there, moving from one company site in the desert to another and sometimes to their offices in Muscat. There, he grew accustomed to sharing his evenings off, either with his Omani colleagues or with the foreigners who worked there, Englishmen and Indians. Gradually he took to drinking. Zayid was the first to bring alcohol to the village, and the first to become addicted to it.

Coming home on his short holidays he brought drink with him—whatever he needed to get himself through the time he would be here in the village. On these days off, he was at the farm every evening, drinking and intermittently humming songs, like the tunes of Abi Bakr Salim that he had learned by heart and those of Salim al-Suri al-Muqayyami, Omani singers famous since the eighties. He usually roasted a little meat for himself, to take the edge off the harshness of the drink.

He had learned how to play the oud while working in the desert. He was taught by an oud player from the northern shore, al-Batina. He bought his own oud and began carrying it with him wherever he went.

His activities were noticed and talked about in the village. People came to offer him advice, generally counselling him to leave off this behavior they had observed. He didn't want to listen. He pushed them away and it angered them. M'allim Marhun came to him accompanied by Khalfan and his cousin Sayf bin Hamud. It was morning when they showed up. He had already started drinking. They talked at him and tried to tell him what he ought to do. Silently he gazed at those mouths moving so energetically above their beards. He waited for them to go silent; their chatter was meaningless to him. When they finally stopped speaking, he simply got up from where he was sitting, refilled his glass from the bottle of whiskey, and raised it high as he spoke.

Here—this is my Paradise and my Fire.

He didn't say anything more. He sat down and began to strum on his oud. Discomfited, the three men muttered *All might is God's alone,* trudged down the steps, and went home. Whenever he recalled the encounter Zayid bin Marzuq broke into laughter. Decades passed and he was still telling that story. Even after he stopped drinking and travelled to Mecca on Pilgrimage—by now, he had gone on the Hajj several times—he would still tell that story.

Back then in the village, people forbade their sons and relatives to mix with Wad Marzuq. Fathers threatened their sons, saying, I'll kill you if I catch you with him. When Wad Marzuq was at his farm, on a break from his work, everyone was in a state of alert. The villagers feared he would appeal to one or another of the young men and get them to start drinking with him.

In actuality it was the melodious sound of the oud that entrapped so many of them. They came to the farm drawn to the music and oblivious to the threats of their fathers. So many soap-bubbles, those expostulations! Rising to the surface, getting bigger, and then bursting. Young men and boys began watching Wad Marzuq surreptitiously, from the heights of the jabal, from the bends in the wadi tributary, sometimes coming nearer to better hear his tunes. The evening sessions wound on and went late into the night. He found companions who began to drink with him. Shamefaced at first, over time they gave in to the alcohol.

People began calling them the *law-farees*. Their numbers began to swell like an epidemic; soon enough there were twenty-five of them coming to his soirees. Some of these lads were not even yet eighteen but they tagged after their friends, wanting to be part of those evenings when the music sailed across the quiet night-time sky. Their voices could be heard all the way down in the wadi and in the village lanes and quarters that were nearest to Zayid's farm.

On whatever day Zayid bin Marzuq left the village for his distant workplace, quiet would return. Under a blanket of shadows the place became newly deserted. His companions scattered but often they were engaged in a desperate search for anyone who might give them a swallow of alcohol they'd been able to smuggle in or had carried from the clubhouses where the military officers gathered.

And then somebody discovered cologne. It became their evening friend on the nights when they had no whiskey nor bottles of beer. There was plenty of cologne available in the village store thanks to the proprietor, Salfiraj the Indian. He ordered it from the souq in town, tens of cases at a time, now that he had found a booming local market for it.

These companions invented affectionate, crazy nicknames for this beloved cologne to which they were dedicated. Al-Shambirisha they called it, or al-Mihantini. They began congregating further afield, on high plateaus and wadis further away from the village. They stayed until they had finished whatever they had on hand and then they returned home—or, just as often, they fell asleep where they were and went home early the next morning.

Over time their number grew. Quite a large crowd congregated now, on a weekend evening or a state holiday. After the break they were suddenly no longer there, scattering to their separate workplaces most of which were a good distance away. They left the village, and they left it prey to the stories and rumors that circulated feverishly now, passed on by the peasant farmers and younger boys who remained here week in and week out. These stories imagined an era when all the village youth would be stolen away and driven to the pits of hell.

Azzan bin Said found his own way to al-Shambarisha, and he began imbibing it. Hearing about it, his father couldn't believe it. He went immediately to the place where his son—so he had heard—had fallen off the sheer cliff of right conduct. When the father smelled the scent of alcohol rising from his son's mouth as he slept there, Said left the boy where he lay. From that day on he would not speak to his son and he would not listen to anyone who tried to raise the subject of his son.

Azzan's dedication to alcohol appeared limitless. The effects on his body and mind were seriously frightening. Whatever the time of day, he could no longer walk in a straight line. He staggered from point to point down the village alleys. He slept wherever he happened to be in the moment when he dropped to the ground, because he was too drunk to stand up again. As soon as he woke up, he went off to buy another bottle of cologne.

Azzan had been a sweet, good-looking, intelligent boy. He had a calm disposition and you had to strain your ears to hear his voice when he spoke. When he had to walk through the village he would do so with his head bowed out of sheer shyness and embarrassment. No one ever had a bad word to say of this boy. Indeed, village women instructed their sons to follow his example as they praised his noble qualities. Until this happened. His addiction seemed so sudden and so thorough. No one could figure out what it was that had turned his life completely upside down.

Al-Shayib Salim bin Ali did have an explanation for it. Praise be to He who alone knows the ways people's hearts can tip over! he would exclaim. This boy has been diseased with people's envy and it's only because of the way some people talk. They don't fear God, they don't keep His power in mind. Such people—one day they're praising this boy, and the next day they can't get enough of the gossip. But Azzan's father remained silent. He withdrew from people. Even if he didn't say it out loud, he was accusing the villagers of siding with these boy drunkards; of helping them to commit their evil deeds.

Zayid Marzuq had an easy acquaintance with the English language. When he was exchanging words with other villagers he flavored his sentences with a flourish or two from the vocabulary he had learnt from the Brits. That's why he always referred to himself as a *law-faree*, Yes, he was a 'Law-free' if ever there was one! Zayid was one of those people who live outside of whatever laws exist around him. Laws of the tribe, laws of the village—none of them concerned him in the slightest. And so, *Law-faree* had become his own special name. People would say: Law-faree was just here; or: Law-faree left the village today. And then the label began to apply to anyone who spent time with Zayid, any of the lads who were his friends or drinking companions. Soon it became the collective name for all the young men who slunk out of the village in order to spend their evenings getting drunk in a nearby wadi. The village men and women began using the label to warn off their children.

May they stay away from me and from you! Watch you don't have anything at all to do with the law-farees—otherwise you will become just like them.

The label carried a sinister echo, the sound of an evil that was barely hidden, lurking just beyond the boundaries of whatever it was these young men were actually doing. No one really knew exactly what that was.

But Azzan was never called *law-faree*. Instead he acquired his own moniker. People said it was Nasir bin Salim al-Hatati who came up with it. Al-Hatati referred to any sort of alcohol as 'hill', because he believed that alcohol and hill al-turab—kerosene—were all made from the same natural substance. Whenever he alluded to one of the law-farees, he said, That guy drinks hill.

Except for Azzan: Nasir simply called him Hilliya, the hill-guy. They all began calling Azzan by that nickname and most of them more or less forgot his birth name. Maybe Azzan himself rather liked this new name. Staggering through the village, whenever he encountered someone—and before they could say anything to him—he would declare,

There's no one wants Hilliya, everyone's dropped Hilliya.

One day Nasir al-Hatati took al-Shayib Salim bin Ali by the hand and steered him in a particular direction. Old Salim's other hand gripped his familiar thick walking stick, probing the lane as he went. They reached the point where the clustered houses gave way to open space and they began their slow descent into the wadi. Soon they were following the path that wound upward amongst the date-palms. The entire way there, al-Shayib Salim was muttering prayers and incantations. Al-Hatati stopped and spoke. We're here.

Yes—and don't keep yourself right here—stay by, somewhere close.

Al-Hatati understood. He went a short distance off to sit beneath the date-palms. There he would be visible to whoever came outside. Al-Shayib Salim knocked on the door. In a few minutes Kadhiya—Said's wife—came outside. When she saw who it was she spoke in a voice nearly breaking into tears. She took the elderly man's hand, helped him into the home's inner courtyard, and called for her husband. Said came into the courtyard leaning on his stick, dragging one heavy foot, his lameness more evident than ever.

You burned your feet—with that branding—more lame every day, it looks like.

Got anything to treat it with?

Gripping a tray of coffee Kadhiya came in and sat down near them without saying anything. As usual al-Shayib Salim had a lot to say, spinning his stories ... and then suddenly he stopped. And lowered his head.

I've come to talk to you about your son. Azzan.

Drink your coffee, Salim, said Azzan's father, his voice firm, even hard. Nothing to be said about this boy.

But he's your son.

This lad is not my son. He's a seed gone rotten.

Praise be to He who creates Hearts, He who alone forms humans into what they are! It might be that a word from you would return his good sense to him.

Don't tire yourself out with this—I have nothing to say about him and nothing at all to say to him.

Al-Shayib Salim tried hard to soften the man's heart, his words interspersed with passages from the Holy Quran and narratives about what the Prophet had said and done. But it was no use. Kadhiya was crying silently, her tears hot for the loss of her only son. She tried to hide the extent of her distress but the tears came faster and faster despite her steadfast attempt. Finally, Old Salim could hear her sobbing. She addressed the blind man.

They lost him, Salim. They made him go astray.

If they made him go astray, you could bring him back. He is your son, your only child.

Al-Shayib Salim bin Ali returned to his trellis, his walking stick tapping out the way and his guide, Nasir al-Hatati, at his elbow. Unusually for him, he did not say a word more. Al-Hatati did not ask him about the conversation, remaining as silent as his companion until he had seen the blind man home. He headed for his own enclosure, chewing over a new morsel as he went.

Al-Shayib Salim bin Ali felt very tenderly towards Azzan. Whenever the boy happened to pass by the area where he sat to receive guests, if Old Salim was alone he called out to Azzan to come and sit with him. That boy so wild in his drunkenness would turn into a submissive snuffling child, his breath rising and falling like waves playing with a little boat. Al-Shayib Salim would murmur a few verses from the Quran, a prayer of supplication or two, and the boy would grow quiet again, laying his head in the old man's lap and dozing off. Old Salim had no choice but to sit there, unmoving, until Azzan woke up. When he did, al-Shayib Salim would ask him to open a chest that sat at the edge of the trellised space, fetch a jar of black honey, pour a small amount into a cup and swallow it. The interior of that old mandus was lined with jars. Like a young child listening to its father's orders Azzan did exactly what he was told. At some point, he would get up suddenly and leave the old man, to resume wandering through the village streets. Usually he fell asleep again beneath the Ghilala mango tree, choosing the side that faced away from the lane and folding himself up behind the tree trunk to sleep through the rest of the day.

If the old man encountered Azzan when he was in a particularly severe state of drunkenness the boy would sob out his laments about his father to al-Shayib Salim bin Ali, tears flowing like the falaj's little waterfall as it rushed downward to the southern side of the village.

His hand ... Azzan would sob. I miss his hand on my head, I even miss his stick against my back. If only he would speak to me, if he would just give me an order to do something, anything, I would do it.

What had happened to Azzan? Who could explain it; did anyone really know the story of the sudden reversal he had undergone? Who could describe the ways by which he had sunk into this pit of alcohol, this bottomless abyss? Everyone in this village had a completely different story to tell about it and each of them swore to the truth of their own narrative—I saw it, I heard it, yes, they insisted. One didn't know, listening to these impassioned tales, who might have really witnessed anything at all. Who amongst them had really and truly heard any of this with their own ears?

Umayr bin Khalfan, one of the law-farees on whom Zayid bin Marzuq relied to get the site ready and procure the necessary accompaniments to their evenings, had his version. Azzan came to us, he snuck in on us, directly from the jabal. He wanted to spy out what we were doing. He sat watching us, watching what we were doing before any of the others arrived. There were only three of us there—me, Zayid, Mismar. Zayid was plucking on his oud and I was salting the meat and rubbing spices into it. Mismar was telling us a story and making up the skewers. When I lifted my head I saw that boy standing on a little rise above us. He was smiling at us. We knew his father, we knew how pious and devout the father was and how fond people were of him, and so the sight of this boy gave me the shivers. Believe me, it was like an angel from heaven was suddenly there watching us. I couldn't move, I was so stunned—my mouth wide open. Finally, I managed to say something, but in a voice so low that only Zayid bin Marzuq could have heard it.

There is no power and no strength but—

Hearing his words, Wad Marzuq looked around. His back had been to the jabal side. He reacted to the shock by dropping his lute as if suddenly it had turned into a huge live coal. Go on now, boy! he shouted. We don't want any problems. But Azzan stayed right where he was, silent and smiling, studying the three of us.

So I said, Come in here. Wad Marzuq scolded me for it. Come in? he snapped. Have you lost your mind?

Azzan came down towards us. He said hello and sat down without saying anything more. He sat down on the very edge of the mat. He spoke to Wad Marzuq.

I want to drink.

So Zayid waved at the thermos of water. Azzan brushed that attempt off with a sign that he wasn't looking for water. He pointed at the bottle of whiskey.

That—I want some of that.

Wad Marzuq's eyes bulged. Surprise, irritation, fear. He shouted again. We don't want any problems! You curse the devil now and go away.

Azzan picked up the bottle and poured some whiskey into a glass he saw nearby. I went over to add some water. He drank it all down in one gulp. He pushed his empty glass back towards me and said, Give me some more.

Wad Marzuq's reaction was to grab for the bottle which he seemed on the point of flinging away into the mountain gullies. Mismar had been watching and now he came a little closer. That's not the way to do it, he said to Azzan. Just a little at a time. But Azzan's arm remained extended, waiting for his glass to be refilled. I couldn't really do anything except take it and refill it. I diluted it with water and gave it to him. He drained it. After a few more he was on a roll and we simply couldn't stop him. He drank until he couldn't stand up. He vomited all over us and soiled himself and collapsed. Unconscious. We were afraid for him, and we were afraid for ourselves—afraid of his father that is. Who knew what might happen now? Maybe there was some curse against us, maybe God's wrath had been called down on us and we were in for a disaster. Mismar went over to him and wiped his face clean. He poured a bit of cool water through his hair and tugged him into a position that would be more restful. Azzan slept for a few minutes and then suddenly he sat up. Then he stood up and tried to start walking towards home. He walked out of al-Quwayra, and after that, he turned into the fellow people got to know.

As for Wad Marzuq, he never spoke of Azzan or of any of this. He was terrified of Azzan's father and he believed an immense curse would follow him forever after and would surely catch up with him one day. Before closing his eyes to go to sleep he would mutter to himself. 'Fraid of your curses, Said; indeed I am. Who would want to give *you* a reason to get angry? And whenever anyone started talking about Azzan in Wad Marzuq's presence he would go silent immediately, no matter what he'd been talking about. He would stop that talk from going any further; he always insisted that no one say anything about Azzan when he, Wad Marzuq, was in earshot.

The villagers heard an entirely different narrative from Mismar. Abdallah bin Hameed—recognizable by his long white beard and always tousled hair, and never linked to any questionable stories whatsoever—was called Mismar because he reminded you of a nail; he was that tall and thin.

Azzan is a smart enough boy, Mismar said. But on a certain day he went out with his mates to the edge of the village. These friends of his had brought some hard stuff with them. They hid it behind the hilf grasses and they took turns creeping back there to chug down a glass. Then they would come back to join the chatter and Azzan wasn't any the wiser. I was there with them; I saw what they were doing. I saw they were ganging up on him, pouring some of the booze into orange juice that he was drinking until it began to play with his head. They didn't stop until he was dead drunk. They came back from that evening and just dropped him in the middle of the village. He couldn't move. Everyone knows what happened after that.

Every law-faree had their own story about how Azzan got mixed up with drink in the first place. But his drunkenness wasn't like anyone else's. After a few glasses he turned into a wild man and no one could stand up to him. What was even stranger was that when he was sober—even if that wasn't very often—he quickly reverted to his usual quiet self, the calm and deliberate soul everyone knew so well. Without the smile they knew, though. All they observed on his face was a terrible sadness.

Everyone began to avoid Azzan Hilliya—whether he was drunk or alert, for it hardly mattered. The alcohol seemed to have taken him over. His conversation was slow and halting now, his tongue heavy even when he wasn't inebriated. The cologne he drank had acute effects on his body and mind. He looked emaciated; he shook; and he didn't have the strength to keep away from the drink for even one day.

He didn't always have a ready supply of alcohol. Nor did his buddies. That's why he resorted to cologne—khamrat al-fuqara, the drink of the poor as it was called. They didn't have the money to buy real alcohol. It was hard to find, anyway. It only appeared when an army officer or someone who had connections with the English could put his hands on some cases of beer or wine, or a few bottles of whiskey. Then it was like a major festival day in the village. Everyone showed up and no one departed until the last drop was gone.

There was always someone to measure out the drink so that everyone got equal shares. Often the job fell to Mismar. It was his responsibility to open the bottles and pour out measures, using the bottle top to keep everything equal. He passed the glass on and whoever got it would dilute it with water or juice as he pleased. In a little notebook Mismar recorded the number of 'covers' each man had gotten, the number of glasses they had drunk. He wouldn't give anyone an extra pour—no more than the others had had—unless someone else gave him permission to deduct it from his own share of that round. And so the drink went round to all in equal measures. When a person finished their glass they were meant to wait until their companions had finished their glasses too. That's how it went throughout the evening and until the bottles were drained. If it was beer they had, the bottles were passed out at the start of the night. A fellow might get three or four bottles and he was free to drink them at whatever pace he chose.

When Azzan Hilliya was amongst them, though, the evening usually ended in a fight, with shouting and blows. After a few glasses Hilliya always demanded more, paying no attention to their law on sharing out the booze. At first he would trade words with somebody and then it would escalate into a fistfight, and usually a gang would form against him and pound him until he lost consciousness. They'd leave him there and go off to a different location. Later on, once they had regained some measure of sobriety they would come back and check on him. What had happened would be forgotten—and then it would begin all over again.

One day, when Azzan Hilliya lay on the ground with blood oozing from a wound on his forehead, half awake and partway drunk, his vision clouded, he saw a vague figure, it seemed to be a woman with her long battering staves over her shoulder; perhaps she had just been trying to coax down the fruit from some high trees. She was standing over him and murmuring something. He could hear the voice but he couldn't make out the words. She was cursing whoever it was who had done this to him. She began wiping his face to clean off the streaks of blood. Her daughter stood nearby. The older woman ordered her to go and look around for some sweet basil sprigs. Almost immediately they were in her hands. She crushed the basil and rubbed it over the wound.

His eyes were fixed on those eyes: the honey-brown eyes of the girl, this pretty girl who stood near her mother.

He wasn't dreaming; he would remember later those few moments of clarity when he could see her staring at him apprehensively. Something in her gaze sobered him up; the fog of his drunken state receded and he sank into the bewitching pools of her eyes. Then he closed his eyes and withdrew into one of his long spells of absence.

Sawwaada bint Khalaf the herdswoman had been on her way into the wadi with her daughter Thamna. They had been living there with the herd for some time. Passing along the village lane she had seen him lying there flat on the ground, bleeding and moaning softly. She knew who he was. But, seeing him in this state, her heart wouldn't let her go by. She couldn't abandon this boy whose forehead was oozing blood.

Umayr bin Khalfan always said that his grandmother, Maymuna bint Syuf, used to reminisce that her grandfather Raashid bin Syuf made alcohol from dates. He had a grove of palms he called al-Mandasa. At the very center of the cluster of palms he had dug a deep hole that no one knew about. He fermented the dates in a baked-mud kharas after submerging the fruit in water and blending into the mixture a large amount of honey. He lowered the basin into the pit under the palms and left it there for several days until it fermented. Lifting it out, he could strain off a drink with a real bite to it, tipping it into an earthenware jug that he kept for this purpose.

Raashid bin Syuf's coffee had been known in his time for the pleasure it gave. Everyone went to see him just to have a cup or two. It was famous near and far, and everyone tried to find out how he made this very special brew. But Raashid bin Syuf always kept his secret in that subterranean well whose whereabouts no one knew.

After the passing of Raashid bin Syuf, his wife told his story. She had known everything, but she had kept it to herself. He would take a little of what was in the jug and pour it into the coffeepot. It was this strong-tasting and highly concentrated alcohol that brought on the state of ecstasy, the pleasure the coffee-drinkers experienced without knowing its source. Some of them tried to get his wife to tell them his secret—how exactly he had made it—but she insisted that she had no idea.

On a day that Umayr bin Khalfan tells this old story, it means he's already getting drunk, laughed Ahmad bin Shannun, hearing the story of Raashid bin Syuf's drink yet again. He went on saying to everyone sitting around him that every time they sat drinking—glasses going round—there was one sign, only one and always the same one, that Umayr bin Khalfan was pretty far gone. He would begin shaking his head and he would mutter for a few moments until everyone got quiet. They were waiting in suspense—even if they had heard it tens of times already. He always launched into it as if he were telling the tale for the very first time ever.

Haaayy, haayy, where are you now, you khamr of Raashid bin Syuf?

Then he lifted his head to address his drinking buddies directly. He always began by saying, *they say* ...

Ahmad bin Shannun or Ahmad th'Lame—or you could call him Wad Shannun, for he was a young fellow no older than thirty—worked in one of the Ministries in Muscat. He carried internal mail from one office to another and poured coffee for senior officials' guests at the Ministry. Or he did whatever else there was to be done. He dragged his lame foot across the tile floor of the Ministry, coming and going through the hours of the workday. He came back to the village only for the weekends. As a small child he had contracted polio, though not the worst case of it. It had made his left leg heavy and slow; hence his limp. The lameness crept into his name like it had seeped into his body.

Ahmad was that rare person on whom alcohol seemed to have no effect. He could go on drinking all day long and into the night without any discernible alteration. If it were not for that smell floating around his mouth no one could have told when he was sober and when he'd been drinking.

He always closed out those sessions—always the last to speak and the one who dragged the drunks out from their hiding places and got them to where they needed to be. It was Ahmad who intervened when a severe argument broke out. He inserted himself between the adversaries and pulled them apart. It was Ahmad who treated the wounds incurred in these drunken brawls. But whenever Azzan Hilliya was involved Ahmad backed off, saying, I have nothing to do with this fellow, deal with it yourselves, don't get me involved in it.

Of that group of drinking companions—the law-farees, or the dead-drunks, or whatever they were called by various villagers—most worked outside the village in distant and scattered places. Most came back only on longer holidays or weekends. No sooner did they reach their homes, having brought with them foodstuffs and other things their families had asked for, then they scurried off to one of their meeting places: in a wadi or in the orchard at al-Quwayriya; at the farm of Zayid bin Marzuq, spending their first night there and sitting half the next day with their families but coming back to meet up again. And so on until the break was over or the drink was gone and there was not a single drop to be found.

The measurer—usually Mismar—was the one who had to screw the lid back onto the empty bottle and put it aside. Every empty bottle, every finished bottle, meant the beginning of another. He would toss it away with a ritual cursing. Why have you consumed us! Silent for a moment, he would add: *Wa ma ta'kuluna ila al-khamr.* It's only booze that can eat us up.

Someone else would always speak up when he uttered that phrase. Don't blaspheme us, Mismar! And don't say it wrong—in the Quran that verse says *Wa ma yuhlikuna ila al-Dahr*—Only Fate and Time destroy us.

Mismar would laugh and say, Now listen to this lad speaking about the Quran. Just drink and shut up, boy.

The empty bottles were tossed into the gullies in the vicinity of where these companions spent their evenings. They were flung away in all their variety of shapes: long necks or short, different colors, different sizes. For their useful life was spent now that their contents had spilled down these throats and into these bellies. Through the height of the summer the bottles burn hot to the touch beneath the implacable sun. The leaves fall and stick to them and the dust congeals on the glass over which the piercing smell of aged alcohol still hovers. Then another hand appears; a fist closes around the neck, ready to return this old bottle to beloved status once again—but a different status. The beekeeper's hand cleans away the filth of all of those days and revives the sparkle of the glass. Carefully, that hand fills the emptiness with honey, clear and beautiful behind the newly transparent glass—pure, delicious, fueling the hunger of those who seek it.

Chapter Seven

Locked mandus ...
what stories do you hide, what tales
of long ago ...

AS THE DAY GOES ON, the sun's glare hardens. The higher it travels in the sky the further it sends its scorching heat across the heights. At this morning hour—it was about nine o'clock—the companions were still searching the caves and crevices amidst trees and bushes and amongst the boulders as well as the smaller rocky outcroppings. They were still hoping to find the beehive that must be secreted somewhere out here.

The sun soaked up their energy and sucked away their hope even as they went on searching. The westerly wind seemed to char them even now, at this early hour—earlier in the day than one would expect. It seemed to burn hotter against their skin—through their clothing—the closer one of them thought they had gotten to their goal. Surveying each promising spot, though, they would soon feel defeated. And baffled, not knowing where to try next.

But Abdallah bin Hamad never seemed to flag. He didn't know the meaning of the word *lethargic*. He was absolutely certain that the honey was there and he was determined to find it now, during this excursion. He had knocked into challenges harder than this in his life, had encountered puzzles more elusive than this beehive, and in the end he had always found what he was looking for.

Yet another time, they sectioned the mountains among themselves to embark on another round of solitary searches. Al-Hatati sat on a high perch overlooking the far-off wadis; from here, he could see all the way to where they had made camp in Aqabat al-Nakhla. He took out the packet of tobacco wedged under the belt wrapping his izar, pinched a wad between two fingers, and stuffed it into his mouth. He felt his head grow lighter. The tobacco lifted him out of the heaviness of this day's fatigue and the sweat soaking his dark undershirt. He moved over to the shade of a large rock to attempt escaping the sun's glare—for a few moments at least—as he savored the light dizziness still mounting into his brain. He studied the thin trickle of water—the only moisture that remained in this dried-out wadi. In his head he sketched out the beeline flight as Abdallah bin Hamad had witnessed it: it would come to precisely this point on the heights.

Al-Hatati knew well that bees did not stop flying to a particular water source simply because it was at a great distance. But if they discovered another source, they would easily change their route. He asked himself: What if there might be a very small stream down in the wadi directly opposite to where they've got their hive? And they know they can find the water they need there? He stared down as far as he could see to the bottom of Wadi al-Nimarat. The air appeared dust-laden above the normal surface of the watercourse itself. Any water it had held had dried up completely. From up here it would take him at least half an hour to get all the way down into the wadi bottom. But the thought consumed him because he was completely persuaded now that there must be another water source somewhere in the area that the bees were using since it seemed they had stopped going to the original one, perhaps because they had encountered one of those pesky human beings there.

The effect of the tobacco had worn off by now. He spit it out and got to his feet to begin walking down the other slope. He had decided to head for the point where they had stayed even though that meant going all the way across the wadi and not ending up at the meeting point they had agreed on.

Climbing down these slopes was perilous especially at this time of day. The stones on either side of the path down had taken in heat through the day and he could no longer press his hands against them to steady his descent—not for any length of time, anyway. It was too hot out on the jabal to be undertaking this, he knew. But he was determined that he had to either find the new water source or convince himself thoroughly that on the face opposite to the crevice where the bees had made their home, hidden away somewhere in the vast body of the jabal, there was no site where they could have found water. He had to either put that possibility to rest or confirm it. Experience had taught him that figuring out how the bees seemed to be traveling and then confirming their path by finding their sources of water, and knowing how they behaved in flight, were the keys that unlocked the honey. But he also knew, to the contrary, that working all of this out according to what you thought you knew could lead you to search in all the wrong places until you were utterly exhausted.

At times as he groped his way downward, the air was completely still. In this heat al-Hatati's body itself seemed to make rain. His undershirt was as wet as if he had just emerged from a deep pond. His hair was dripping and sweat covered his body. There wasn't a breath of moving air to ease the torpor of the sun's heat or to lighten the excruciating difficulty of making his way along the jabal. Sometimes there were obstacles in his way that meant he had to drop to his knees and crawl like one of the mountain animals, his back bent double and his hands clutching at rocks he could only hope were firmly lodged in place as he made his way down toward the wadi bottom.

Often in his life al-Hatati had gone alone into these mountains; and sometimes he had gone with others from the village. On one particular day that he remembered well, on his way through the village he had encountered Abdallah bin Hamad and had quipped, My heart's up there, you know—like yours.

Abdallah had laughed. D'you want to go up? We can go right now.

Al-Hatati's eyes had widened in surprise. God forbid any evil come upon us!

Abdallah's joy at this coincidence was indescribable. Though he had never accompanied al-Hatati on one of the older man's excursions he had heard often of the man's endless yearning for the mountains and his determination, the ever-retold stories, his quips which (after that day) they all became accustomed to hearing. Al-Hatati quickly became his companion on every outing. And then they were joined by Azzan bin Said who asked al-Hatati rather shyly if he could go with them. It would break the sharpness of the loss he had suffered. By then, he had stopped drinking.

If I don't *do* something, he had said to al-Hatati, I'm worried I'll start on the stuff again.

Al-Hatati thought of Azzan as more or less his youngest child. His strong affections led him to respond with a threat that was also a reprimand—but all said in a light enough tone. If you go back to drinking I'm going to kill you with a bullet between your eyes.

That evening, after the final prayers of the day, al-Hatati knocked on Abdallah bin Hamad's door. He told him that Azzan was hoping to go with them. Abdallah shrugged and gave al-Hatati a little smile. No problem, let him come along, it's the mountains that test men and harden them.

Ever since his first trip with them Azzan had proven that they could rely on him. Of the three of them he was the strapping young lad, his build strong. He could carry more stuff than they. It was Azzan who usually fetched the firewood, laid the fire, and got it going. He filled and carried the big water containers and he washed the dishes and pots after they ate. And above and beyond all of that he appeared to have particularly good luck searching for honey—and happening to find it.

Azzan was calm by nature. He was still a person of few words, as he had always been. He listened to his two companions as they pulled on the threads of one story after another: tales of what had gone on in the village or the adventures they'd had in their many excursions into the mountains, as well as the problems and setbacks they had encountered. Their old memories intermingled with more recent accounts. Listening, Azzan would laugh softly, enjoying this companionship which had compensated for the company of his drinking buddies who were still trying to get him to rejoin their raucous evenings of revelry.

On the morning of their departure for Aqabat al-Nakhla, as he lay beneath the big sycamore fig tree in their home's courtyard, al-Hatati's nose picked up the aroma of baram honey, the best. His wife was sitting nearby, occupied with her mending.

He opened his eyes and took in a deep breath, allowing the fragrance to flow into the depths of his lungs, and then he exhaled slowly. It was just like relishing the taste of honey in his mouth. But this came through his lungs, the pure scent alone.

His wife gave him a sidelong glance. Recently, she had noticed with concern, he seemed to be passing through states of mind or body that she could not explain. The man's getting old, and he's beginning to lose it, she thought; but she kept her thought to herself.

Asal! Honey! Where is that beautiful honey smell coming from?

Al-Hatati asked his wife this question as he was sitting up and shifting his body to support his back against the tree trunk. Again he sniffed hard at the air and arced his head, wanting to follow the trail of the scent. He darted his eyes right and left, stood up and then sat down again, came closer to his wife sniffing her garment and then her neck and then her chest. He descended all the way to her lap still trying to catch the scent that had made his head go dizzy. He was all over her, like a dog. Kneeling, he put his hands on the ground and lowered his head to sniff at the soil. He stared at his wife, his eyes rolling, unfocused. Now, she thought. It's happening now. He is really going over the edge.

All we need is for al-Hatati to go crazy, she murmured uneasily. That'll be it for us.

He sat down directly in front of her so that his eyes were on a level with hers. He went on staring at her. Asmaa bint Nawfal's eyes were light-colored—honey-colored in fact, giving the impression that at any moment they might drip honey onto her cheeks, softened and smoothed by her use of a cream made from shurana and myrtle leaves. He touched the tip of his forefinger to his lips and knotted his eyebrows, and he kept on staring at her, the pupils of his eyes sometimes as high in their sockets as they could go.

A feeling of terror came over Asmaa and a shudder went through her joints and rose into her shoulders. If he had not broken that moment's silence with his next question the poor woman would surely have begun sobbing from sheer fright. She really was starting to believe he was mad. The specters of it danced through her head and tossed her to and fro, and now she feared even the sight of his hand reaching for her. She could only imagine him gripping her neck and pressing on it, and pressing, choking her so hard that she could no longer draw a breath.

Where's the honey? Where? Where's it coming from?

She shook her head hard. The look on her face would have told anyone how odd she found this question.

There's a honey smell, it's coming from your clothes—tell me, where's the honey? Where is it?

She shrank back. He put his hand out and undid the pin that held her overgarment together over her chest. The embroidered bodice panel flopped open and fell towards her right arm; the pale skin of her throat gleamed and he could see where her breasts began to part. He edged nearer until his nose was brushing against her throat. He took a deep breath and slid his nose lower until it was buried in the folds of her undergarment. He had his hands pressed against the tree trunk against which she sat, as though he wanted to embrace the tree and her both, or as though he was trying to hug the fragrance that was coming from his wife's body.

He knew for certain that his wife was going to go on hiding the truth from him. Maybe someone had given her the honey or maybe she had swallowed some mouthfuls while over visiting with her neighbors. But a question hung unanswered in his head. If she had eaten honey then the smell would be coming from her lips; it would be on her breath. But this honey fragrance was rising from the folds of her inner garments, precisely from where a pair of breasts sat tense and wary beneath the light translucent turquoise chemise she wore.

He jammed his face against her chest until his nose was as deeply embedded as it could be. The further he pushed into the deep softness between her breasts the more strongly he smelled mountain honey, the fragrance taking possession of his senses and overpowering his mind.

His strong hands ripped open her sudayriya. Her dark-blue dishdasha tore across the glinting silver threads of its embroidery which ran from her throat halfway down her chest. Her breasts were visible now, small and curved like a pair of mountain-bees' spherical hives, hanging on a stone polished by watercourses, the surface smooth and gleaming. From such a hive, the aroma of the honey would rise into the air as the bzzzz of the bees spread softly across the area.

He brought his head close again and took in the scent of her chest; he moved back slightly and the smell grew less pronounced. Whenever he came close again the smell of baram honey grew stronger and with every step back its thick, hazy presence broke up little by little but did not disappear completely. It toyed with him, playing hide and seek. He gripped his wife's bare shoulders, thrust his head closer, and breathed deeply again.

I've never tasted—I've never smelled—any honey with an aroma like this. Where's the honey? Where is it coming from? Where?

He didn't wait for an answer but took a deep gulp of air as though to fill his lungs from this liquid source. But his lungs were not yet full. As if he were drinking from a sweet, abundant wellspring after suffering a thirst so intense that it could not be satisfied. He lifted his head and looked into her honey eyes and repeated his question.

From where—this honey?

Asmaa was half-lying under the tree, her head against a large, bulging vein protruding from the tree trunk and her body flat on the sand that covered the gritty soil. She stayed in that position, unmoving, for some time. She had closed her eyes and dropped into a half-faint. She had not yet emerged from it when al-Hatati was closing the door to their house and setting off to where his companions waited for him. This business of the honey-smell had made him late—this scent that still played around his nose.

Al-Hatati made it his home, this enclosed plot that he had purchased from Harith bin Shiikhan for three hundred riyals. From the start he called it the maqsura—a garden, even though it was barren land with no growing plants and no trees except for a couple of sorry-looking date-palms. The watercourse descending from the wadi tributary had filled the land here with pebbles and it was beyond the capacity of Harith bin Shiikhan, who owned many orchards, to deal with it. So he sent the village auctioneer and deal-maker, Haashil bin Masoud, to al-Hatati to negotiate a sale. Although three hundred riyals didn't amount to much money, it did mean several months-worth of food to al-Hatati and his wife.

At least the maqsura did have the right to draw water from the falaj. It got a lot of water, in fact: its regular share of five lots from the collective schedule set by the sundial, according to the shadow creeping across the clock from late morning into late in the afternoon; and two and one-half parts from midday on the sixth day. The maqsura was situated in the more remote palm-grove area nearest to the jabal, and thus—and as was known and agreed on around the village—the lands bordering it and the tributary were considered to be assigned to the maqsura as well.

When the offer came al-Hatati gave it some thought and asked his wife for her opinion. They were living in the house called Bayt al-Gharifa then; three-fourths of the structure was crumbling and much of the roof had caved in. Al-Hatati didn't even have the right to repair it, because Bayt al-Gharifa was collectively owned by the Bin Shiikhan family and no one would give up their share to anyone else such that repairs could be agreed on. So it stayed in the condition it was, deteriorating stone by stone, and clay brick by clay brick.

How much do you have? asked his wife.

He rubbed at his head. About enough to keep us from going hungry one day to the next.

She got to her feet and went over to her chest. She took out a small green metal casket from inside the chest, opened it and pulled out a roll of fabric. Inside were some coins. She counted them as he watched. Four hundred riyals.

Selling the jewelry—if this money isn't enough, that's what I will do.

Nasir bin Salim al-Hatati took three hundred riyals from the fabric roll and handed the rest back to his wife.

Asmaa bint Nawfal was about twenty years younger than her husband. He had been something under forty when they married. A girl of fifteen or so, she had just had her third menses when he spoke to her mother through the matchmaker Saada. She came back to him the same day. Get yourself ready to marry, she said. No more than a month later, Asmaa bint Nawfal was living in Bayt al-Gharifa.

Although she was so much younger than he was, Asmaa was already a hard worker. She worked all day long at many tasks, and after that she would sit down to embroider the delicate headgear that she sold, keeping the money in the metal box that she locked inside her chest. Every riyal that went into that box stayed there. Asmaa had spent most of her life fatherless. She had been very little when, one day, he had fallen from the top of a palm tree. He lay unconscious for days. Then he came out of his coma, said a few words to his wife, and died. Asmaa could remember his face just a little, like a face in a dream; she remembered his bushy beard and a crease between his eyes. What she remembered most of all were his hands caressing her hair and her face fondly.

When she got married her mother gave her a cow, three ewes, and a ram. She began her adult life like any other village woman, trying to come up with what the household's many living creatures needed to get through each day, using what she had and whatever life would bestow on her.

A mudbrick wall enclosed the maqsura but it had worn away over time. Sections of it had crumbled and fallen. Al-Hatati demolished what was left of it and built a new wall on the foundations of the old, a stronger and higher wall. It's not a maqsura unless it's got a proper wall, he said.

After a year of hard work the place regained the glory it had lost. He worked hard. He got rid of the pebbles and rocks, the heaps of old dried-out dung, the rotting trunks of fallen date-palms. He brought in new tree shoots and planted them after thoroughly turning the soil. He planted the enclosure with beans and varieties of forage such as ghashmar, with its small heads of corn, and barley.

Opposite the orchard's tributary, mango trees flourished along the whole length of the wall. Those trees had been neglected but they seemed to respond happily to all of the attention that was now being lavished on their home. That year the trees were heavy with fruit and he sold a lot of it.

The enclosure harbored a giant lush sycamore fig tree. Someone advised him that he should cut it down and level the trunk because the tree would bring harm on the place and was useless. But he did not touch it. One burning-hot day he was seated beneath it resting, when Harith bin Shiikhan came by. He echoed the suggestion of taking the sawqam out by its roots. This sawqam is my home, al-Hatati replied, though he had never said or even thought this before.

From that moment, the tree did become his home. He built two small rooms nestling close to it and erected a wall around it that also enclosed the two original rooms, all inside the larger maqsura. When he had done this, he and his wife left their old village lane and the dilapidated Bayt al-Gharifa behind and moved into those rooms. He built a roofed open shelter beneath the sumar trees in the small level expanse of ground that abutted on the orchard.

A few tombs were dotted here and there in the space between the gum-acacias and the jabal. When they were on the point of moving into the new rooms inside the maqsura his wife's mother had suddenly faced him with a question. You're taking my daughter to live in a graveyard?

He had smiled. The people in there are like our uncles, they are good, pious people, and no one among them would bring harm on us, as long as a person makes friends with them.

She said nothing more about it and he never added anything to that explanation of his. She could see the contentment in her daughter's eyes and when it was time to move, she helped them, along with the other neighbors in their alley who carried their belongings out to the new homestead.

And so, a maqsura that villagers here had viewed as the embodiment of a wild, frightening place where jinn played their tricks and pursued their fun in every crevice and dark corner, coming out by night to rove about and show themselves to terrified humans, became a human dwelling. The place had been haunted, people were certain: they heard wispy half-conversations or worse, terrible sounds emitted from amidst the density of the sumar trees. There had been many stories about what happened to the tenant farmers threshing grain out there. These were stories that would make a listener's hair stand on end and consequently, no gab session in the village could be without them, no evening story-telling to their children could fail to include these terrifying tales of happenings on the edge of the village. Someone would concoct a tall tale about what had happened to him, and the children who were listening avidly would shrink into themselves, rolling up into balls under their blankets or in their mothers' laps. An old woman would declare, in their hearing: That maqsura! It belongs to the folk of the netherworld. Then they would hear a blind old man insist, I saw them with my own eyes before my sight went—and maybe it went because I saw them. Old Hamdun's thresher said, You don't find a day going by spent in that maqsura without a new story the jinn have made.

But after all of that—after all of those stories—now the maqsura had become a place to which everyone came: neighbors from the village and folks who lived further away. Asmaa bint Nawfal suggested to her husband that he might buy the lemon harvest from landowners who had lemon trees on their properties that they couldn't harvest themselves. Well—once she had said it, what could he do? He went to the broker who managed sales of fruit harvests. He wanted to take over the lemon harvest—he would rent all of the trees, he said. The fellow arranged it, writing down the sums in his notebook—the debt al-Hatati would have to pay to the owners at the season's end.

That year and in the years to follow al-Hatati bought the lemons ripening on the trees. He picked them, dried them in the sun, and stowed them in burlap sacks. There they would stay as he waited patiently for the beginning of winter. At the souq he could sell a sack of dried lemons for many times over the cost of renting the trees as the fruit ripened.

Asmaa plotted out what he should do, and then all he had to do himself was to put her strategies into action. He did it because he was so fond of her and also because he had great respect for her opinions. He knew the serious bent of her mind. When he came back from the souq he gave her all of the money he had made from selling lemons and she locked it in her chest. For the hard times.

Nasir al-Hatati had left his home heading for the lane that went towards the source of the falaj. He walked parallel to the palms until he was past the orchard called Rahina. He followed the course of the falaj as far as the end of the long stretch of low-lying land. He ascended along the mountain path towards where his companions would be. They had grown a bit tired of waiting for him. The fragrance of honey was still whirling around at the top of his skull as he recalled the sudden flare of ecstasy in his wife's eyes as she gazed at him without a word. Bliss—and anticipation of more passion, of madness; take as much honey as you want, she would tell him.

Al-Hatati arrived at the river bottom of Wadi al-Nimarat. In the long and narrow cleft, always shaded because it was so deep, he sat down to rest from the fatigue of the descent. The area was completely dry except for some stagnant pools of water, darker than they would be in the rainy season and giving off the smell of moss. He remembered long ago coming along here, making his way by clinging to the steep sides of the jabal so that he would not fall into these ponds which had been filled with water back then. In times of abundance when all was blooming, human beings couldn't even cross this area. The waterfalls poured into this cleft, the water tumbling down from the heights to fill those rocky basins carved long ago into the wadi's bottom.

Light gusts of wind swirled around him and batted his face gently, absorbing some of his fatigue. He looked at his watch. It was about nine-thirty. Yet he still had to walk the length of the wadi, upward, searching for any water sources that might be nearby. Although the long dry spell had consumed all the water in these wadis, al-Hatati had enough experience to know that there were still some rare spots where water welled up between the rocks, thin trickles perhaps but always there, providing enough fresh water to quench the thirst of a traveler in these parts, or a mountain animal.

At the point where the wadis intersected—where Wadi Waala came up against Wadi al-Nimarat—he decided to swerve off to the right, going into Wadi Waala. He remembered a small spring running by a small palm tree on the wadi edge. If there were a water source around here, he said to himself, it would draw the bee to it.

He arrived at the spot that he'd held in his memory. He examined the spring; it had left the surrounding rocks damp. He studied it intensely, hoping to catch sight of a bee dancing over this wet patch, but he couldn't see anything. He didn't want to come too close lest his presence startle any bees that might be there and cause them to fly off. He inched forward until his body was pressed against a boulder that half-hid him, all the while staring at the moist area which lay slightly higher. He couldn't hear any buzzing, no droning, not even the distinct sound made by the red mountain wasps that made it their business to chase bees. But he was certain now that the three of them had been searching in the wrong place. Abdallah bin Hamad thinks he knows this terrain inside out, he mused, but he got it wrong. There's nothing at all on this peak. But he wasn't completely certain.

Maybe there was another site nearby where the bees were getting their water.

He had to return to Aqabat al-Nakhla. He would take the descent through the wadi to the point where it joined the larger canyon, the major watercourse. There, he would head upward as far as their campsite. But first he went over to the little trickle of water since he needed to moisten his own dry throat. The water was collecting in a tiny depression, like a little bowl; at most it held three cupfuls. He swept away the thin layer of moss covering the surface, cupped his hands, brought a few sips of water to his lips and drank. He took another portion and tipped it into his mouth, enjoying the sweet coldness running down his throat. Another dip; and then only a slight amount of water remained in the stony bowl. He scooped it up and wet his face.

At that moment he thought he heard a buzzing but maybe it was only in his head. He listened harder; the buzzing was fainter, almost non-existent but then he heard it again. He looked to his right and then to his left, trying to figure out where the sound was coming from. The buzzing stopped suddenly. Al-Hatati was as motionless as a mountain rock; his eyes had just fixed on a single bee. It was very close to him and it appeared to be unaware of anything but the task of taking in water.

Surely he had stopped breathing; all other creatures had grown silent. All that existed in the world was the faint sound of trickling water and the louder sound of his heart beating.

The bee was there. He would retrace his steps but only after making certain that otherwise there were no bees in the immediate area. Where had this solitary bee come from? He thought hard. Maybe one of his companions was already there at Aqabat al-Nakhla, near the watering spot they knew, and so the bee would not go there but had come here to drink instead, as if it knew that this little trickle would do for emergencies only. Al-Hatati smiled. He loved the intelligence of these mountain bees.

The mountain bee, the wild bee known as Abu Tariq—Wayfarer, as they customarily called it—was the sort of bee a human being could not tame or raise in a colony as they did other bees—the ones the villagers knew as Persian or foreigner bees. But those strains of bees too might be found in the mountains. More than once al-Hatati had happened upon a watering place that these now-familiar imported bees were using. They were inhabiting a nearby cave, he had discovered.

In recent years these Persian bees had become more widespread in the mountains, while the wild honey—Abu Tariq honey—had grown rarer. Over an entire season, al-Hatati might find only a single hive or maybe two. Often, after an exhausting search he returned empty-handed with no honey at all to show for his efforts.

Two years ago, when he and his companions had gone into Khabb al-Ghafa, what they had found was Persian honey. The beehive was in a large cave with an entrance so narrow that only bees could come in and out. Azzan bin Said had returned to the village and fetched a tool used to penetrate and widen clefts in the mountain—basically, a large hammer and a nail. He also brought a box from his bee colony big enough to hold five frames. He intended to remove the hive from its cave after they had extracted the honey and to tend this new hive as one of his own.

They had taken turns trying to open up the entrance, which was no more than a crack down the rock. To protect themselves against the likely bee stings they made a small fire and directed its smoke towards the opening. Trying to escape the smoke, the bees flew further into the cave. The three of them continued pounding and chipping at the rock face, widening the opening gradually until they could see the hive. The worker bees had built up fifteen spherical nest-hives in a tightly adjacent series, and every one of them was bursting with honey and sealed over with beeswax. As they removed the hard shell surrounding each hive, Azzan examined the contents closely looking for the queen bee. When he found her he placed that little hive carefully in the box first, after they had cut the honey away from it; then he put the other hives inside along with it.

He had cut off a good number of palm leaves to bind and cushion these wild hives as he set them inside the hive box. The three of them were working together like clockwork as if they themselves were worker bees in a hive. With his knife Abdallah bin Hamad cut the hives from their moorings in the cave. He drew out each one carefully and handed it to al-Hatati who removed the honey and gave the hive to Azzan. In turn, he would tie it up and fix it firmly within the box.

When they had extracted all the honey Azzan set the box down outside the cave's entrance, having made certain that the cover was tightly on. The difficulty in this operation—in trying to hold onto the bees—was that when those bees smelled smoke they would flee as deep into the cave as they could go. Most of these caves were cylindrical and narrow, and their interiors were out of reach to a human hand. The crucial tactic—if there was to be any hope of hanging on to the hive itself—was to look first for the queen bee and to make certain she was held securely inside the box so that the other bees would follow her in. If they picked up her scent they would leave the cave and fly into the box. To allow plenty of time for this to happen Azzan left the box in place for a full day and then overnight as well. The next morning he could see that indeed all of the bees had abandoned the cave and were now in the box. The operation had succeeded. They left for the village carrying the box carefully between them. They had secured a lot of honey and Azzan had gotten himself a fine cell of calm domestic bees who produced honey in abundance.

Stumbling on that Persian honey had been a massive stroke of luck. These bees tended to build their hives in high and inaccessible places, spots that were most often treacherous when they weren't impossible to access. In addition to being located in the most remote stretches of terrain, these hives were evidence that the bees chose caves that were practically sealed shut already. Beekeepers could search for days at a time hoping to come across them. It was worth it: in the time it might take you to harvest one or two jars of wild honey, coming upon a colony of Persian bees could yield ten or even twenty.

This subspecies of bee had not always existed in Oman. The Persian bees arrived in the seventeenth century along with the rule of the Ya'aribah dynasty, both coming from the Persian lands. In that era, efforts to settle these bees in the villages of al-Rustaq and Wadi Bani Awf included carving out homes for them in the trunks of date-palm trees. There the bees thrived and grew numerous; and this work of centuries before had bequeathed the cultivation of Persian bees to the next generations. At least this is what al-Hatati had heard from Old Salim bin Ali who had spent long stretches of time in those villages.

What al-Hatati knew for certain—from his time living in the mountainous regions and his indefatigable search for honey year after year—was that Persian bees did not take quite the same level of precautions about locating and using water sources as did other types of bees. Their wariness lay instead in choosing where to place their hives—that is, solely in inaccessible locations. Most people weren't capable of finding them because it was almost impossible to even reach the hives. Some honey searchers had tried to scale these forbidding heights using ropes, but when they actually got to where the hives were they found they couldn't break open and widen the cave entrance sufficiently to get at the honey.

But now, his eyes were fixed on this one bee who was wholly absorbed in the water. In the slanting rays of early morning and this clear and still air, he should be able to see where it would head next. He waited and waited, his hope reviving. He would note the path it was taking and from that he could calculate its destination. It trembled, moved, crept a few centimeters, and stopped. He watched as it flew westward but then came back and headed towards the east on a spiraling path. Shading his eyes with his hand so that the sun's rays would not blind him he followed the bee's route.

It was hard for bees who inhabited these crevice-ridden locations, al-Hatati knew, to trace a straight path home from a drinking place as they rose out of the deeps and toward the summit. The bee had to follow this spiraling zig-zag way upward until it was on a level with the spot where the hive was suspended. Al-Hatati knew also that such behavior meant the hive really was situated in a very high location. The knowledge gave him some hope that he would not have to even bother with searching along the lower slopes. He and his friends could aim directly for the mountain's greatest elevations.

But he sat there waiting for another bee to show so that he could better confirm the direction these bees were taking. He waited for a long time until finally the sun's terrible force consumed his waiting and his body. He got up and left his lookout, following the contour of the wadi and heading for the campsite where his companions would already be resting.

Chapter Eight

I left my desire on the mountain summits
far from the eyes of humans
and tried to forget

ABDALLAH BIN HAMAD—THIS TALL, hard-sculpted man whose graceful agility clambering up mountainsides never deserted him whatever the time of year—was the character at the core of the village's best-known tale when it came to the honey search. The story bestowed on him a special and unique moniker of dubious worth which spread far beyond the village.

Abdallah bin Hamad owned a donkey on whom he relied to ferry necessary belongings and supplies from one place to another in these mountainous parts, including his plot of farmland which no wheeled vehicle could reach. When his donkey had made one of these excursions, Abdallah's usual practice was to leave it in one of the wadis—often quite a distance from the village—to graze on small shrubs and wild grasses. He might leave it there for weeks at a time or even months. And then there would come a day when he set out and tried to find the donkey by looking for the tracks it had made. Most of the time the donkey didn't stray far from wherever he had left it.

After the government issued new regulations prohibiting the hunting of mountain goats and other wild animals, many of those who hunted were reluctant to tell their fellow villagers that they were going off into the mountains—just like the honey gatherers. They didn't want rumors about what they might be doing to circulate. And so they began making these excursions in secret, doing the best they could to conceal their comings and goings or at least their destinations. The most secretive amongst them would say simply that they were going off somewhere. To the capital city, perhaps, or to the markets in larger towns.

Generally wary of humankind, Abdallah held the conviction that a person who tended to suspect others' motives ought to be the first to shield himself from willy-nilly involvement in people's problems and quarrels. The way he saw it, people were either enviers who didn't like what you had and didn't want anything good to befall you, or they were outright enemies who—to your face—showed you a gentle hand while behind your back, they worked to destroy you. Repeatedly al-Hatati had exerted himself to erase this belief from Abdallah's mind. In the end, though, he came to believe himself that it would be easier to move one of these enormous mountains that surrounded them than it would be to change Wad Hamad's outlook.

So—let's hear what you think of *us*, then? he once asked Abdallah. The younger man was training his binoculars on a far-off white patch sitting high on a peak.

Without turning to his questioner Abdallah had snapped out an answer. So-so.

This response did not please al-Hatati at all. He stood up immediately, intending to leave. But Abdallah grabbed the hem of his cloak and yanked it. His hold was so strong that al-Hatati could not move. Abdallah turned toward him with a smile playing on his lips.

Except al-Hatati, he said.

Wavering between irritation and amusement, al-Hatati exclaimed, Get out of here! And they both laughed.

Abdallah bin Hamad was an eleven-year-old on that long-ago evening when he chased after a magpie, his air rifle in hand. The bird was flying from one rise to perch on another. Abdallah was fairly close by but not close enough that his air rifle could reach the magpie. But it didn't go very far and so he still hoped he could bag it.

The bird kept deceiving him. As soon as he came near enough that it seemed within range, the magpie flew off only to alight on another spot that seemed close enough to lead his pursuer on again. Abdallah was focused on the pursuit and wasn't paying attention to where he was. But the moment came when he realized he had left the village far behind and was heading towards Attab. The magpie came to rest atop a small cave. As soon as Abdallah got closer it flew off, a longer flight than before and this time without a pause, circling overhead and finally vanishing into the mountaintops.

He stood there for some moments downcast, his hopes disappointed, ready to retrace his steps with a firm promise to himself that he would never again try to hunt a magpie. But then he noticed bees flying in and out of a cave opening. He would go and investigate, he decided. He would learn something about what these little creatures were up to. It was the first time he discovered a beehive all by himself. At the cave opening he peered in and saw the hive hanging there, filling the aperture almost to its edges. Thrilled, he ran home and told his father. The next evening the two of them went to find it. But he lost his way. They couldn't find the cave.

His father was very annoyed with him. The boy must be dreaming things up, he hadn't actually found anything at all. But Abdallah insisted he had seen the hive. When his father calmed down and stopped rebuking him, Abdallah tried to focus on that moment, to rewind the tape of his memories. When he had stumbled on the hive he had been following the magpie, and so ... He set out again and followed the same upward path he had taken before. His father was shouting after him to come back. But finally there he was, standing at the opening in the rock. He called back to his father.

It was his first experience observing how one extracted honey from a hive. Even though he was the one who had found the honey, his father's cross words were alive in his ears the whole way home. Perhaps this is how the passion began: like a little seed falling in an unexpected place that happens to have been moistened by a few drops of light rain. This was the substance of it—of why one felt such a passion for this activity: coming upon honey when one didn't know where it might be. The exultation of the search itself—not out of need but for the joy of the adventure, looking for a wild and elusive beehive when everyone else who had been searching for it had come back utterly worn out and empty-handed.

Aged fourteen he had gone with his cousin Hamud to Raddat al-Rawgh. The low-lying basins there were full of little sadd fish, like freshwater sardines, the boys knew. That had been a tremendously fertile year: the trees were green and full and luxuriant, and flowers bloomed everywhere. When he told his mother where they were planning to go she said to the two boys, If you want to fish for sadd, go over to Shiraj Saaduh first and cut yourselves some branches of aytman to take along.

They cut as much goat's rue as the two of them could carry and headed for Raddat al-Rawgh. They left their supplies beneath the ghaf tree and began trying to fix the goat's rue branches in the watercourses above the basins. They had chosen a spot where the fish were abundant. Moments later, they could see the tiny sadd fishes bobbing on the surface of the water and swimming about as if dizzy.

They harvested the little river fish and dropped them into a small container of water. The effects of the aytman were astonishing to see: it intoxicated the fish and made them lose their bearings. The catch was a large one. They made about fifty palm-leaf packets of fish and set them on the coals they had prepared. It was still early in the afternoon—and then Hamud stumbled on a spot where bees were coming to drink. The water source was in the wadi to the west of the big ghaf tree. Abdallah was asleep. Hamud tried to figure out where the bees were coming from; he watched as they headed westward. He came back and woke up his friend. Get up, c'mon, I found a musaqqi, I found where the bees are drinking, c'mon, let's go search it out.

They did have a good look around. But they couldn't find anything more in the area. After the morning's work they were tired, and they knew they must head home before sunset. They packed all of the grilled fish into a palm-leaf basket and left. That evening Abdallah told his father about finding the bees' drinking place.

What direction were they going?

West, from the big ghaf tree.

The honey—you'll find it in a crevice over there. Over on the eastern slope.

Early the next morning they retraced their steps, almost. They made their way to the spot his father had described. Exactly where he had located the crevice they found the honey, inside the rocks. Hamud was more practiced at cutting down hives. Abdallah watched him and tried to help. When they got home he asked his father how he had known where the honey was—when he was sitting here, in the house? His father told him that he had come upon that same water source some years before. He had trekked directly east from it and had found the beehive in that very crack in the mountain. A place where you cut down a hive, he said, and you take the honey—the bees will go back there. They'll build again.

After that trip he began to learn how many places there were where you could find honey. They were scattered throughout these high elevations. Some of them he came upon by chance while searching and others, he had been told about. The wadis were full of honey; wherever you turned you would find a hive. Others searched near the village; but Abdallah went further afield and higher, to the peaks between and above the wadi canyons. This was the terrain where the wild-animal hunters also ranged. He found many hives where large stores of honey were secreted and sealed.

One morning, coming from the mosque where he and the other men had completed the dawn prayers, he tossed a few dates into the big leather bag he used for gathering honey and headed towards the mountains. He was aiming for Dukkan al-Khummas. From there, he scaled Aqabat al-Rafaas and walked along the ridge that separated Wadi Ya from Wadi Qaabat. He climbed further, reaching Wadi al-Rayaan, and made the descent to Shaghaf al-Habbasa. He was heading towards Wadi Sarid. There he found many watering spots that suggested bees might be nearby. He searched further, found some of the hives, and filled his leather receptacle with honey. He returned home as rapidly as he could, taking the same path down. He arrived just as the late-afternoon call to prayer was piercing the quiet air. He hung the leather bag in its usual place and went off to pray with the others.

Where did you go today? Uncle Khalfan asked him.

I made it as far as Wadi Sarid. I found some watering spots there and so I looked around and found the bees. Came back with a full habban of honey.

At these words Amm Muhammad screeched. You're lying! Just fibbing …

He didn't say anything; he just smiled. Amm Khalfan turned to Amm Muhammad. No, he isn't lying. He's a young fellow—and these young'uns can do it.

Amm Khalfan's words only made Amm Muhammad angrier. Young'un? Getting to Wadi Sarid—just like that! And then finding a musaqqi—just like that! And 'looking around' and he finds it and cuts it down and snap! he's back here to pray the asr with us? Who would believe that? Not unless he flew through the sky.

Everyone laughed at Amm Muhammad's enraged words. From that day on they described Abdallah as *the lad who knew how to fly*. He acquired a new name, too: Honey-Fly. Dhababat al-asal—that was Abdallah.

He always remembered another day—on which he had set his sights for some particular, distant wadis. The surrounding plains were bone-dry but when he located his honey source, the hive was overflowing. He filled every vessel he had with him. He had made himself a large saddlebag that could hold about ten pounds of honey. He would cut down one hive and slice the wax off and pour the contents into the bag—and so on until it was full. He was also carrying a much smaller leather bag that usually held drinking water, but he had to fill that with honey as well. He hung both bags from branches of the giant lathab tree in Mahallat Bint Saad.

But then two women came along. They were looking for wild grass shoots to feed their cows. Instead they found the leather bags hanging there. One of them shouted to her sister, Yallah! Here's some fresh water! She opened the mouth of the larger bag eagerly but it wasn't water that she tipped into her mouth.

Honey! It's honey! she shouted this time. Her companion opened the smaller bag, but no water there, either—a little pool of honey poured into her palm. They were thirsty; they weren't interested in honey right now. No honey hunger at all. They longed for fresh cold water.

Often he altered his route by heading to the rises of the great White Mountain range. Looking for honey there did not mean searching for bees' water sources, for there was no water at all on the Jabal Abyad now, except perhaps the negligible trickles near the summit. On the White Mountain heights, the honey quest meant searching amongst rocks and trees without any particular sense of direction or guideposts to steer you. Or if you had previously come upon an old bee fortress from the past, and you could see the traces, you might try to find it again, just in case the bees had returned to inhabit it.

When you did find it, honey from the White Mountain range was out of this world. And a single hive would fill a whole saddlebag. Abdallah would go on his searches, would figure out where the hives were located, and would return a second and a third time with his equipment to harvest them, one hive after another.

One day as he was on an ascent and searching for clues amongst the boulders he heard the song of a herdswoman rising from a nearby slope. She would be tending her animals. From where he stood he could not see her; but she could study him from the higher elevation where she stood. He kept to his upward path and went on poking between boulders and peering inside trees and bushes. Her voice grew sharper and he could hear the song more clearly. If he heard her, she had thought, surely he would turn back or change direction. But her songs didn't put him off. Or draw him on, either. All his attention was focused on the hunt for honey.

The herdswoman stopped singing. Her voice vanished abruptly and completely from the heights. He didn't know where she had gone, in what direction. Perhaps she was descending into one of the wadis and seeking shade for herself and her animals. Or she had decided on another route.

He kept climbing, jumping from one rock to another. On the heights the sumar blooms had opened—finally. It happened here later than in most areas: the colder winds at this elevation kept the buds tightly shut. The lovely fragrance of baram—the flowers of the gum-acacia—was everywhere here. These flowers gave their name to the honey that everyone hungered for most.

Nearing a huge white rock, now he saw the bees. They were alert, wary, circling around the boulder, and he understood right away that recently, someone had harvested the honey that had been here.

The young woman had been monitoring his ascent anxiously; she was worried that he would snatch away the honey before she could get there. She nestled the circular hive with its contents of honey into her head wrap though some was oozing out, dripping down and checkering the stripes on the wrap. As she walked, more of it trickled out. Drops fell onto the rocks. He followed the drops. He walked far; he stopped only when the path made by the drops came to an end. That's where he found her, crouched in the shadows, miserable and irritated, her eyes red from crying. He saw the head wrap lying on the ground next to her. He couldn't repress his laughter. She glared at him.

All your fault.

You lost the honey.

At least I lost it with my own hands, I didn't lose it to the hands of a stranger.

He had been seventeen when he had that encounter. His ties to the mountains were strong and fierce by then. He went up often during the honey-harvesting season and usually with his brother Sayf. Most often, they went to Khabb al-Ghafa and Wadi Qaabat but they also began searching in earnest in Wadi al-Ghaybar. He remembered how as they were crossing the depression at Bu Sarwala they had come across a water source they were convinced the bees must know. The water was welling up from beneath a large rock—at least at this early hour of the morning. They put their bags down in the shade near the water and climbed higher in search of the hive. They didn't find anything. Hungry, they returned to their campsite. As they sat in the shade eating, they saw it. Less than a meter away was the hive, hanging off a large, smooth rock.

Those were the beginnings of their regular expeditions, which continued every week throughout the months of May and June. The year was 1991 and no one but them had penetrated this site, at least not that year. They would search high and low. For each trip they singled out a particular wadi and did not leave it until they had found all the honey it held. When their rations ran out, they returned home to spend a day or two resting before they set out once again.

His bond with Khabb al-Ghafa wasn't simply about the urge to hunt for honey. His spirit seemed to have lodged itself there, as if he had now found a pasture he had been seeking. Or as if on a certain day, he had turned himself into a sapling or a seed and had burst forth, splitting the ground in Khabb al-Ghafa. Now he was simply returning to it. Coming home.

On one trip he thought of bringing his rifle along. Maybe they would find a bird or a mountain animal they could kill and eat. After spending his day with his brother in patient search for honey, he decided around three o'clock in the afternoon to reconnoiter the larger area. He took the rifle and headed upward following the contour of the wadi. He walked for a long time without really being aware of how far he had come in hopes of finding something to stalk. By now the sun had dipped toward the west and the shadows had lengthened. He heard the braying of goats on one of these summits. He stopped, trying to figure out where the sound was coming from. He raised his binoculars and saw her climbing the jabal.

Sometimes animals escaped from their home pens and fled into the mountains never to return, eventually becoming creatures of the wild akin to the wild goats. They grew skittish and afraid of people and their owners lost hope of ever getting them back. Recapturing them was too difficult. At some point it became understood that they no longer belonged to anyone. He knew all of this and he also knew that at this time of year the herders would have left the wadi because they needed to take their animals to lusher pastures. They abandoned these parts but they would return after some time away—they would regain these places where they had erected shelters beneath the sumar trees near Wadi al-Ghaybar or in

Riddat al-Rawgh or Manzilat Bint Saad. The remains of their stays here—their fire pits and their little shelters—awaited their return.

These livestock—the ones he was studying now—did not belong to any shepherd. He could tell the difference easily between their animals—calm, stolid, familiar with people—and these creatures. If anyone still had any rights over these animals, by this hour late in the day they would be near their pens. He knew that the domesticated animals always returned home on their own shortly before sunset. They knew they would find their carer waiting there and ready to give them some dried dates to conclude the day.

So he would hunt one of them, he decided. Because they didn't belong to anyone and he had every right to pursue them. He quickened his pace to follow them, wanting to get to the summit before they did; he even ran, and reached his high lookout panting. Everything was utterly silent around him. He could no longer hear those bleats and he did not know where the animals had gone or how they had managed to vanish from his line of sight. He stood still in that soundless landscape and tried to listen, hoping perhaps he might even hear the sound of their hooves clacking against the rocks. Or the sound of scattering pebbles rolling away under their feet.

It was almost dark, and it was a long way back to his brother. Just as he was deciding to turn back he heard the soft rumble of a goat somewhere nearby. He scurried toward the sound. He stopped suddenly and raised his rifle. He fired, there was a drawn-out scream and the kid goat fell. The echo seemed to resound the length of the wadi. The animal struggled to get to its feet and escape. He lifted his rifle again and this time, he nailed the animal.

He pulled a knife from his belt and slit its throat. He tried to pick it up but he couldn't. He didn't know what to do. The sun had gone down. He left the goat where it lay and hurried back to find his brother. Sayf could help him to carry the slain animal. It took him some time to reach the spot where his brother was waiting for him and readying their campsite. He recounted his adventure and they hurried back, hoping to get there before the darkness swallowed the wadis completely.

They reached the spot where he thought he had felled the kid goat. He had not even tried to drag it down from the mountain slope into the lower wadi. In the darkness they searched for it but they couldn't find it. They had one torch between them; the batteries were nearly exhausted; they could not search any further. Thoroughly tired, they set out empty-handed to return to camp.

They were walking in utter darkness with only the very weak light of the depleted batteries to help them. Sometimes the flashlight flickered out completely. They decided they would turn it on only when they came upon particularly narrow and difficult passages. Reaching the wadi at Khabb al-Ghafa, the hissing of snakes near the pools of water made their hair stand on end. But they couldn't do anything to lessen their fright since the flashlight was completely dead by now.

It must have been about nine-thirty before they reached their campsite. They were so drained that they did not attempt to cook. The next morning, they woke up only when the sunlight began to slap their faces.

They made their coffee and then they retraced their steps looking again for the dead goat. In the daylight they found it, the corpse swollen and the smell of death already rising. They could no longer use it but they couldn't simply leave it here on the slope. Another honey-hunter might come by and suspect they were the killers. They tried to hide the goat carcass somewhere but the whole area was so rocky that it was impossible to dig a hole. They had the idea of interring it by heaping stones over it and that is what they did, until the body was almost completely hidden from sight.

Coming down, they could see a man walking along the wadi with two younger men who must be his sons. They were going towards Manzilat Bint Saad. The traces of blood from the dead goat had left spattered stains on Abdallah bin Hamad's shoes and he feared encountering the man face-to-face. The man might ask him why he had blood on his shoes. When they reached the wadi he tried to rub out the spots of blood with some water. He managed to get most of it out and he thought the discoloring that remained was not so obviously blood.

The man was someone they knew. He was from the village of Naqsi. They did come upon him and his sons resting under the big sidra tree at the point where Wadi al-Nimarat ran into al-Wadi al-Kabir. They sat down for a round of coffee and drank some water from their thermoses. The man asked them about the honey thereabouts and they gave him a terse answer. He was a man of about seventy, still healthy and vigorous and fully capable of scaling the heights here. He wanted to tell them about his life, spent in these mountains. How he had met their father. How a firm friendship had grown between them. The man's stories went on and on. Abdallah and Sayf were anxious to be on their way. Finally Sayf managed to stanch the meandering stream of the man's chat and they said their goodbyes, adding a barely sufficient helping of apologies, and headed off to Khabb al-Ghafa.

A single excursion might go on for a week and perhaps another two or three days beyond it. Abdallah bin Hamad and his brother Sayf ventured to the truly far-off wadis. Sometimes they walked the entire, level length of the wadi and other times they took grueling shortcuts upward and across the mountains. The ascents were difficult but they preferred the mountain routes because these gave them more time to spend once they reached their destination.

To get to Khabb al-Ghafa—the locale he liked best of all—Abdallah bin Hamad would climb to Aqabat Sam, the mountain pass that took him directly to a point not far from Khabb al-Ghafa. But to do this he had to take his jeep, leaving it in the village of Bu'd and then entering Wadi Sam on foot. From there he climbed and climbed. But the ascent took only an hour and a half and then he would be heading down to the wadi on the other side.

Previously, he had heard much of Aqabat Sam but he hadn't yet attempted it. Instead he would ascend through Aqabat al-Rafaas and from there climb down to Wadi al-Jarif and then directly into Khabb al-Ghafa.

But he had wanted to find a different route. Aqabat al-Rafaas was a very high and difficult pass. It drained his energy just to get to the top.

When he tried this new route, he believed his journey would be more or less completed when he scaled the pass even if he had not yet reached Khabb al-Ghafa. The remaining distance was short and easy because it was level ground. He would walk along the ridge dividing Wadi Ya from Wadi Qaabat, moving from one height to the next along a level path. He had tried the ascent to Aqabat al-Rafaas several times but when he discovered the route through Aqabat Sam he was happy to find it easier. Or the distance seemed shorter, anyway.

True, he did not need his vehicle if he were taking the Aqabat al-Rafaas route. And the new alternative meant he did have to take it as far as that village, Bu'd, which was about seven kilometers from home. Sometimes he asked an acquaintance to take him there. He certainly preferred getting a ride there which meant he could avoid having to leave his vehicle in Wadi Sam. Anyone who saw it there would know he had gone into the mountains.

He found another kind of enjoyment on the Rafaas route, though. Reaching the summit he could survey all the wadis laid out below him. He could see the villages in the distance and run his eyes along the slopes and down into the valleys. And the fresh, gentle breeze up here seemed to lift away the exertion and strain of his ascent. Ever the energetic spectator, he loved to contemplate every detail of these surroundings—the peaks in their ever-changing features, the array of colors, the vast distances he could traverse and see, the shifting landscapes and curves of the mountains in every direction, the wadi bottoms and the sloping climbs, the villages and tiny lanes far below. He loved to listen for all the sounds coming to him from afar. He wished he could just stay on here, floating in and through the world these heights made.

He scaled Jabal Rayyaan early one evening in search of a honey-filled beehive whose inhabitants had been getting their water from a deep crevice directly below. The bees took a spiraling path because they had such a sharp ascent to get home. He had tried all the usual methods of figuring out which way they were going; he lay in wait just above the crevice to see whether he could track even one bee with his binoculars. The bees had gone in a generally westward direction and this posed difficulties for any bee-hunter. For one thing, the sunset came on rapidly and the final blaze of sun rays from low on the western horizon would not reflect against the wings of a bee. The evening gusts of wind, stronger than they were earlier in the day, threw the bees off-course. This meant they would not follow a straight path as they did in the early mornings when it was still and quiet—a time of day that honey-hunters preferred too.

He had been here since morning perched on the lookout with his binoculars pressed against his face. He concentrated on the large cleft in the rocks into which the bees vanished as he was watching their ascent from his location below. He stayed where he was, squatting and motionless for a very long time until finally he saw two bees ascending into the air together and heading directly for the summit of Jabal al-Rayyan. He followed them. That evening he did find the hive, mounted in a large isbaq growing on a slope near the mountain's highest point. He tried to remove the honey without injuring the tree but it was no use. If you so much as scratched an isbaq, he knew, its sticky, milk-white sap would run and drops of it would blend into the honey. He knew exactly how difficult it was to pick off the sac of honey from an isbaq. Especially when the hive was as large as this, occupying virtually all the tree branches. But he was able to get the better of this hive—like others, so cunningly interwoven with the tree—by cutting the branches themselves and pasting a length of cling film over the cuts to prevent the tree's milk from flowing.

But he couldn't avoid some isbaq sap, and it made him itch terribly. His fingers and hands stuck together and he knew they would bond to anything he touched because the sap was so sticky. He knew that every drop of sap falling into the honey meant a bout of diarrhea for the human being who swallowed it. He wanted to keep this honey pure. Even one drop of sap and it would lose its quality.

The easiest harvest was when honey hung in a tree—any tree but the isbaq, that is. Whenever he found a hive hanging in a qafas tree or a hindbub or even within the leaves of a date palm, he was delighted because it would not require great effort to extract the honey and return the hive to its place. He could tie it back up to the tree branches as he had found it. The operation itself was straightforward but it did require painstaking work to guarantee that the hive was hanging firmly in place once again. It was even trickier when the hive sat in a cave or hung from a rock. He would usually look for an appropriate tree nearby. He would saw off a branch and break it in two, and insert the top part of the hive between the two lengths. He would do his best to fix the split branch firmly in place, ideally hanging between two rocks if he could manage that. Or he made a sort of scaffolding using more branches, to hold the hive in place firmly enough that it would not topple with the first gust of wind.

Before, he hadn't cared about returning the empty hive shell to its previous usefulness by fixing it in place after he had gotten the honey out. But he had come to understand how necessary this was. Besides, one could return to the same hive later on, fairly certain that it would be there. The business of replacing the empty hive, and finding it re-used, usually succeeded. But sometimes the makers of wild honey did not welcome having the sanctity of the hive invaded. They found a new refuge instead.

As was well-known around the village Abdallah bin Hamad hailed from a family of skilled mountain climbers with profound knowledge of how to search for honey. Every man in the family had their memories—their own stories with the mountains. They had their own routes, too, which might or might not converge with the paths others chose. Abdallah had gone into the mountains just like all the rest of them. But then there came a time when rumors and insinuations seemed to be eddying around him from every side. He was afraid that someone would catch on to his mountain sallies and divulge his activities to the province's governor even if he did not use his rifle for anything more than hunting foxes or mountain birds—pigeons, sand grouse. But caution was crucial, as they said. He didn't know who was his friend and who was his enemy. If rumors reached some interested party they would conceal the name of whoever it was that had told them the tale while opening an investigation, little by little, looking into whatever bits of news they could pick up from others. It might put him in difficulty, which he certainly did not need in his life.

That was why Abdallah began leaving his donkey on the mountain slopes for periods so long that it almost grew wild. He told everyone he knew that his donkey had gone missing. He was looking high and low for his donkey, he would declare, but he still hadn't found the animal. At first people believed the story of the missing donkey. Some villagers even scolded Abdallah for having neglected the animal, allowing it to stay long enough out in the mountains that it forgot the comforts of living with him and began associating instead with the wild donkeys on the slopes. Some villagers were so sympathetic that they too began looking out for the donkey wherever they happened to be. Maybe they would catch a glimpse of Abdallah bin Hamad's animal somewhere or other and if so, they would let him know where it was. Others advised him to call off the search and buy another donkey. But he always told them that his heart couldn't bear the thought of it.

Every time he went into the mountains on a wild honey search, he told folks that he was going off to look for his donkey. If a person stopped by his home to ask for him the visitor was told that he was on the hunt for his donkey. But then someone happened to cross his path as he was returning to the village and he couldn't prevent them seeing that he was carrying honey. A lot of honey. The story grew stale; gradually, everyone knew the truth behind it. Years passed and Abdallah was still announcing that he was going off to find his donkey. The villagers knew he had pulled the wool over their eyes. Eventually, the deception itself became a joke. Whenever anyone encountered him now they would ask, Found your donkey? And Abdallah always responded with a laugh. I'll find him soon.

From being a tale about Abdallah bin Hamad and his donkey the fiction became a badge adopted by anyone who was going in search of wild honey. We're going off to look for Abdallah bin Hamad's donkey, they would say. When they returned to the village people asked, Did you find Abdallah bin Hamad's donkey? If they had found the elusive prey they were after, they said yes— meaning honey, of course. Or they said no. Sometimes their answer echoed Abdallah's own usual response: Soon ... soon, we'll find it.

Abdallah was branded with this for years but eventually the village lost memory of it as people moved on to other stories and new parcels of news about this person or that. No one really remembered it now apart from a few individuals who were susceptible to living on their memories; or it might be churned up as an occasional joke. In the past, whenever Abdallah bin Hamad had found a beehive and opened the collar around it to see whether any of the honey had already been harvested, but instead found the honey still sealed in wax, and knew the hive was mature, he simply cut it down. If it was not ready for harvesting, he would cut some reeds, bunch them up just below the hive, and place a stone on top. This was a sign to all that someone had found this hive. It would not be right for someone else to cut it down. This was a longstanding practice amongst honey gatherers. Even if someone was returning fatigued and empty-handed, searching for that hive and finding it—but finding it marked as a hive someone else had already found—his hand wouldn't obey him when it came to cutting down the hive. He wouldn't want to break that long-respected understanding.

In recent years though, people's respect for this practice had dwindled away. No one trusted any more that tokens like this would be honored. They figured that the next person here, coming upon the hive, would not respect these older practices anyway. So when they found a hive they siphoned off the honey even if there was very little of it to take. Whenever it came up—this issue of marking the honey one had found—Abdallah bin Hamad would observe that no one trusted anyone else these days. And that it was a big reason why wild bees had nearly vanished altogether—why they were so rare in the mountains these days. That it was a punishment from God. When corruption spreads across the land, he said, the people's God-given income vanishes. The gifts of this earth are no longer. Creatures die and new illnesses spread. Sickness afflicts people's bodies just as it has spread through their souls.

Chapter Nine

You seized my mind from me
your beauty from the prophet Yusuf
what recourse have I before this magic?

AS A LITTLE BOY, AND as he grew older, he inspired the women's adoration. Seeing him, one or another of the village matrons would declare her hopes to all who were within hearing: that when he grew older he would marry her daughter. If the woman didn't have a daughter, she dreamed that she would have one and when that baby girl grew up he would be her destiny.

Sawwaada bint Khalaf, the herdswoman known to all because of her intermittent visits to town, sewed and embroidered kummahs. She was commissioned to make one for his little head. It would be embroidered with stars as his mother had requested. When she came back, bringing the splendid headgear with her—stars glittering across its surface—Sawwaada bint Khalaf called the boy over for a fitting. Setting it on his head—he was eleven years old at the time—Herdswoman Sawwaada said to him, Hurry up and grow! Thamna's keeping her eye on you.

Sawwaada's ten-year-old daughter was sitting next to her mother, still and silent, staring at the magnificent sight—that gorgeous kummah set atop a face shining with earnest beauty.

In their late-afternoon women's gatherings, mothers drank their coffee together and rounded out their social time by breathing in yet another lungful of sandalwood incense. They rubbed local saffron across their foreheads. They cut and sewed and embroidered the stories they had always told. Said had a boy as beautiful as the moon whose body already gave off the scent of manhood as he scampered through the village lanes. Any woman who happened to be walking along there when his form appeared would come to a halt. Women standing up would sit down. Women who were already sitting would slap their hands smartly against their cheeks in wonder and appreciation. Every one of them dreamed that his hands were held out to her.

He might as well be Yusuf, he's so beautiful, chuckled Subha bint Jamil.

Fatima al-Amshaa chimed in to add a folk hero everyone knew to Subha's prophet Joseph. He's as straight and tall as Abu Zayd! she exclaimed.

All they knew of Yusuf—or of Abu Zayd for that matter—came from the books that Wadha bint Hamad had in her possession. For Wadha was forever reading those wondrous tales to them—and they loved listening to her read. She was the only woman in the village who could read a book without stumbling over the words. She was just like the men of learning—like the teacher-preacher here, M'allim Salim bin Ali.

Wadha had learned these skills from her father, Hamad bin Saud. From a very young age she had been close at his side whenever he began to read out loud. She memorized the poetry that he read or recited in her hearing. She learned the odes of the famous maddened love-struck Majnun Layla and those of the venerated poet al-Mutanabbi. She knew poems by the great medieval poets Abu Tammam and Abu Nuwas, and others among the ancients. She had even learned by heart a goodly portion of the long didactic poem that taught precepts of the faith and its laws, *Urjuzat jawhar al-nizam* by the Omani scholar Abdallah bin Hamid 'Nur al-Din' al-Salimi. When her father lost his eyesight, it was Wadha who read to him. Whenever a new book came his way he asked her to sit next to him and read it out. Every morning and over several days, she would read a section to him, until they had read the book cover to cover.

In the late afternoons the women sat together in the outside space created by the enclosed alleys, spreading out their mats. The women brought fruit if they had it to share along with the afternoon coffee. In her pocket every woman carried a new story: it would be something that had happened that day. Wadha carried her book and that was all she cared about. She didn't have the same wants and needs as the other neighborhood women. Her coffee—her energy—was enfolded in her book. Her caffeine was there in her clear voice which listeners found so pleasant to their ears. As she read, the timbre of her voice rose and fell exactly as the men's voices did when they read. No voice could compete with hers and everyone got quiet when she began to read.

She read the *Mustatraf* to them. She read the magnificent *Book of Songs* with its stories of medieval entertainers. She read out the life of the sainted Hasan al-Basri and the epic of Bani Hilal, narrating the tribe's trek across the north of Africa. She gave them the poems of the famous Antara al-Absi and his life story as well. And—there was the story of the Prophet Yusuf, may God's peace be upon him! She read from the collected poetry of al-Sayf al-Naqqad, from *Tuhfat al-'ayan*, and from the mystical poetry of Ibn al-Farid. And there were many more.

They listened to her, bent in the submissive attitude of persons at prayer. Even the children grew silent. The entire space was still and quiet. From homes nearby, the men listened too. In one sitting she would read about three pages—in these old large-format and small-print books; or sometimes four. She ended her reading with a pious supplication. And then the coffee was passed around, and along with it, a vial of perfume. Someone would wave a stick of frankincense around each of them and the samgh incense made locally, a blend of spices and fragrances. The women applied kohl and oil to each other. Just before the muezzin called the late-afternoon prayer their session would break up and they would all go home.

Sarah bint Sultan bin Abdallah rarely left her father's house, which sat in an outlying hamlet of the village. But she had been steeped in the fine words the women had when it came to describing Azzan bin Said. Secretly she fell in love with him, in the way that village women would when passion and imagination grew feverish, and then melded and mounted together. Sarah asked her friends to come along with her on a foray to the quarter where he lived but she didn't tell them why. All she said was: I want to see the village, I want to see what it is like.

Nothing more divided the community's two tiny clusters of homes from each other than the wadi and the lane snaking between the palm trees. But Sarah had never crossed the wadi. She knew nothing of the houses standing on the other side of it except the descriptions she had heard from the women in their gatherings.

Now, Sarah's pace was slow as they made their way through the village on the wadi's other bank. Whenever they encountered someone she studied the face surreptitiously. She was trying to square the descriptions she had heard from women with the features of the men passing by. She gripped her friend Safiya bint Sulayman's hand and squeezed it even harder every time someone came by; she was signaling to her friend that she wanted to know who this man was. Safiya would tell her. But they hadn't come across Wad Said. Sarah could only spend a certain period of time away from the house and she tried to make the most of every moment, hoping against hope that she would catch a glimpse of the boy if nothing more.

But it didn't happen. She didn't cross his path that day even though they walked by his family's house. She did see his father, who was on his way home. When he saw her he began immediately to guess who she was, assessing her features. He asked her what her name was and told her that she looked just like her mother and her mother's brothers, more than she resembled her father. When she heard a moment later that this man was Azzan's father, she whipped around to look at him again, trying to study his form before he disappeared from sight, further inside the quarter.

There seemed to be many occasions for asking Safiya to accompany her into that part of the village. She always came up with a different reason for making yet another expedition. And finally she did come across him. He was sitting under the mango tree. She knew immediately who this was. She tried to get a good look at him, but only with a quick sidelong glance and then another, hoping that her friend wouldn't notice. He looked at her; their eyes met; he averted his gaze and gave all his attention to scratching at the ground with a small stick. He was tall and well-built—she could see that, even if he was sitting down. He had long fingers. That's what Sarah was able to see in this first chance she had had to see him in person.

Her eyes flashed and watered; almost savagely, she flicked a tear off her face before it could betray her. All of her attention had been focused on just creating an opportunity to see him. Now—how could she hurry off so quickly? Her heart spoke to her: You haven't had enough. She spoke back to her heart: *Enough* is what brings on ruin.

At home, Sarah grew stiller and quieter. Much of the time her mind seemed to be wandering. Her long silences bewildered others. When she did speak her voice was hoarse and barely audible, as though something was keeping it imprisoned inside. Anyone who tried to have a conversation with her had to listen very closely and carefully to gather in her scattered, fragmented words.

Yet there was a story Sarah began to weave together, even as she seemed oblivious to her surroundings and to other people. Reading to Sarah and others from the famous treatise on love by the Andalusian scholar-poet Ibn Hazm, *The Dove's Necklace*, Wadha would declaim: Love—and may God help you!—love begins in jest and ends in gravity. Love is too magnificent, too glorious, for human description. Its reality will become perceptible only through suffering. Love is not prohibited by the religion; love is not frowned upon in the Sharia. After all, our hearts are in God's hands, Mighty and Majestic is He.

Sarah pressed her hand against her head and said to Wadha, Aunt, read that part again.

So Wadha repeated it. Love—and may God help you! ..., and Sarah said the words after her, all the way through 'in God's hands' ... and then she asked Wadha to recite it yet again until she had the passage firmly in her memory. Now she could say it to herself; as she murmured it, her fingernails dug into her embroidered dishdasha and traced the letters and words of the passage hard across it.

Wadha just smiled and praised the girl for her intelligence. Addressing the group of listening women, she urged them, Keep these words in mind, now—because you've all heard them and you've learned. Life isn't just the work we do at home, the husband, the children. Life is more than that—keep this lesson in your heads. Read it; repeat it to yourselves.

They went home from their taasira—the women's late-afternoon gathering. Ibn Hazm's words in *The Dove's Necklace* were echoing and re-echoing through Sarah's heart. Her mind soared away to unknown grottos, the darkest, deepest spots in these cave-pocked hills. Sarah was no longer the girl they knew. And then Sarah fell ill, very ill. Her fevered ravings went on for so many days and nights that her family believed an alien and hostile spirit must have come to inhabit the body of their beloved daughter. Her eyes looked completely different, now—glazed over, fixed in a bewildered stare.

In this village nothing could remain secret. Hearts that might appear sealed tightly against the outside world, closely guarding a certain passion—or a particular rancor—could not shield themselves or others against these late-afternoon conversations amongst the gathered women. Trying to guide her thread through the eye of her needle, Safiya bint Khammaas observed, A person's mind is like the tiny hole in this needle; it is nigh-impossible to push a heavy cord through it. The mind of this girl—well, look, a virus has got into it and has begun tunnelling through it, and then consuming it, getting bigger and bigger until it takes over her head. I saw her with my own eyes talking with Wad Said! Why, yes—she was there, clutching her water-jug at the bridge over the falaj. He had his hands on his hips and he was standing there talking to her. The shame of it! That's what I felt. How could a girl stand out in the middle of the road just like that talking to a man who isn't one of her family?

Your tongues will land you in the Fire, my dears! It was Old Kadhiya speaking up. Ahh, these tongues that never go quiet, never stop wagging on about others. Leave the girl alone, can't you? And, aren't you worried her mother might hear what you are saying about her?

Rahma leans against the wall in their gathering place which is adjacent to Kadhiya's home. Rahma tips her head back and goes on speaking, but as if she is speaking only to herself or perhaps saying the nonsensical things that one babbles in a dream.

What is the lover but a soul that carpets the ground, and tries to come out of its body, to rise and to circle in the heavens far above. May God freeze my tongue if I am lying to you! I heard her once, when she was by herself, giving in to her aloneness. I heard her say, Ya Rabb!—Lord, the heart of the lover is an earthenware jug, one that is cracked and chipped.

Everyone has thought of Sarah as the most brilliant flower of the quarter, Rahma went on. When she leaves the house, she is always perfumed with the sweetest aromas and the most fragrant incense. Her father hasn't stinted on anything. Sarah always has a new set of clothes. Even on an ordinary outing she looks like she's about to attend a banquet or is on her way to a wedding.

But now it's all passed into those legendary tales that you swear you don't really believe. Women! sitting here in your afternoon gathering and so weary of your usual stories. Because our everyday stories are like the heavy loads we have to carry on our shoulders. The weight of them never grows lighter. The burden sits there forever, like a sin that's never forgiven. But legends, now—they send us into the air, flying, freeing ourselves. They let us dream that everything is possible in the future.

Who will believe it, seeing this crazed young woman wander through the lanes and amongst the date palms? Who would believe that this stumbling figure was not so long ago that lovely girl so fetching that whenever she came near, her presence commanded people's gaze in spite of themselves? This beautiful girl who could say a mere word and everyone's ears would strain to hear it? Will she even recognize herself if she looks in the mirror now? She'll see a young woman with unfocused eyes, uncombed hair and an unending trickle of tears down her face.

Sarah was on her way home when she heard some noise and saw a knot of people gathering. She came a little closer to the commotion and mounted a small rise in hopes of seeing what it was about. People were clustered around a body lying on the ground. She stood still and stared but she couldn't tell who it was. She was about to leave when a young boy, about ten years old, rushed by. Without being asked, he called out. Wad Said is drunk!

She froze. She didn't believe this boy's words. She remained where she was until she saw that the figure who had been lying there had gotten to his feet and was trying to make his way through the crowd of people taunting him. She stumbled away, waves of fever coursing through her body. She reached home but fell in a faint on the threshold.

Day by day, Sarah's condition worsened. Her father took her to Muscat but she was no better when they came back. He took her to one place after another in search of treatment—seers, chemists, sorcerers. But Sarah had lost her mind for good and she never got it back, even for a brief spell. Her father bought honey—a lot of honey—to nourish her. Various medications were mixed into it, and herbal remedies that were known to have beneficial properties. But the spirit's hunger surpasses any other. Sarah had no interest in eating and did so only when forced. Her mother tried constantly to get her to take a swallow, a bite or maybe two.

Salma bint Khalifa, who had maintained her silence as she listened to the women's talk around her, spoke. Mercy to Sarah bint Sultan, mercy be upon her for the day she was born amongst you, as you watched, and inspected, and refused to avert your eyes. Mercy be upon her for the years when she grew, and grew beautiful, her torso as slim and fresh as a sapling, a countenance worthy of praise. Mercy be upon her as your eyes consumed her even as you wouldn't invoke God's name in her guarding—God who created her. You did not beseech protection from Satan—that devil who accompanies you in your comings and your goings. Mercy be upon Sarah—may she be spared your tongues that did not sound in prayer for the wellbeing of one of God's creatures.

And you—with your hateful, ugly self! How could your heart and mind persuade you to slander this poor girl? And hint that she's committed the most awful deeds? How can an innocent heart that is truly wrapped in goodness and protected from falling into error fall into passion? We are the daughters of the generous and the noble: and we do not need passion in order to live fully. That sort of passion is a shame and a disgrace. We were raised well and we know that passion degrades the body and the soul. No—what afflicted this poor girl was your envy and nothing more. So ask mercy upon her—or at least stop your tongues and shut your mouths. Leave her alone. Maybe with the grace of God she will stand again on her own feet. Maybe the veil of this tribulation will be lifted from her vision and she can once again be healthy and whole.

Sarah is her father's daughter—a lovely bearing and a beautiful character. She was raised among us and in our care. We watched her grow like a beautiful flowering tree, as the branches of her being arced and blossomed. She wore clothes that aren't like yours; clothes of carefully chosen and vivid fabric which enhanced her natural beauty. She had fragrances that gave bloom to her femininity. Wherever she was, the entire place was immersed in her scent. She filled whatever space she came into—no one else would be noticed or listened to.

Every story she heard, read by Wadha bint Hamad, she memorized, making your eyes widen in amazement. But you wouldn't make mention of the Merciful as her fine voice intoned the poetry that Wadha had recited first.

> If only Layla al-Akhyaliya had greeted me kindly
> when around me there lie only cold slabs and stones
> I would welcome Layla with a most cheerful smile
> or send an echo from the grave to ring out or moan…

Do you remember how old Kadhiya wept hearing her singing those lines of the great Sufi poet Ibn al-Farid?

> My heart tells me now: loving you is my ruin
> but my heart's ransomed to you, if you notice or don't
> I would never erase this love's presence, were I one
> who cannot suffer sorrow—for I'm one who is true
> I have only my spirit—and exerting the self
> in love of the adored is never undue

And Shannuwa bint Burayk—do you remember when the jinni entered her body and she began to shake, and then she became so agitated as we sat watching and listening? Shannuwa, whose body is as wide as a sawqama tree trunk. Even a man with very big hands and long fingers can't span her waist! Shannuwa shook until we thought the earth wouldn't hold beneath us. You saw with your own eyes how Salima bint Ghufayl flung herself to the ground out of fear that the earth would split open … that day, you recited out loud whatever you had memorized—the holy verses, the prayers, the supplications—so that the spirit that lived inside of her wouldn't come out and invade one of your weak bodies instead!

Shannuwa, who was possessed by jinn when she was little, and those spirits made her wander in the open plains at night. She would be asleep at her mother's, but when her mother woke up, the daughter was not by her side, even though her father always shut the door tightly and locked it from the outside. Shannuwa still found a way out. How? No one knows—the jinn would take her. Like them she could turn into a gust of wind and get out through the cracks between the wall and the door.

Get out! and go distances. One time they found her in a cave at the very top of Jabal al-Maqsura. She was sound asleep. They woke her up and she said she didn't know how she had gotten there. That was the way it was, night after night: she would be gone from inside these locked rooms guarded by some bold young men ready for a little adventure. She would disappear all of a sudden—as soon, it seems, as whoever was with her got sleepy enough to doze off.

On one particular day, her Aunt Moza settled into the girl's room, believing she could keep an eye on her niece and could avoid falling asleep; but only moments passed before she dozed off. She woke up several hours later. She told the lads standing guard that she had sensed a cold and aromatic wind sweeping in from the corners of the room. She had tried to overcome her sleepiness but she could not.

The spirits took the girl to a new locale every night. Her family put on an elaborate and costly zar ceremony to appease the spirits. The particular jinni who was riding her quieted down. He no longer spirited her off but he did reappear now and then, giving her such strong convulsions that she would lose consciousness. We had to fetch the oud-oil concentrate and put it up close to her nose before she would come to her senses.

Envy—it's eaten up your insides, all of you! And there is nothing more to this life, in the end, than the dust of the earth! What did you do for that girl besides devouring her mind and the years of her young life? Just like your tongues devoured Wad Said. Who would ever believe that this well-brought-up, steady and thoughtful young man—if the respect due him were weighed against that of the entire village, he would outweigh them all—who could believe he would go this way, losing his mind? His father's careful training going in vain, his mother coming to me in tears, distressed and complaining.

I said to her, Your son has been bewitched by someone. The wretched woman cried so hard that her face veil was dripping wet. How vile, how disgusting—what you have done to these young ones! Do you even know what a mother's heart is—you who are mothers? Aren't you afraid that what happened to them might happen to your own boys and girls? Do you have any feelings at all in your hearts besides malice? Envy, malice—that's what you use to mess up everything.

Azzan was a little sparrow-boy, warbling and hopping from branch to branch, a playful, heedless little bird who had no idea what the passage of time was holding in wait for him. He did not realize that a hunter was in ambush there, ready to chop him down—to topple him from the highest tufts of the date palms or to lead him into the very lowest gorge in these parts. A hunter of no mercy who doesn't care how weak the sparrow might be, this creature with no fat on his tiny body and nothing to keep him from eternal hunger. The hunter thought only about the instant in which he would strike his prey down. That magnificent plunge! The hunter would enjoy the sight of the little bird dropping all that distance and he would pat himself on the back. Only one shot and I brought it down, that devious target—a tiny bird who was hopping from branch to branch!

Have your hearts gone completely cold? Envious women, do you feel victorious at the fall of others' children, whether it's sickness or bad behavior? His mother went searching for him all over the village. If she came upon him in that drunken state she would bend over him and rub his head until he got quiet and began crying, huddled there in her arms like a little child who has gotten lost all of a sudden but finds his way back to bury himself in his mother's hugs. He said to her, Tell my father to understand, tell him to forgive me. She tried to get him to come home with her but he refused, he would not go back there. For the malice that envy brings destroyed his mind. It is all because of you, envious women, whose tongues work and work on God's creatures—and then you talk about how this and that happened, oh dear! You spin new stories for each other—and then you believe them.

Salma bint Khalifa got to her feet and left them, calling God's name down on their wrongdoing. They were silent. They stared at each other, each one asking herself the question, reciting incantations and the Verse of the Throne: asking themselves, Who is the real source of malicious envy among us?

Another time they were sitting together when Rahma bint Sulayman observed the change that had come over their gatherings. Ever since Sarah bint Sultan fell ill, Wadha bint Hamad no longer sits with us, she said. And she has stopped carrying her books when she goes on visits around the village.

Someone else said, Well, she was the witch.

It all happens, you know, said another.

Wadha reads books, yes, but the books she reads to us are poetry and beautiful sayings and religious rulings. They say she has many, many books, of all different sizes and shapes. One of the women told us that someone saw her reading from al-Ghazali's book, and that she has that book *Shams al-ma'arif*. It's been said she has two faces. The one you see is all mercy; and the one you don't see, somewhere beneath the first one, is all punishment. And that mad Sarah is simply absent, that's all. It was Wadha who took away her mind and her life and left her like a dumb animal. And it was Wad Said, too.

Who is her next victim? someone else asked. After all, they thought, Wadha's character and her habits seemed not to be what they had been. She no longer came out of her house—or not very often. She did not sit with the women when they came together to talk. She shut her door and stayed inside and avoided everyone.

In her coma, Sarah muttered lines from the poetry of the 'mad lover' of Layla, and lines by Ibn Farid, and she repeated these lines over and over.

> O, dear departed, a patient soul traces your wake
> but is there a path to you, one I will find?
> My tear-heavy eyelids were unjust to your being
> and my heart was untrue as it burnt to ashes
> my mind!

Her father felt keenly the weight of what his daughter said, or didn't say, in her ravings. She did not mention anyone by name. The poetry she recited all summoned the venerable lines of the ancients. Her disconnected words and mutterings seemed those of a wholly distracted mind. The impact of her illness was very painful to him. He loved Sarah, and he respected her, too, and he felt much more for her than he did for his sons. Sarah was his only daughter. He was ready to go to whatever trouble and expense were necessary to cure her. But there was nothing he could do to bring back his beloved child's mind—this rose of his, whose sweet fragrance had perfumed his life.

If he had not had the usual occupations and worries of a man prominent in his community, he would have shut the world out and sat at his daughter's side, trying everything he could think of to solve the riddle of what she had become. This beautiful painful poetry of love—these lines she would suddenly blurt out—cut him to the heart. If only he could know who it was who had broken her heart—who it was who could return her to life. He knew nothing at all about the passion that had crazed her, for even in her distracted state she never uttered a name. As if the mention of that name would land her once again on the path of all that was right and proper—where she did not want to be.

Days went by when Sarah was entirely silent and calm, going quietly into her room and in general seeming a different person, someone who might emerge whole from her illness. She would take a bath, comb her hair, perfume herself, and sit down before the mirror. She stared at herself for hours at a time. Then she would rise, go over to her bed, and sleep peacefully and soundly. As soon as she woke up, she would hurry to take another bath, followed by another long session sitting in front of the mirror. Days and days went by like this. She did not say a word. The ravings subsided. She did not cry and her eyes seemed focused once again. As if her well-being had returned. She never left her room. Her mother brought her choice dishes, the tastiest fruit, bread rounds slathered in samna and honey, and she ate, sitting in front of the mirror, not leaving it for a moment, staring calmly at her own image. There seemed to be no time for anything else. No one knew what she saw in that mirror, because she didn't talk to anyone, didn't even babble or rave. She didn't make a sound.

But then, after one of these periods of calm, Sarah would return to her state of madness—neglecting herself, coming out of her room and into the courtyard but only to sit under the trellis to one side for hours at a time. Day after day she would refuse food and she wouldn't drink any water. She recited her lines of poetry over and over and mumbled deliriously about the beloved and never once got up from the spot beneath that trellis. The courtyard was spacious; there were many places to sit. But that one corner was her spot, night and day and whatever the season. The cold air did not keep her from sitting out there for hours. Afraid that she would fall ill with a cold, her father tried to put up a thick tarpaulin around the trellis to keep out the harsh winter wind. In the summer they opened the courtyard to the breeze as fully as they could so that Sarah could catch her breath.

Chapter Ten

Don't blame my eyes: your love is like a storm
destroying all in its path
The storm came up
and snapped away my branches

LIKE THE UNTROUBLED, EVEN JOYFUL, cries of a little child, al-Hatati's voice could fill his ears and keep on echoing there. Long ago he had become attached to this old man—since the beginnings, since childhood, since he remembered seeing al-Hatati scuttle through the village lanes bringing his glee with him—a sense of fun and enchantment along with a certain oddness and an appealing air of unconcern about whatever was going on around him.

Hearing al-Hatati at the door calling out his name, he would try to drag himself up from the mat where he lay, moving his body as if it were a deadweight coming slowly back to life and surfacing from a pond of heavy, sticky silt. After it had happened, time itself had become so heavy, so unmoving.

But now, having been finally jolted awake, yanked out of his constant drunkenness, Azzan bin Said was coming back to life. Years had passed; a blur, as if those years had existed only in a dream. He had missed important village milestones and solemn commemorations. People had died; people had gone away; and if they came back they found him exactly as they had left him, his fingers tight around the neck of his cologne bottle. Sprawled somewhere on the village outskirts he would be taking desperate sniffs, sucking in the aroma sip after sip. With every sip a wave of it reached his insides and off he went, fleeing to another kingdom, another existence; crossing seas with no end, dying and coming back to life thousands of times each day.

Now he had no one. Suddenly, amidst these uncountable voyages into oblivion he found himself really and truly alone in this world. When he heard the news—in a state between slumber and wakefulness—the impact of it was tremendous. He couldn't move. He remained absolutely still and crumpled on the ground, hearing nothing but a loud ringing in his ears.

At first no one had dared to tell him. They were afraid to come anywhere near. And so it was Nasir bin Salim al-Hatati who came finally to wake him up. He found Azzan huddled in one of his isolated spots and as usual, the bottle next to him was empty. As the older man came closer Azzan tried to poke the bottle into a space somewhere behind himself. Al-Hatati sat down and put his arm around Azzan's shoulders.

When are you going to leave off this poison?

Azzan didn't say anything. He didn't know what he could say. But al-Hatati didn't wait for an answer anyway. There was no point in prolonging the silence. His parents were dead, he told Azzan.

For one of them to die was catastrophe enough. But both parents dying at once—and then, to learn this from someone who had little idea of what to say, of how to break it to him gently. What could remain of life for him when this had happened?

Through those long years Azzan had blundered on, struggling with himself over whether he could wake up one day and return home. Not once did he see his father's face or exchange words with him. What led him to drink more and more, day after day, was precisely that voice still echoing through him—in his dreams, and when he was alert and sober, and when he was drunk to the point of near-unconsciousness. The voice of his father. The hoarseness in his throat that Azzan's ears had grown up learning to recognize, hearing it when he was deep asleep so that he would wake up with a start, searching all around for that voice, overcome by forebodings and worry.

In his final year of school Azzan had dreamed of being accepted into one of the government-sponsored study missions abroad. He yearned to go and study in the West, in one of the countries that fellowship students could opt for. His degree was good enough to qualify and he chose to study engineering in America. His dreams—day and night—were all about that moment of departure and voyage.

It never occurred to him that he might not be accepted. Not once. His marks were at the top of the range for those who got scholarships. But they did not take him. And then he learned that some school graduates who had been accepted for the scholarships had marks lower than his. The possibility of going to university locally had passed him by as had choices elsewhere. It was too late now to apply. When he returned to the village and told his father what had come to pass, his father rebuked him soundly. There were many harsh words said and his father blamed him for neglecting to register himself at the university in Muscat or in any of the teacher-training colleges in which one was all but guaranteed a place. Blamed him for how he had risked everything and had lost the gamble, and now the only choice before him was to find work on the basis of his secondary school diploma or to join the army as a regular private.

The voice of censure was powerful—so strong indeed that he left the house and never came back. A few days later he went to al-Quwayra for the first time and his long journey with the cologne bottle began.

On this morning that al-Hatati had to tell him about, his father had gone to the souq in the city of Ibra with Haashil bin Hamdun. The man had a taxi and went to that market most mornings. Still at home, when Said sat down for his morning coffee his chest felt heavy and constricted and he had a pain in his right shoulder. But he was determined to go. His wife tried to change his mind about the trip but he was insistent and she had no choice but to stop arguing. She knew instinctively that a tree that has grown in its own way and has never had to bend or stoop cannot be budged at such an age as this.

At the market, he and the taxi driver agreed to meet at ten o'clock to head back to the village. Said went toward the fish market. As he stood there talking with the fishmongers, asking them about today's prices, he felt a strong twinge in his chest and his shoulder seized up. He tried to take a deep breath. He began to cough. Right there he fell to the ground amongst the throng of people. Dead.

Some folks carried him immediately to a nearby hospital but all they could do there was to confirm his passing. Meanwhile Haashil bin Hamdun waited and waited but his passenger didn't show up. Haashil bin Hamdun looked everywhere in the immediate vicinity but he found no sign of Said. Time stole itself, the day rolled on, and there at the taxi stop he stayed, faithful to his promise to take Said home. Surely the man would be here any minute now. And then an acquaintance from Wadi al-Taiyyin happened to pass by.

Someone from over your way just died. At the hospital.

When Haashil bin Hamdun's car came to a stop in the village quarter the ambulance had arrived ahead of him. The loud siren had drawn a crowd. Kadhiya, wife of Old Said, came out of her house and at the sight she fell on top of the corpse. Another body going cold. Instead of one dearly departed on this day, the village had two. And from the same household.

Because Azzan had no other family, no relations— no uncles on his father's side nor on his mother's—there was no one else who could lead the mourning rites that had to be gotten through. He had to be there. He had to see all of it through—the burial and then the mourning period with all of its ritual moments.

First to go to him, and breaking the news to him, al-Hatati had to take the boy by the hand and drag him along because the death rites would not wait. Azzan picked up his feet heavily. Even after some sleep, the alcohol was affecting his sense of balance. Al-Hatati took him to the maqsura. He handed him a fresh—new—set of underclothes and a clean izar and told him to bathe. Al-Hatati waited a long time, every so often anxiously calling out to Azzan to come out of the bath. But the young man stayed inside and poured water over his head time and time again as the tears poured from his eyes. Asmaa bint Nawfal waited there too, leaning against the trunk of the sawqama, her head wrap veiling her face. She was crying and mourning, though as quietly as she could manage. But every time she heard sobs coming from the bath her own tears responded. Her keening went on as al-Hatati's eyes moved back and forth between Asmaa's face and the door that remained closed.

Finally Azzan emerged, his face red and raw. He meant to go over to al-Hatati but he stumbled on some smallish rocks and nearly fell. His alcoholic abandon had mostly worn off only to be replaced by the agony of death: the debilitating grief that came in its wake. Surely he was destined for unending sorrows; the road to the cemetery lie in wait for him. That familiar space where he would have to stand tall and bid farewell to his parents who had taken a voyage from which they would not return.

Between the two corpses he sat motionless, one hand on the forehead of each departed parent. He did not really know what he ought to be doing. From every direction there were eyes trained on him. Some gazes were genuinely sad; these were the people who could see his grief. Others shook their heads in sympathy for him in his bereavement even if they didn't know what to believe.

There were also sets of eyes that he knew were viewing him in mockery and scorn, silently taking some kind of revenge. Wordless it might be but their glares pierced him. He had been the lad who didn't have a care in the world and who had not paid attention to things. He hung his head. His tears stopped. At some point al-Hatati gave the word and the two bodies were lowered into the ground.

He had not reached out a hand to help wrap them in their shrouds. He did not scatter soil over their bodies. With his gaze he raised them from the soil and placed them inside his heart. After the burial rites were done he stayed at their gravesite as everyone else went home.

The next morning in the village majlis, Azzan bin Said was there to receive the men who came to pay their respects and to mourn. Al-Hatati sat next to him and so did Old Salim bin Ali. Azzan had tried the evening before to go to the house and sleep there. But he couldn't. Standing at the door he reached for the latch but some powerful force repelled his hand and it dropped to his side. He stood there for a long time staring at the large old keyhole and latch. He noticed the cracks and how badly the wood had been eaten away. He sat down on the ground next to the door and leaned his head back against the wall and began to cry soundlessly, remembering the warm moments he had lived in this home.

He fell asleep. He dreamed that the two of them were opening the door and calling out to him. Come in! Between dreaming and wakefulness he heard their voices coming to him from inside the house. He heard his father's laugh, faintly, and his mother's characteristically tender voice.

He woke up. He got to his feet and stood facing the door. Again. He reached for the latch and lifted it. The door opened and he stepped inside. For the first time in years he could smell it: this fragrance of the place, of his parents. Inside everything was there as he remembered it. Alive, clean, orderly, as if the two of them had left the house only to go and pay a visit to a relation, and would soon return here in their normal way. The ceiling fan in the front room was turning slowly and the hens were pecking at whatever seeds or grains they could find on the ground. The inner courtyard—his mother had swept it clean just the day before, he could tell. She would have gathered up the fallen leaves to throw them under the hooves of her cow out in the pen. The date-palms and the other trees looked fresh and alive—as if the news hadn't yet reached this house. In the rooms, though, there was a dense silence: the mute presence of dead people who had abandoned this place. He felt the silence creeping over him. He felt it pressing on his chest and constricting his breathing.

For three days he was there in attendance for the usual period of mourning. Three days of receiving people and shaking their hands and listening to the words of consolation on their lips. Some were truly moved as they witnessed his return from that other life he had led. They embraced him, crying. Others simply shook his hand and did not meet his eyes. But he did show them all that he was truly intent on mourning these two people whom he had lost. On these three days he returned to the house only after the evening prayers.

On each of these evenings he went into the inner courtyard and spread out a small mat on the sandy surface and fell asleep. On whatever night it was, he heard meowing close by. He woke up and found his mother's cat lying very near, looking at him and meowing. He put out his hand and gently dragged her over and put his arm around her. He could feel the heat of her body, her breaths sinking through his skin. This cat had spent years in the household and had given birth to many kittens. All of her children were gone—as soon as they had grown up a little, they scattered across the village and never came back. She had remained alone here. As a little boy and ever since, he would find her nestling into his bedcovers and sleeping. He pushed his nose into her fur and took in this smell that he had been without for so long. Smells stay on in a place. The smells were what was left after the two of them had gone away. After all of the years that had passed, here he was, opening his nostrils and waiting for the smells to come gradually back to him.

All of those years, yes ... and now here he was, in this house once again, pulled back to a place whose every corner he knew so thoroughly. Yet he tried not to let his eyes focus on anything in particular. A few nights, and he had barely gotten beyond the courtyard. He sat down again there, his face lowered so that he saw only the packed-dirt surface. He was afraid to lift his gaze. He was afraid of seeing anything that would prick his heart with the pain of remembrance. But as the days went on, Azzan began to discover what was in these few rooms, the things his parents had had.

There was a picture hanging on the wall. It was a photograph of the three of them. His parents were seated and he stood between them. There was a rich green background, waterfalls in the distance, and a few birds circling in the blue sky above. He had been nine years old when they sat for this photograph in a studio in Ibra. He remembered it very clearly. How they all waited for this photograph, waited outside the shop and for more than three hours. Waited for it to be developed and made ready for them. And he recalled that the hunger erupting in his little tummy had been disruptive enough to get his parents to order some lunch in the restaurant nearby.

Memory opens up onto all of the tiny details that time's passing has submerged. He more than anyone had relished his position there at the center of that picture on the wall, standing between his parents. Now, as he took a step into their room he couldn't keep himself from staring at that picture again, drawn to it and marveling as though what had happened was beyond anything his mortal mind could take in. The portrait stood as a completely harmonious whole, perfectly finished—especially the fable-like details of the background.

He had no memory at all of his father ever speaking roughly to him as a child, or spanking him. He had grown up in that man's home without ever hearing a word of rebuke from him. Even as a little child he had been quiet by nature; this was the person he had been ever since. He didn't complain or whine, didn't make the little but insistent demands that children normally make, never cried unless he was ill and hurting. And anyway, he didn't encounter his father very often in the house. Either his father came home when Azzan had already gone to sleep or he saw him for only a few moments in the morning as the man was hurriedly preparing to leave the house yet again.

His father was the sort of man who is always occupied with the property he has acquired. He had land throughout these parts. He liked to work alone in his orchards and came home only when it was time to take a rest or to eat the midday meal. Sometimes his wife took his meal to him, wherever he was that day. Azzan grew up accustomed to his father's absence. At a distance he often saw his father in the company of other men who were equally focused on their business. His father never asked him to accompany him to the fields or to one of the souqs. He had grown up at a distance, physical and emotional, from his own father.

Every year, he earned the highest marks in his class. He was the academic star. Returning home with his yearly school report, he would hand it to his mother. She always said the same thing: she would let his father know. He must not bother his father with anything, she would add, for his father was a very busy man. And indeed, through those years his father became ever more immersed in work while Azzan grew ever more accustomed to his father's lack of interest. That was so until the day came when the sense of failure and disappointment weighed on him heavily like a dark raincloud about to burst. When his father flung those words at him he had left and it had all gone terribly wrong from that moment.

For many weeks after their deaths Azzan did not leave the house. He did not even move position, really. At some point he began to hear the three knocks on the door once a day. Opening, he found food—prepared meals, sitting on the threshold. Someone was making and bringing his food but without waiting to see him. He didn't make any attempt to spy out who this doer of good deeds was. He just opened the door, picked up the tray crammed with small dishes, and returned it all later, and clean, to the threshold where he had found the tray.

It was some time before he could feel his hands emboldened enough to try opening the mandus that sat in their room. The lock resisted him. He searched all over, everywhere in the house where he remembered keys possibly being kept, but he did not find a key to the lock on the mandus. In the end he had to break the lock, to strip it off entirely. He opened the lid expecting to see very little inside the chest. He reached first for the mound of silks piled on the left side where his mother had put them. These must be fabrics she had not yet used. His mother always built up a supply of cloth and then made her own clothes. He took out the lengths of silk and piled them on the floor. Next appeared a honey pot, less than half full. Its color, he noticed, was very dark. He opened the lid and put the jar up to his nose and took a long and deep sniff. The fragrance of it filled all of him.

He remembered how he used to squat next to his father whenever the man was opening this mandus so that he would be given a small helping of honey poured into his open palm. His father would put a little more of it into a cup, sprinkle some shaynuz over it, mix the honey and shaynuz together with a finger, and drink it, licking the sides of the cup until he had gotten every bit of it out.

He set the jar down next to the heap of silk. He scrabbled his fingers along the floor of the chest and came upon a stack of folded papers tied in a bundle with a length of fabric. He undid the knot and began opening the papers. He wanted to read the contents but the light in the room was faint. He took them out into the front room. He began to read.

Five sheets contained legal documentation concerning date palm sales; his father had bought these in lots, in various locations around the town and over many years. Two others were official, signed records of debts owed to his father by two men, one for the sum of five thousand riyals and the other for fifteen hundred riyals. For the first, the debt was scheduled to be paid very soon; the smaller sum carried a more recent date of transaction and hence a later due date.

He returned the documents to the chest after retying them into the bundle exactly as they had been. He rummaged in the bottom of the chest again but he didn't come upon anything more that was significant. His father's reading glasses, an amulet folded into a scrap of leather which he thought was probably his mother's, and a knotted thread attached to a rusty key.

One evening soon after, as he was stretched out in the courtyard he heard knocks on the door and a voice calling him. He opened the door and found his drinking companions clustered around it. They had brought their bottles along as well as their drums. It was Mismar who spoke up.

No one's happy to see you in this state—not your friends and not your enemies either. You've got to get back to being your old self.

We've come to take you back to paradise, Wad Marzuq added.

He made way for them to come inside. There were seven of them and they had shown up determined to have one of their convivial nights—but this time at his place and on this very evening. He was silent. He didn't volunteer anything even though he had let them in. They formed a circle and put all of their kit in the middle. But before they could launch themselves into their evening they heard another knock at the door. Al-Hatati and Old Salim bin Ali were here. Azzan let them in too. When the lads who had gathered inside saw the two older men they hung their heads; they were clearly as embarrassed as they could be.

Al-Shayib Salim was blind but he could sense that something doubtful was afoot. He asked his companion what was going on but al-Hatati didn't respond. Instead he went directly to Wad Marzuq and whispered something into his ear. Wad Marzuq stood up immediately, one hand grasping his walking stick and the other his bottle, and scurried out of the house. His companions followed.

What had al-Hatati said to him? No one knew. Later on, and several times, Azzan bin Said tried to find out what he had whispered but al-Hatati always repelled these attempts heatedly. One year on one of their trips to Wadi al-Mazaari', in the course of one of those evenings when memories are revived and aired and stories are shared, they were getting close to sleeping when Azzan bin Said repeated that old question to al-Hatati. Abdallah bin Hamad was there too of course, and he was listening intently. Al-Hatati laughed. Wad Marzuq is afraid of his own shadow, he said.

Al-Hatati knew Wad Marzuq well. The man was terrified by death and by the specters of the dead.

Accounts of wizardry invariably scared him. Tales of jinn too. He believed that every dead person left a curse in the place where they had been living. The curse would pursue those who had harmed them when alive. Al-Hatati didn't have to whisper very many words into his ear.

You've come to spend the evening in *his* house? Fine, then you'll find he is watching you, over in al-Quwayra.

Al-Hatati laughed at the memory of Wad Marzuq's face sagging with fear. From that day on none of the law-firees came anywhere near Azzan and they never made another attempt to draw him back into their drinking sessions. In fact, they made a complete and total break with him, as if they didn't know this fellow personally and had never even met him.

When the room was quiet—after Wad Marzuq and his foot soldiers left—Old Salim bin Ali spoke first. My boy, he said, we all know your father loaned money to many people and we know he would have had the documents to prove it. Now you've got the right to that money and you're going to have to stand up for yourself and deal with all of these loans.

Azzan fetched the legal documents from the mandus. He read them out loud, one after another. Every time he came to the end of one of them, Old Salim verified the truth of what it said. The money that had been loaned against people's property as security was there in the village; he knew where it was, in such-and-such a location. Al-Shayib Salim vowed to stand with Azzan however long it took to get what he was due from these debtors. In fact he would go to them on his own, he declared, and he would urge them in the strongest terms possible to take care of their debts to this boy.

Azzan listened hard to every word he heard from this old man who long ago had tried so hard to return him to his home and family. He felt some reverence towards Old Salim, from whom he had never heard a harsh word throughout his long absence in those netherworlds of intoxication. Getting to his feet, Old Salim bin Ali said to him, Your Lord loves you, my boy. God tests his servants and He purifies them through calamity.

The two men departed. Alone in his house Azzan had nothing to do and no one to be with but his cat, who prowled the room and meowed at him. He lay down on the mat again and stared at the stars as they appeared and vanished between remnants of cloud, light shadows in the sky. Finally his eyes closed and he sank into the sea-depths of sleep.

When he woke up the next morning his mind went immediately to the mandus. He got up and opened it first thing. If his father had had some money, where in that chest would he have put it? He rifled through all of the contents and then took everything out. The chest had been built with a hardwood bottom. He studied the smooth wood, feeling clueless. There was nothing more here, he thought, nothing but that polished expanse. But he tapped his fingers along the wood anyway. At the upper righthand corner, the wood seemed to release a different echo. Only then he noticed a barely perceptible fissure extending fifteen centimeters out from the corner joint. He tried to wiggle the wood at the corner but it wouldn't budge. He fetched a knife from the kitchen. He stuck the blade tip into the crack and tried to pry out the wood. Finally it came up and he could see a gap, like a tiny vault below. He stuck his hand down into the dark space and felt around. Yes. It was stuffed full of paper money, and there were more debt statements, too. He began taking it all out. There must be about seven thousand riyals in this mandus.

He also found a legal contract for a large farm outside the village that was mortgaged to his father, and an old marriage contract—his parents'. He found two photographs, one of his mother and the other of his father. They had been slipped inside a small envelope. He found two final wills and testaments, his parents' declarations of their wishes, rolled up together. He put everything back into the concealed vault exactly as it had been; he did not need any of it immediately. He slid the wood panel into place. He replaced the old padlock with another one that he had in the house and hid the keys beneath the knotted rug. He left the house to go walking through the village lanes.

He passed by al-Shayib Salim bin Ali's sabla but he did not turn to go in to the meeting space. He kept going until he had gone past al-Quwayra. He heard some strumming. It was early in the day to hear that sound and so he knew this must be Friday, the day on which all of the drinkers came together, having come back to the village at the end of the work week from their far-flung workplaces. He climbed the stairs into the quarter and then descended, leaving it behind him. He came to Old Sultan's home. As he passed the door he heard whispering, as if someone was calling him. By name. He stopped. He could see a handsome pair of eyes—handsome but wandering—gazing at him from the crack in the door. It was Sarah bint Sultan in her usual vacant state. A chance meeting; their eyes met. The woman started and pushed the door shut. He could hear her hurrying further inside.

He barely knew who she was. He remembered having heard a long time ago that Old Sultan had a very attractive daughter who was also extremely clever. He'd assumed that she must have been married some time ago. He didn't stay there at the door for any length of time; he certainly did not want to bring on a scolding from anyone. He went on towards the edge of the village. He walked a long way that day. When the midday sun was nearly level with his head he sat down for a rest where the smaller irrigation canal leading to people's orchards branched off the wider main falaj. He scooped up some water and splashed it across his face and then scooped again and drank.

When the mutawwa Ali bin Mubarak heard about how Wad Marzuq had left Azzan's house in hurried disappointment, it gave him some hope that the young man would enter his ranks instead. Here was an opportunity that he must seize! A bright and gleaming opportunity as impossible to ignore as a precious stone in a silver ring. It was a matchless opportunity indeed: here was the wounded bird encouraged to return to its safe nest where it would find security and reassurance. That's how Mubarak put it, relying on the Holy Word.

Mubarak did not go knocking on the boy's door. He didn't approach Azzan directly. Instead, he sent a messenger to deliver a set of cassette tapes that held lectures on prayer, the Day of Reckoning, and the torments of the grave, plus a few didactic anthems. Along with the cassettes there were some glossy booklets setting out the punishments to be expected when one abandoned one's prayers.

The man handed Azzan the tapes and books—all of them encased in a large paper sleeve on which were embossed verses from the Quran and sayings of the Prophet explaining the importance of calling people to the faith gently and amicably.

Shaykh Ali sends you his greetings, the man said. He hopes you will welcome this simple gift from him.

Azzan took the packet and set it down in the front room on the shelf built into the wall where it stayed for several days. He forgot about it, in fact. He hadn't even opened it to take a look when, on his way somewhere one morning, he encountered someone he didn't recognize who asked him, Did you like the gift?

Azzan tried to recall what gift could have come his way from this man, but he could not.

Gift? What gift?

I sent you a little package with a few things in it. Maybe it didn't get to you?

Then he recalled the large envelope. His gaze lowered, his eyelids half closed, he was frowning slightly as he tried to reconcile the image of this mutawwa standing in front of him with the words of the man who had given him that package and said something about who had sent it, calling him *shaykh*. It was a perfectly ordinary title to hear: the Shaykh was the local head of the clan. There were no other shaykhs around here, and that was what left Azzan confused. The term they had always used for a man of piety, the person who taught people their religion and led their prayers, was the M'allim. There must be some mix-up. He simply nodded and smiled at the man and went on his way.

A few days later, as he was coming through the passageway into the inner rooms he noticed the packet that he had forgotten about. He opened it and pulled out the tapes and read the titles on the booklets. There was one on disobeying your parents, another on abandoning prayer, and a third on isbal al-thawb—if you are a proper Muslim man, it said, you must not lengthen your garment to the point that it touches the top of your feet. It was not the Islamic Way. There was a pamphlet on the importance of having a beard but shaving one's moustaches; a booklet on communal prayer; another on women's hijab.

He began to read, feeling genuinely interested. But why, he asked himself, was this mutawwa giving him these things? His curiosity mounting, he fished out the cassette player. He listened to one tape and then another. On one was a sermon by the famous Abd al-Hamid Kishk, the popular Egyptian preacher. The man was having to out-shout a lot of commotion and background noise and yells from the audience. Another cassette held a lecture by a different shaykh. The rest seemed to be mostly chanting or reciting and he did not particularly want to sit through it.

There must be some mistake, he still believed—the whole thing seemed so doubtful. *A gift*, the mutawwa had said; but what he'd gotten was nothing more than these little books and taped lectures. The person who had handed all of this to him had gotten it wrong. He left the house at once to look for the fellow, asking those he passed in the lanes where the man lived.

Finally he was knocking on the door. The mutawwa came out and welcomed him with a smile that lit up his whole face with true delight. The message he had intended to send had gotten through to this youth! But then came a bolt from the blue that turned the gleam in his eyes to bewilderment and froze the look of joy in his face. Celebration turned to the cloudy aridity of a desert awaiting a dust storm.

Here's your package, said Azzan. The man who gave me this got the wrong person.
What? Why?
These are your things. I didn't find any kind of gift in it, just a few tapes and booklets.
Did you read the books?
Yes.
What did you think?
I don't know, I don't think I understood any of it.
Azzan was about to turn and leave but the mutawwa opened the door and invited him in for coffee. He took Azzan into the men's sitting room. He tried to explain the idea to him: that he was trying to guide and help him so that he would naturally come and attend the prayer service with the group of them and of course then he would want to listen to the mutawwa's sermons in the mosque.

Coming outside, he listened to the man saying goodbye. The man asked, Will you come and pray with us today?

Fine, okay.

He didn't say anything more. He went on his way and forgot the whole business within minutes. But at a later moment, sitting with al-Hatati, the memory of that series of events came back to him and he mentioned it. Al-Hatati chuckled.

So—that boy Wad Moobiiriik couldn't find anyone but you to persuade? To wear a dishdasha and come kneel and pray?

Ali bin Mubarak had been a student at the old Sharia institute for training religious judges in Muscat. He was the first person from this village to specialize in these particular sciences, and in a time when so many young men were looking instead for some kind of work that was not too taxing once they had got their secondary diplomas. The army, perhaps, or a government agency. It didn't occur to any of them that you could go somewhere and study to become an expert on questions of jurisprudence—on *religion*. That you could attend an institute that graduated future judges and preachers—imams to be employed by the state in mosques. When Ali was appointed after his graduation as an imam in the village where he had grown up, many had talked and gossiped and wondered about this odd form of employment. How could someone agree to take a salary for praying on behalf of people and leading their worship? They had never known such a thing. For as long as they could remember, Old Salim bin Ali had led their prayers on the holy days and whenever they needed to pray for rain. There had been a time years before when someone dispatched from the Governor's office had come to see Old Salim, telling him the Governorate would appoint him formally as imam to the village.

My praying is not up for sale, Old Salim had told him.

He had been summoned to the governor's office. The province's governor himself and an official from the Religious Endowments Bureau explained this concept of the job and the salary that should go with it. But he refused it vehemently. He didn't even ask permission to leave the meeting. He simply got to his feet and walked out the door because he had heard enough. On the Day of Reckoning when God asks me why I took money for praying over you, he had asked them, what am I supposed to tell God? Do I say that the Gov'nor ordered me to do it? Are you going to take responsibility for the consequences of my actions, before God? Bitithaasib anni amam Allah?

When al-Hatati heard that Ali bin Mubarak had been newly posted as imam in the village he had only one thing to say. This is one of the signs that the Hour is nigh. Now religion has become merchandise that people buy and sell—people making money off the faith!

Ali bin Mubarak began by imposing his new principles on the members of his household and then on the wives of anyone to whom he was related. He made them put on hijab and he covered their faces himself whenever they were about to go out into the village lanes. Old Salma bint Sultan, sitting outside in front of her home and seeing her sister walk by in this state, said, Well! The angels of judgment have come down to see us now.

Over the next years the influence of the village's government-trained mutawwa Ali bin Mubarak on the local youth mounted slowly. Eventually, he fashioned a group of supporters who came to listen to his sermons and followed his directives. They started addressing him as Shaykh.

In the months that followed his encounter with the shaykh, Azzan was preoccupied with the declarations of last wishes that his parents had made in writing. He hired someone to perform the Hajj in their names and he distributed alms as they had wanted. With the help of Old Ali and al-Hatati he gave Salim bin Khalaf a sum of money on the basis that he would fast for two months, one month for each parent, as an act of piety. This completed the requests set out in their wills. Now he was free to follow up on the two debtors. They did begin to repay what they owed—but the owner of the large mortgaged farm outside the village wasn't able to redeem his mortgage. Azzan proposed to buy the farm for the sum that was owed and the man agreed immediately. The farm came to him with a new title deed.

Anyone who had known him before and who saw him during those months would have hardly been likely to recognize him. They could not have anticipated this inner transformation. Yet, he was beginning to feel bored and restless. Partly he was a bit afraid that this sudden acquisition of money and property would seduce him and he would go back to the alcohol. Instead he went to al-Hatati to ask if he could join their excursions into the mountains. It was the birth of a new passion. Every time they returned to the village Azzan asked immediately if they could go again—preferably in a very few days' time.

You've got a seed of madness inside you, al-Hatati said to him. It seems you can't do anything without becoming completely crazy for it. That drunkenness of yours was beyond belief. And now here you are, completely mad over the mountains—even more of a surprise!

He accepted everything al-Hatati said to him calmly and openly. In his eyes this man was like a father— now that the other father was gone. He respected and honored this man through and through; anything that al-Hatati said he must do, he did. He loved this man in whom he had discovered a true friend in times of trial, a companion on the road—and the best possible teller of tales on those dark evenings in the mountains.

Chapter Eleven

When the departure comes near
choose your companion well
among those who know

AL-HATATI REACHED THE APPROACH TO Aqabat al-Nakhla before his two companions did. He descended through Wadi al-Nimarat and crossed the valley bottom. It was nearly eleven thirty. Abdallah bin Hamad and Azzan were still off somewhere in the eastern stretches of the jabal.

He touched the heavy fabric water canteen. It was cold by now; it sat in a full pan of water. The only problem with this mattara was that water did seep out of it if you didn't soak the fabric until the threads were swollen. But it was one of the best there was for keeping water cool—one of these new-fangled kinds introduced by the soldiers who depended on it in their movements. He trusted it to fill their needs in this very hot summer as it had done in other summers. The water you drank from its mouth tasted unlike that of any other: it was unusually cold and sweet. You only needed a small cupful or maybe two in order to feel completely refreshed and revived.

His companions would show up soon. No creature had the capacity to stay out in this midday sun, whatever species they were. In these hours of the most extreme heat even the hardy mountain animals fled to shaded spots. Abdallah bin Hamad—that mountain sprite who never got tired—would feel he was being pursued relentlessly by the sun, and he had to marshal all of his energy just to keep going. He would return to their camp with his tongue literally hanging out, desperate for a gulp of cold water to damp down the flames of this blaze that seemed able to reach every recess in his body.

Azzan was more like the desert lizards: he didn't get thirsty and he never complained. All he required, as he made his way through this terrain, was to come upon the smallest pool of water—even if it was seething with heat. If he could hold a bit of it in his palm that was enough to refresh him. His demeanor never seemed to change. He could always be seen walking steadily and calmly along, his gait slow and measured, already carrying some sticks of firewood he had picked up on his way. That was how Azzan was. He would never arrive empty-handed.

He ought to summon them back, al-Hatati thought; ought to tell them it was high time they returned here. The smell of the campfire would be his voice. It would rise and spread and carry far. But in fact, it was the fragrance of the coffee that would get them to abandon the search for whatever it was they were looking for as they gave themselves up to the power of that aroma.

He set the coffee pot, half full of water, on the three flat stones set in a triangle around the fire pit. He lit the fire and slowly, skittishly, it caught, though the tiny flames were almost choked out by the thick smoke arising amongst the branches he had laid. He used some dry sakhbar grass to get it going, but still the fire thwarted him and died down. He took the coffee pot off the stones and relit the kindling. This time he waited until the tongues of flame were constant and strong and danced to the late-morning gusts of wind without dying out. He set the coffee pot over the flames on the athafi and left the fire to do its work before pouring in the finely-ground coffee.

The pot needed all three stones supports—the athafi—beneath it in order to balance properly long enough and close enough to brew the coffee properly. These mountain journeys needed three other athafi, too: Nasir bin Salim al-Hatati; his friend who was as stubborn as the towering mountains were unmoving, Abdallah bin Hamad; and this much younger fellow with his marvelously strong and steady nerves, Azzan bin Said the bee-man, he who completed the triangle of stones that made for a steady cooking-fire.

Any such venture demanded strong and steady companionship. The trek was not an aim in itself; and searching for honey might not be such an important goal; but having companions who shared everything was vital. It was this that created memories for the years to come; this that opened the floodgates of storytelling as they sat in the shade gifted to them by the mountain trees. True, the shade was rather pitiful. In fact, it was weak enough, powerless enough, that any creature seeking it would simply shrink beneath it, too hot and listless to form anything more than a shadow puppet cowering against the tree trunk. The three human athafi shrank into these shadows too, surrounded—or barricaded in—by the heat, the flames, the lackluster breeze, and their thirst.

Between noon and three o'clock, the sun began to slant slightly and the shade crept eastward. The breeze came up suddenly, as if it had been enclosed in its own wind-irrigation channel which had suddenly been opened to release it. Their afternoon rest would be sweet. Al-Hatati's head would nod, oblivious to the talk of his friends. They would all need to stretch their legs out from where they crouched now in the meagre shade. If only for a few moments, they would let their bodies sink into a half-slumber that lifted away the fatigue of the morning's search. Ahead of them was another search, commencing after the late-afternoon prayers and lasting until the sun withdrew from the peaks. In these circumstances a quick little nap was critical.

The coffee bubbled and frothed and its sharp fragrance floated from the pot to hover overhead, reaching the nostrils of creatures huddling from the heat in caves and niches or beneath the mountain trees—luqum, qafas, shawaa. Abdallah bin Hamad was not far away but he was still glued to his binoculars as he scanned the cave openings and trees, looking hard for that hive. No sign of weariness or despair showed on him. But he knew there was no alternative to returning for some rest in that early afternoon hour; otherwise, he would have kept going. A break also meant he was leaving plenty of unsearched spaces for the evening and the coming days.

To find what you were searching for was momentous—but what would you do then? Completing the excursion exactly as planned and taking it to its conclusion were just as meaningful. Would these friends return to the village as soon as they came across the hive? Of course not! They had provisions enough for three days or even four. They would certainly stay out here for as long as they had planned on. And so he was not in a particular hurry to find anything, however strong and immovable was his desire to ultimately find it. The pleasure of the search, of coming up into these mountains, of making discoveries—the insects and mountain creatures, the unexpected moments encountered on the way—were more compelling than was coming upon the specific end he had in mind. And he would find *that* in the end, for it was here somewhere amongst the peaks and plateaus and it would not suddenly change its location. It was his job to reach it, to find it, just as it was his business to read perfectly the behavior of the bees and to interpret the way they flew. To sketch alternate maps of routes he imagined, mounting towards that hive that inevitably existed. To guess what the most appropriate site of it was, or the most likely—and also to know which locales were not suited to hosting a hive of wild bees—although, in the end, they might do so. He must cover every possibility; he must search in places where one would hardly think to look.

As soon as the coffee boiled and its fragrance began to spread, al-Hatati's companions did reappear. The sun had worked its ways on them, depleting their energy. The late-morning wind coming from the west was picking up, slaps so hot that they must surely leave burn marks on everything the moving air passed. The wind siphoned off whatever moisture might still hang in the air, having arisen from the boggy pools and trickle-springs. Its dry whistle growing stronger, the wind rattled the tree branches. Their little campsite felt like an oven roaring at full blast. As the shadows withered under the noon sun, the three of them chased whatever remaining slivers of shade they could find amongst the date palms and lathab trees.

When they had drunk their coffee Abdallah bin Hamad got slowly to his feet. He gathered some kindling to make another fire. Because the wind was at its strongest now he constructed a miniature stone wall to protect the flames which otherwise would have no chance of surviving. Lunch was simple: salted fish with slices of onion and lemon. They ate it with boiled rice. It was just right—a meal to take the edge off the stifling air. It relaxed them enough that they all dropped off into much-needed naps. The drowsiness hit al-Hatati first and rippled across all three of them to finally reach Azzan bin Said.

By about three o'clock the sun had retreated enough to have a noticeable effect on the air temperature. They got to their feet again, ready to attempt another climb. They had sketched out some new maps of where the wild bees might have built the large hive that the three of them—and others—had been seeking. They were going to spread out, each of them heading in a different direction. The wind had quieted slightly and had lost some of its heat—that western wind which no living being could withstand for long; the wind that sent all living things hurrying to find shade, hiding in mountain crevices or in shadows beneath the leafiest trees, or under the rocks until the wind's moaning midday song would dwindle and finally vanish.

He was climbing the path when a sandgrouse suddenly flew up from beneath Abdallah bin Hamad's feet. He turned back immediately to their campsite, took his gun from where it hung on a tree branch, and slung it over his shoulder. He had forgotten all about the gun even though this was the hour when sandgrouse and mountain partridges left their nests in search of water. As he set off again, he felt hopeful that he could bag a fresh evening meal for the three of them, though he was reproaching himself for having forgotten his rifle in the first place and possibly missing his chance.

Abdallah was heading directly for the summit while Azzan had taken a southward route, intending to approach the mountain from the wadi by following a circular path upward. Both paths were broken here and there by fissures in the rock that were difficult to negotiate as well as low-hanging isbaqs where one had to stoop to clamber beneath. Al-Hatati took still a different way, going along the easiest descent into the wadi and then all the way to where the two wadis converged. From there, at the end of Wadi al-Nimarat, he began to ascend towards the point where, on his last climb up here, the lone bee he had followed through the wadi had suddenly vanished.

The villagers found the bond between Abdallah bin Hamad and al-Hatati puzzling. For as long as anyone could remember, if the two of them left the village they always left it together. People called the flirtatious Abdallah bin Hamad *al-Mughizluh*, Dragonfly. His sweet tongue spun such sugar! He took great care to select exactly the right words, the most succulent syllables, those beguiling phrases that would compel whoever spoke with him to listen, to stand spellbound by the throbbing warmth of his manner of speech. That was Abdallah for you. Al-Hatati, though, was a man who couldn't care less about the words that came out of his mouth. Anyone he encountered was as likely to be accosted by oaths as by jokes, or met with curses and ribbing at the same time. There were those who didn't appreciate it. Al-Hatati was so heedless on the matter of his speech that even the mutawwa who made the villagers' piety his business—that man Ali bin Mubarak—got an earful of words from al-Hatati so objectionable that he couldn't ignore what the man had said.

Why couldn't you at least learn how to speak, back in your tender years?! Wad Mubarak sputtered at him.

He spoke with such misplaced fury that al-Hatati started laughing. That was the way he was, irritating people at every turn and never letting up until he could see you losing patience and beginning to release the demons of your anger in his face. Meanwhile, there was Abdallah bin Hamad, that silver-tongued flirt, that sugar-spinner ... if he found a woman in his path he would stop her and keep her there simply with his honey-sweet manner, charming the very earrings in her earlobes. Yes, his talk alone was enough to attract the women. Setting out for her fields, many a woman hoped she would run into al-Mughizluh. Elderly Shamsa bint Abdallah—who was related to Nasir al-Hatati's wife—always said: That Wad Hamad is a devil, he is, a human devil, his tongue would warm a stone-cold boulder!

Little insinuations and even accusations made the rounds among the women. So-and-so daughter of So-and-so was slipping out at night to go to al-Mughizluh ... he was her— ... well, her friend ... and then, sometime later, there would be similar murmurings about another woman. The men were helpless; all they could do was to pass on these bits of news quietly, in secret, so that none of it would reach him. Every bit of the talk did reach al-Mughizluh, of course; but it didn't have the slightest effect on him.

Al-Mughizluh, the Dragonfly, hums and skitters across the still surface of the pond, and the waters ripple. He darts forward and back as though he is spinning an imaginary garment before your eyes; his darting, swooping movements through the air are the words that tell his stories. Abdallah bin Hamad comes and goes in the village, seemingly everywhere, visiting this person and returning to that one. If he has nothing particular that he needs to do he will cross the village from end to end and chat with whomever he finds in his path.

At some point, someone came up with the nickname. At first it circulated quietly within a certain group of young men and then it spread widely enough that he learned of it. When he heard it, Abdallah knitted his brows, thinking about this nickname. He rather liked the comparison to nature's creatures that it suggested, and so he didn't let it bother him. He just nodded his head and smiled.

No woman was completely safe from the traps set by Abdallah bin Hamad. Maymuna bint Khumayis would stand with him for nearly two hours at a time whenever she happened to bump into him on the lane. She started trying to map his movements; she would lie in wait and ambush him. He didn't pay attention to how much time might pass; after all, he got his pleasure from chatting with people and especially with women. During an argument Maymuna's husband raised it. People are talking, he snapped. They're asking why you're always chatting with Wad Hamad. They're guessing at what you are talking about.

Maymuna had a ready response. Go away and learn how to be as much fun as he is, why don't you!

That's why people whispered that Maymuna had become the beloved to whom Abdallah bin Hamad crept off at night, or maybe she went to him. Someone swore a binding oath that he'd seen her going in, well, *there*, looking like she was madly in love and then, just a bit later he saw al-Mughizluh heading for exactly the same spot. Someone else saw the two of them coming out of some concealed byway on the edge of the village, alone, and walking along together.

Abdallah bin Hamad hadn't shown any interest in relationships with women. All he cared about was his work and his excursions into the mountains. But that changed after he had his first experience. Mabruka bint Ahmad used to stop him in the street for long conversations. Things proceeded from there and led eventually to surreptitious assignations. Mabruka had tumbled into a snare from which she couldn't extricate herself. Whenever Abdallah went off to do some job for someone outside the village, staying away for several days, or when he went off into the mountains, Mabruka all but went mad waiting for him.

She was married to her paternal cousin Qays, whose distant posting meant he was away for weeks at a time.

When Qays did come back to the village, he usually joined up immediately with Wad Marzuq's crowd and stuck with them until his break was over, coming home only to sleep or perhaps when he wanted something to eat. Occasionally he lingered there but only because he knew there was no drink to be had with his buddies. His presence—on days when he was alert—was always calamitous. It was like an evil curse placed on Mabruka and her six daughters. He shouted rude words into her face and slapped her girls around. He called them terrible names.

Sitting next to Abdallah one night long after dark, Mabruka said to him, You are my paradise. But Abdallah bin Hamad never found that this sort of talk touched his heart. He really didn't care much about what she was feeling. But he liked new experiences. He enjoyed this novel sensation: that his heart was opening itself up to adventures, each one more intense than the last. He decided to put himself in front of any woman in the village who seemed a likely catch. He would flirt with her until he could get something. But the more he came to feel that he'd had his fill of a particular woman—and meanwhile, another one would have fallen into his trap—the stronger his hunger grew. These girlfriends of his were always trying to out-scheme each other; the secret struggles, which the men had no idea were going on, grew in number and intensity. They all wanted him for themselves and only themselves. But Abdallah went on distributing his favors amongst them according to his needs and inclinations.

He went through periods when he only desired rotund women and so he avoided anyone who wasn't plump. He chased these women persistently and even into their own homes, managing to be alone with them there in the stretches of time when their husbands were away. But then at a certain point, he would dump them and pursue only lean women. Or he would go for the youngest ones, those who had been married only recently. But sometimes it was the older women he was after. He had his way with pretty much all the women in the village. Still, he had an instinctive sense of danger hiding in certain women he encountered. He read it in their eyes and saw it in the jittery way they reacted whenever he happened to come across them and tried to start a conversation, or merely when he passed one of these women in a village lane and saw how she started, how quick she was to move away from him, how tersely she exchanged words with him. He didn't persist. He was not about to humiliate himself by heading down a path that would lead him nowhere.

A woman who wanted him would come to him on her own, after all, without any effort on his part. They were there wherever he turned. First a simple exchange of greetings. And then the long story would begin, with an inevitable ending that he already knew. Every woman had her own nature, of course. He would infuse their spirits like a beautiful soft perfume that never faded; that entered them so gently that they didn't even sense it as a foreign scent. The aroma of him seemed like a part of themselves and they never could get enough of it.

But with Asmaa bint Nawfal he was otherwise: immediately, he was still and said almost nothing. If he did speak to her, it was in the hushed tones one used to address a lady so highly respected that she commanded everyone's awe. When he was in her presence he was afraid to raise his voice at all, fearful that it would break this sanctity. She knew his story with the village women and she avoided him. Whenever he knocked on the door looking for al-Hatati, she wrapped her headcovering over her face before answering, and spoke from beneath the litham over her mouth, in curt and rapid phrases. If al-Hatati was at home she opened the door; if not, she told him to go to the men's majlis adjacent to the house. He could be served his coffee there. He always excused himself and went away, to come for his friend another time.

When Asmaa learned that the villagers had come up with the sobriquet al-Mughizluh for Abdallah bin Hamad, she laughed. Someone's outdone you on the nicknames! she exclaimed to her husband. But al-Hatati didn't appear to worry particularly over the talk going round about his friend. Even that time when someone asked him, Aren't you going to give your friend some advice? He's like a billy-goat in heat always hitting up another nanny goat!

Al-Hatati replied offhandedly. Well, he's a man—if you fellows were men your wives wouldn't go anywhere near him.

The man walked away, muttering back at al-Hatati. No one sees eye to eye with you.

Both al-Hatati and Abdallah bin Hamad had their limits and their defenses. Neither one stepped over the boundaries when it came to the other. Their relationship seemed to have no truck with advice-giving or blame-casting. They accepted each other as they were and as though they'd had some prior story together that still wasn't over. They never got into conversations about themselves except when it concerned their mountain excursions. If one of them said or did something that irritated the other, they resolved it without impinging on sensitive territory, most likely by avoiding the other's company for a time and doing their best to swerve away from such issues. That was why al-Hatati always tried to shield himself from what other people were saying about his friend so that he wouldn't have to respond or make anything up.

Even with all of this going on no one in the village actually challenged Abdallah bin Hamad over any of his doings. Indeed they looked to him trustingly when there was a fight to break up, between brothers and their cousins or between any two of the villagers. Whoever was involved in the dispute understood that there would be no avoiding some kind of truce if they found Abdallah bin Hamad knocking at their doors. Faced with his incredible tongue they could not but agree to every word he said.

And so, accounts of al-Mughizluh's illicit liaisons spread but only in whispers so that he would not hear nor would the woman in question or her husband. But the whispers had made their way to him anyway, and to his wife as well. The situation angered her. When he had asked her what was wrong and tried to find out why she was so upset, she started crying.

People are saying you're with a hurma from the village.

So—what do you say?

She hadn't answered but had just kept silent. She was the only one who could not abide listening to his flowery words. She thought they were contrived and insincere. But she had a certain respect for him anyway, a real respect. And she had gone on living with him for the sake of her children.

Abdallah bin Hamad had married Badriya bint Saud at the age of eighteen. She was fifteen, an attractive girl whose eyes sparkled with intelligence. She did not have a lot to say but when she did want to express herself on a certain matter her words could be sharp. She wasn't hesitant about making her views clear and she would speak without worrying about what the impact of her words might be. From their very first months together, a silent struggle marked their marriage. He was trying to tame her so that her sharp tongue wouldn't lose her the affection of others. He wanted her to speak gently with them. But every time he besieged her with his words, every time he tried to absorb and change her, all she said was, I don't know how to play up to people the way you do.

They were related but not closely; still, he was bound to her by some sort of family tie. She hadn't grown up in this village. She was his mother's kin: they lived in the Sahel. When she came to live in his village she dealt with people the way her family had done—with their usual liberality of word and behavior. But the things the village people said, the descriptions of her their tongues crafted—it all put her off. She began to withdraw into herself. She spent more and more time alone, shutting others out except when absolutely necessary. When she spoke her words were invariably terse and sharp. Her father visited one day and found his daughter so changed that he began to regret the marriage—although it did cross his mind that maybe this was simply part of her maturing into a woman.

She gave birth to four sons; she had hoped the fourth pregnancy would give her a daughter. She felt her loneliness strongly, felt a need for feminine company to nourish her days. When the fourth son arrived she wept, so strongly had she dreamt of a girl. She hugged this fourth infant close and gazed upward. Everything from You is a blessing, she whispered.

The fifth one was a girl. Badriya's life changed completely. The baby girl gave her back her spirit—gave her what she had despaired of ever regaining. Her life to come had felt so arid, as though she lived deep in a barren desert where the wind swirled and kicked up the sand until it blinded the eyes and filled the soul. Day and night she had counted the days likely to remain in these sterile years of her life to come.

But now at last she felt newly fertile. She began to forgive her husband for the agony he had brought on through his questionable attachments to so many village women. She began smiling, even when she looked at him, speaking to him affectionately, and singing in his presence. Of course he noticed the change and he didn't criticize her for anything. He had sensed how she was feeling and now he sensed her gradually coming out of the isolation which had been her companion for nearly twelve years, since she had rarely even gone on visits to her neighbors' homes. Now her life was colored springtime. She began to seek out what was pleasurable or intriguing without caring what people might be saying to each other about her. She began attending weddings, singing in the bride's procession and dancing in the beautiful way she had, which the other women envied and tried to follow. They couldn't match her. Some of them asked her to teach them how she did it. She smiled, and then laughed. It's easy, she said. You learned how to swim. Dancing is like swimming—after all, when you're afraid of drowning, you learn how to swim.

Badriya swam in a universe of magic as she had swum before in the deeps of her interior. She danced inside a circle formed by the clapping women. First she established the rhythm with her own hands and then she began to move, her elegant figure quivering lightly. In spite of those five pregnancies she still had that bodily grace which the village women could not believe. They sighed over it.

One day Abdallah bin Hamad said to her, They say your dancing is the envy of everyone at the weddings. She dropped her head, her face reddening. It was as though he was looking at her for the first time in their lives. He saw a feminine presence that seemed completely different to the woman he had been living with. He felt her femininity fill the house and life flowing into all its corners like a budding flower. When he asked her to dance for him—and he had just closed the door to the room—she began trembling because he had so confused her. She was reluctant to do as he asked. At first she refused. She felt very shy with him; he had never seen her in such an act as this. In this village wives never danced for their own husbands. They danced in the closed-off spaces where no man would ever come in. But he tugged at her heart when he said, Do it for Zahra.

She had named her daughter Zahra. Now, she stood up and tied her head wrap around her middle, leaving her hair to tumble down like the waterfalls in Wadi al-Mayabin. She began to dance.

At first her face was crimson with embarrassment. But she closed her eyes and felt herself voyaging, making a path in her mind through the green meadows. She danced to the beat of her own handclaps, shaking her torso, and every hair on Abdallah bin Hamad's body vibrated. But he remained as still as though he were praying before the mihrab in the mosque. He was sitting on the floor, half-kneeling as though ready for the final creed he would utter in his prayers, receiving the beauty of this dancing and the beauty of his wife opening little by little in front of him like a row of desert flowers giving off their fragrance to scent everything around them.

That night Abdallah bin Hamad took her into his arms and embraced her lovingly. She was crying, as though she had just returned from a very long voyage.

As Zahra grew so did her mother's heart. The little girl crawled around the courtyard and in her mama's eyes, brightly hued little birds cheeped and fluttered. Zahra took her first steps and that big heart leapt in her chest out of fear that the little girl would stumble and fall and get hurt. It was as if this was her first experience at motherhood. As the girl grew older, she became her mother's companion in everything. Every day, Umm Zahra waved incense over her. Fearful of envious eyes, she recited talismans. She taught her the verses that saved a person from danger. She sat at the little girl's head and told her the ancient tales she'd learned by heart until the little one dropped off to sleep.

Abdallah bin Hamad al-Mughizlu had remained his same old self: roving through the village and chatting, heading upward on the mountain paths, knowing every track as well as he knew all of the clefts and canyons, all of the narrow, perilous mountain passages, reading the gazes of the women he encountered on his forays, seeing their desire or their discomfort as they crossed paths, reading apprehension in those eyes—the fear of his relentlessly seductive ways. If he was sitting with old Kadhiya bint Marhun he wouldn't leave her to herself until he had her gasping with laughter. When he did get up to leave she would be repeating the same words, always in his hearing: You came to me when I'm an old biddy, yooo, you wicked man!

But something began to hold him back after that evening when his wife danced. It was as though he had tasted all the many kinds of honey there were and only now had he found that rarest sort. Suddenly his eyes and heart were opened to a honey-source that had been hidden away yet had always been very close by. A honey-source, a beehive that had been saying to him all along: I'm here, I'm right next to you, come find me! Close he was but he hadn't paid attention, until he discovered the flavor of which legends are made.

Something akin to this had happened to him once. He was on Jabal al-Dharwa hunting for honey, searching painstakingly amongst the rocks and scrubby trees as he went higher. As he was accustomed to doing, he had gone on this search just before the arrival of spring—looking for winter honey. He usually found it. It would be sealed in wax and waiting for the hand that found it and reached out to take it. As he climbed his eyes roved across this particular patch. But he didn't find anything before he got to the summit.

There, just beneath that great sharp rocky peak, he sat down to rest from the rigors of the ascent. He had begun his climb at dawn and now the hour hand on his watch pointed to one o'clock. The weather was balmy, closer to winter chill than to summer heat, especially up here on this rocky height. He was sitting just next to a humid crevice off of which shrubs of mountain thyme were growing. The leaves were already green and the piercing scent of thyme hung in the air. He had decided to cut as many branches of it as he could and carry it back with him: it was quite rare, and he knew its nutritional and medicinal benefits. As soon as he felt rested, he got to his feet to lop off whatever he could reach. He spread the bunch out on the ground to dry in the sun. He spent two whole hours on the task and covered a large expanse of ground with the thyme. He had decided he would stay here until tomorrow, when the thyme would have dried out and he could stuff it all into his turban to carry back.

He cleared enough space to lie down comfortably, ready for a good long rest. He listened to the creatures around him, his eyes closed. A bevy of quail passed by, close enough that he could hear the rustling of their wings. A shannaa bird was trilling somewhere below. Around his ears he heard the drone of mosquitoes, a mountain dove cooing, and the dry chirp-chirp of crawling insects in the crevice. And then he heard the bees, faintly. Just for a second; and then, silence. Then he heard the sound again.

His eyes were still closed but even so his pupils darted. He listened as hard as he could. Somewhere here, this told him, lived a colony of bees. It must be very close to where he had made his bed. He wasn't imagining that sound: his ears could distinguish the various calls and buzzings around him. He was certain now that the zzzz was coming from a point directly overhead. But the sound was very weak, or faint. He opened his eyes and tried to crane his head back, studying the body of this mountain peak. Then he saw the hive, hanging right there, close above the crop of thyme bushes.

It was a very large wild bee nest, the hard shell of it nearly a meter in length and half a meter wide, almost filling the crevice where it hung. He got to his feet and went nearer. He picked up a green thyme branch and tapped it against the wall of the hive. The tiny bees flew out and fled, giving him room to peer in at the mounded honey cached at the top of the hive where the bees had produced it.

He fished a bottle out of his pack and filled it with honey. This was a honey different to all of the other varieties he had tasted in his life. It was white—a milky white—and especially thick. Never had he seen honey like this. How could honey be such a pure, clear white? When he tasted his fingers, the fragrance and the taste put the image of various flowers in his mind, yet he couldn't quite guess which nectar the bees had collected to make this honey. He filled his lungs with the smell, trying to recall where he had ever experienced this particular scent. But suddenly he caught sight of the nearby face of the mountain and remembered.

As he had climbed, the same fragrance had come rolling down to him from the slopes where the sarh trees grew. He had found their smell odd, unfamiliar at first, until he recognized the blossoms and could figure out where the smell was coming from. But as he climbed higher and began to search more intensely he forgot all about it.

He had never stumbled upon this white sarh honey before. He filled the whole bottle with the pale substance. He had heard al-Hatati's tales but he hadn't expected to find that this particular story was actually true. Who would have thought, up on this high, rocky summit, to find that secret that so few people knew of?

There were so many different shades and hues. He had seen yellow honey, and brown and red and black. Some honey was a greenish yellow. For the first time, on that day, he saw the astonishing white substance in the heights of the thyme mountain. And now Badriya was his rare honey that he had never expected to find at such close hand.

After the night when she danced, that luxuriant night which returned a sense of balance he seemed to have lost, he decided that he would give his wife something rare and it would be a surprise to her. He left the house early in the morning, heading for Wadi Maqdisi. He began cutting branches of every bush he could find that had a strong fragrance: mhadhidi, sakhbar, germander, basil. He gathered a lot of branches and bundled them up together and hurried back. Before she could come out of the house he went in to her. She had just finished making bread. He handed her the bouquet and said simply, Smell it.

As she sniffed it, Badriya opened as though she were one of the trees on the face of the mountain. Her face lit up and she smiled.

You are the fragrance like no other, he said to her.

Her face reddened at his words. He felt his chest expand to encompass whole worlds of joy, of fragrant blooms. He heard the songs women sang at weddings in her breathing, as her eyes gave off magic, and bursting flowers, and rare honey.

Chapter Twelve

Our secrets fence in our ascent
that was so boisterous beforetimes

AL-HATATI RETURNED FROM HIS HUNT empty-handed. By the time he got back to their meeting point the sun had departed the wadi. Only a pale daylight played against the summits all around. He was the first to arrive, and in order to make the most of the time before darkness fell he began moving their packs, still full of provisions, to the place they had slept the night before.

On the summit he had heard the echo of a gunshot somewhere on one of the closer mountains. He guessed that Abdallah bin Hamad had shot down some kind of fowl. It was only one shot, the whistle of one bullet that reached him and the echo continuing for several seconds before the whole area returned to stillness. All that could be heard now were the little melodies of the wind as it played with the dry bushes and grasses on the mountain faces and plateaus.

The wind coming through the wadi was at its strongest now, shaking the trees violently, uprooting dried-up plants and shrubs and tossing them hither and yon, leaving them to bounce across the steep wadi walls and rest momentarily suspended whenever a rock outcropping entangled them. Then the dislodged flora would be swept along again by the currents of wind until they slammed into the enormous looming boulders, the force of the collision shattering them and scattering bits across the land.

Al-Hatati rested, leaning on his pack, and tugged his pouch of tobacco from beneath the belt over his izar. His fingers compressed some of it into a wad and stuffed it into his mouth. He waited a couple of moments until he could feel it in his head; every chew restored his balance and lessened his sense of fatigue. He was the older man among them; time had bequeathed him nothing much more than his chewing tobacco. He held onto the pleasure of it like a dear friend.

His first memory of tobacco in his mouth: he had been fourteen years old. He remembered the details of that day. Impossible to forget! Sitting with Old Huraymal he saw him put the chaw of tobacco in his mouth and asked if he could try it.

Son, my tobacco is the kind *men* hanker after.

He understood Old Huraymal's words as an insult because he saw himself as already belonging to the company of grown men.

Give me some, I need to try it.

Al-Shayib Huraymal took a small measure of the tobacco and put it in the boy's open palm, instructing him on where he should place it—between his lower lip and his teeth. Al-Hatati took it and did exactly as the man had said. The effect began to invade his head and then his entire body. It felt like ants were crawling all over him.

His limbs began to go numb and his head felt heavy. But at first he tried to make light of the man's words.

Hah, it's not doing anything to me, this stuff of yours.

But soon he felt dizzy and he couldn't see straight. He tried to change position thinking it would stave off the dizziness, but he lost his balance entirely. He collapsed. The man was giving him a very stern look and it was clear what he was thinking. His gaze mocked this child who had thought he could match him in his chewing—when not even grown men could always endure the force of this ghalyun.

The tobacco Old Huraymal habitually bought was called al-Hatati because it was farmed in Wadi Hataat. It was amongst the highest-quality ghalyun known in those days, and one of the strongest strains. Old Huraymal liked to use it in a particularly concentrated form. He only mixed a small amount of ashes into it, just enough to cut the sharpness slightly. But then he got used to the bitter taste and began hardly diluting it at all. After all, the concentrated form gave him a nicely strong high.

Many men who had asked him at one time or another for a chew stopped asking. They understood that they probably couldn't keep up with him and so they left him to his preferred chew. Trying it, every one of them had gotten dizzy and so numb they felt momentarily and horrifically paralyzed, unable to move their limbs even an inch. And then, whatever they had in their bellies surged out, and so wretchedly that they felt their intestines must be springing from their open mouths too. Tears down their cheeks mixing with the snot, they were completely undone by what they had ingested.

Huraymal was one of the herders who usually stayed with their flocks near the village. In the hot afternoons he came into the village quarters to sit and pass the time with other men. At the end of the day he returned to wherever it was he was spending the night. Like the other shawawi, he moved with his animals, always in search of the best pasturage and following the rains as they moved from area to area.

In some seasons Old Huraymal went to Wadi Hataat to settle there for a while and then he would come back and stay for a time just outside the village. Or sometimes he went to wadis further away. But when he was staying in the vicinity of the village, he was always around. He liked the company of the villagers and he enjoyed his ability to spellbind them with stories of his travels and his adventures.

Old Huraymal never pushed away the hand of anyone who asked for a bit of his chew. He was always keen to see with his own eyes what it did to them. It usually meant he could have a good laugh and indulge in a fair amount of mockery. The only response for those with a wad in the palms of their hands was to try it out. That's why he permitted Nasir bin Salim al-Hatati to have a go.

The boy was trying hard not to lose his balance as he walked away, swaying and stumbling, completely intoxicated by the chew he had had. He tried to keep the nausea down. He felt like a great weight—the weight of the very world, surely—had slammed down upon his shoulders. He fell to the ground and his body ejected everything that was inside and the man just went on looking at him without saying a word.

He stayed where he had fallen, flat on the ground, for several minutes before he could regain any sense of balance. He spat out the wad and wiped his mouth to get rid of the remaining flakes of tobacco. He clambered to his feet and washed himself in the falaj. He sat there for a while longer, near this man, taking one deep breath after another. His mind had been turned upside down by this experience and he was stunned by what it had done to him. But he got a certain pleasure out of it, too. As soon as the dizziness and nausea began to fade he asked Old Huraymal for another hit.

Huraymal laughed—mostly because he was so startled. It was the first time anyone had ever asked him for a second round.

You trying to kill yourself?

But the fellow who would become known as al-Hatati had his hand extended and his palm open in expectation of another wad. From that day on he was never satisfied with any other strain of tobacco. In fact he challenged Old Huraymal to bump up the concentration of hatati tobacco even more. But the old man just shouted in his face. Get out of my sight, you jinni child!

Thus it was that he acquired the name that stuck to him throughout his adulthood and into old age. No one could ever match him in his tobacco chewing. Al-Hatati's habit was to keep a heap of ghalyun leaves in the shade away from the sunlight but just touched by its glow. He always said that direct sun damaged the stuff, draining what made it so good for the mind. It would retain no flavor or fragrance. When the leaves dried he pounded them, only a small amount at a time and very carefully. He mixed the paste with a bit of palm-leaf ash which gave it a particular aroma on the nose and tongue. He tried it once without adding in the ashes: it ate into his lips and gums and gave him sores. Now he understood why it was always blended with some kind of ash. He had to get through several days without it until his sores were gone.

Al-Hatati had grown up in the village. But he was one of those inhabitants who had begun life there on the margins and had always remained so. He was little concerned with what went on in village society or with the fact that people didn't see him as a particularly important man. This way he could live as he wished without attracting attention; his status gave him a certain freedom which not many of his generation enjoyed. He was able to stay apart from the bonds of socially imposed shame which dictated the behaviors that were generally expected and approved of.

He had his own tobacco schedule. First thing in the morning and after a few cups of coffee, he pressed the tobacco into his mouth and closed his eyes for a few seconds until he could feel the effect at the top of his brain. Then he would go to work. He wouldn't have another wad until around midday, after a short rest followed by several more coffees. Then he wouldn't give it another thought until late afternoon when he would have his third and final hit. Then he would forget about it until the next morning.

Three times a day was enough to keep him in balance. Night times, he would always say, were not for chewing. Tobacco opened the fissures in one's head. If you chewed it at night your eyes would stay open, counting the stars and watching for meteors. You'd be unable to sleep and then dawn would be upon you.

Al-Hatati had worked as a grain thresher on the outskirts of town and in people's orchards. He didn't have any date-palms of his own before he married Asmaa bint Nawfal. It was because of her that he acquired palms and some other assets, when before his marriage he had been entirely dependent on the generosity of those who employed him on their properties—dates to eat, and money enough to get by. He had been on his own with no family to depend on him.

People said he had always been an orphan. His father had died, they said, several months before his birth and his mother passed away a few days after he arrived. He lived from house to house in the village; he was kept but never adopted. As an infant he was taken by Khaalisa bint Salim who nursed him for several months. But when she decided to accompany her husband to the city of Muttrah she left him in the home of her neighbor Sabiha bint Umayr, where he stayed for three years until she had a raging argument with her husband over him.

He's an orphan, it's not right to just toss him out.

But her husband was adamant. Walking out of the house he said, I don't bring up a child who isn't mine, not in my own house.

So she picked him up and left the house. Outside the village she set him down by the door of a tiny mosque-shrine, placing a handful of dates next to him before going away. Fairly soon one of the herdswomen came close enough by that she could hear the little boy crying.

His face was smeared with mud because he had taken a spill at the edge of the falaj. Her heart softened at the sight and she took him with her. She lived near the village. She raised him on the milk her goats produced. But when he turned ten she had no choice but to abandon him, leaving him on the verge of a lane leading into the village before she went off with her herd to a distant wadi. She had said to her husband, Let him stay with us, he can be useful, he can help us with the animals. But her husband had his head full of forebodings. When he gets a bit older, he'll steal from us. There's no trusting any of these orphan boys—no trusting him.

Yet, fortune did not abandon Nasir bin Salim al-Hatati. He did not die of hunger. The boy was sitting beneath a big sidra tree at the entry to the village when Salim bin Ali happened to come along, on his way from Bilad al-Rustaq and Wadi Bani Awf. He saw the small figure crouched there, a little bundle beside him on the ground.

Where are you heading, boy?

I don't know, Uncle, my mama Khusayba left me here and went away.

Where'd she go?

Went to the jibal, that's where she told me she was going. She said, Go back to your village and live there with your folks.

The boy was in a pitiable state in every way. Salim bin Ali didn't have any family himself, no children. He took the little boy's hand and led him home. That's how Nasir bin Salim came to live with him. Salim bin Ali asked the other villagers about this boy and they told him what they knew.

How can you pray and fast and recite the name of your Lord when an orphan boy is here amongst you and not one of you reaches a hand out to him?

And so al-Hatati grew up in the home of Old Salim bin Ali, who lost his eyesight after some time. All he had left in life was his storytelling, those tales he'd fashioned from his own experiences, what he'd seen and what he'd lived. Because Salim became blind in old age and people respected him and esteemed him and thought of him as one of the village's shaykhs and notables, al-Hatati's attachment to him was an attachment to the village. He was Old Salim's eyes, after all, whenever the old man had to walk anywhere. When Old Salim went to the majlis, al-Hatati was there beside him. He carried the man's secrets, too; he was a trusted keeper of the problems that people took to Old Salim when they needed some help.

When al-Hatati married he did not abandon al-Shayib Salim bin Ali. He visited constantly when he was in the village, sitting with the old man every day. If he had to be elsewhere, as soon as he returned he came to see Old Salim, ready to recount everything he had seen and heard.

Al-Hatati was a man of strong build, his muscles hard and visible. Even now in his older age he retained the brawny body that the mountains had burnished. If he gripped your hand in greeting, you would feel as though he were crushing it. Everyone had a certain sense of awe towards him. Someone told him one day that the mutawwa Ali bin Mubarak had been mentioning his name in sermons where he attacked the vices of intoxication. He was aiming especially to draw the attention of the young men in his audience. He warned them against taking up chewing tobacco—so that, he said, they wouldn't end up like Nasir bin Salim al-Hatati.

Nasir bin Salim showed up one day outside the mosque. Ali bin Mubarak had just begun preaching. Al-Hatati waited out there, thinking that this fellow would allude to him in some way and maybe even mention his name, hopefully before he got too far into his sermon. But the mutawwa went on and on and al-Hatati got bored. He was sitting close enough to the window that he could hear and watch. The mutawwa cleared his throat and resumed by reciting from the Holy Book—the Chapter of the Bee. *Verily God forbids you acts that are shameful, and that which the faith rejects, and all that oppresses.*

Al-Hatati's ears perked up. It wasn't long before the man mentioned intoxicants and began scolding the young men against taking that road. And then he intoned: Some people believe that chewing tobacco won't lead them into deepest Hell. One of those people lives among us here without any sense of embarrassment or remorse, and his mouth is full of the wicked substance. Instead of using his mouth to recite the names of God he stuffs it with what God forbids.

Nasir bin Salim al-Hatati had never in his life hurt any creature, not even an ant. But these words were too much. Just as the mutawwa was uttering his name he burst in through the door and seized Ali bin Mubarak by the collar. He dragged him off the pulpit and into the courtyard outside the mosque where he released his hold and pushed the man to the ground. He rubbed the fellow's head in the dirt, took out the tobacco he was chewing and stuffed it into the preacher's mouth. He poked his finger in between the mutawwa's teeth and lips and rubbed the tobacco into his gums. He stuffed more of it into the preacher's nostrils. Ali bin Mubarak began to vomit. As al-Hatati straightened up he spat in the mutawwa's face. Next time I'll make you drink a whole cooking pot of boiling tobacco, he said. He stood there at the doorway of the mosque, popped a fresh wad into his mouth, stared around at the mosque-goers who had gathered silently outside, and headed home.

People speculated that the mutawwa would surely lodge a complaint with the governor and escalate the whole thing. But nothing of the sort happened. The mutawwa never again referred to ghalyun in his sermons. In fact he dropped out of sight for several months, staying at home until the village—abuzz with the story—settled down. Gradually he began to reappear, believing that people had more or less forgotten the incident.

But nothing is ever forgotten in that village. Sometimes young bullies sitting in the streets would yell taunts—hey mister preacher, Ali bin Mubarak!—when they saw him coming. Al-Hatati got you good. Al-Hatati got you got you.

Al-Hatati himself just laughed whenever the story came up in conversation. He always had the same response. That boy—Wad Moobiiriik, that lad, he wanted to shove me straight into the flames of Hell, to drag me there himself. What's wrong with the riffraff in this place? Why do they despise me? Do folks really think I'm just a bit of stubble in their eyes?

Despite it all, al-Hatati had his own special view of what he had been through; of his repeated expulsions as a child. It was a positive view. He had started off with one mother and one father, and then he had had many mothers and fathers, and he had also acquired uncles, paternal and maternal. He got into the habit early on of addressing anyone he encountered as some kind of relation—including the kinship formed by nursing. When the herdswoman who had abandoned him returned to the village after an absence of many years, he went to her immediately and addressed her as Maah. It had a strong impact on her. Squatting, she put her arms around him and cried and cried. Wordlessly she asked him to forgive her, in her remorse at abandoning him beside the village falaj.

Al-Hatati waited for his two companions; the sun was going down but they still weren't in sight. Darkness was falling fast when Abdallah bin Hamad showed up with a young goat draped over one shoulder. He greeted al-Hatati who looked him up and down without commenting on this evidence of the hunt. Abdallah sensed what he was thinking and didn't meet his gaze. In a tone of voice tinged slightly with rebuke he said, I thought you would have gathered some firewood by now.

Al-Hatati didn't shift his gaze. Firewood's nearby, he said. Plenty of it around. He waited for Abdallah to reveal something. But Abdallah didn't say anything. He went about gathering some kindling, piled it up, and lit a fire. He poured out a cup of water from the mattara and downed it in one gulp. He came over to sit near al-Hatati, still breathing heavily from his exertions. Al-Hatati's expression hadn't changed nor had the focus of his gaze. But the younger man's irritation was mounting at the questioning glint in those eyes.

Why are you looking at me like that? he finally burst out. I bagged it. God's gift to us, a billy-goat that was roaming around on his own, gone wild, no one knows what family it belongs to—and here we are wishing we had some meat.

It might belong to one of the herding families?

You want fresh meat or not?

They both went silent. Al-Hatati started laughing, the sound loud enough to ricochet through the empty expanse. I'm going to start calling you Mihna, he said. You're a real trial for us.

Abdallah looked around. There was no sign of Azzan bin Said. He was very late getting back. But before Abdallah could ask or comment he heard footsteps in the wadi. In moments, Azzan was there and standing next to the mattara. Three big cups of water it took to open his parched throat. They waited for him to recover a bit before he could tell them where he had been. But their focus was really on what Abdallah had shot, which was now hanging near their sleeping place; and on the fire, which was strong enough now to throw off some light. Azzan looked at Abdallah.

What's that?

Al-Hatati began to chuckle again. And then he was laughing until tears were rolling down his cheeks. He lowered his head trying to stop. Abdallah bin Hamad was trying to resist the outbreak of hilarity by channeling all his concentration into sharpening his knife against a smooth stone. But al-Hatati's laughing fit was contagious and Abdallah exploded into guffaws, in the end collapsing flat on his back on the sand. Azzan's eyes were moving from one man to the other. He didn't get why there was all this hysteria. When it looked impossible to stop them he spoke.

I found the honey.

They were so taken aback by his statement that they choked on their laughter as they swiveled their heads to look at him. It was dark but he pointed towards the summits. Up there, way up there.

Now al-Hatati started laughing again, so hard that he began to cough uncontrollably. Abdallah bin Hamad's laughter sounded more muted but his whole body was shaking as he made efforts to stop. Azzan didn't say any more; he lay down in his sleeping place and stared up at the sky. And then suddenly he began laughing too, a few stray chuckles at first but then like a waterfall of sound, the waters spurting out to plunge into the wadi.

The infectious laughter was not only of this moment and this lone spot. It had been with them at other times and in other places on these mountains. It was the sign of their crazy exhaustion, physical and mental—these three men who spent long periods of isolation, savored and sought out but never easy, in the most inaccessible locations and in almost unbearable heat. And at this time of year, the worst. When the extreme dryness up here had bent all creation to its will it was not well-advised to venture into these parts. But that did not deter these three. Sitting at home tired them out; listening to people's laments and complaints, their same old narratives, the grumbling and grousing that never seemed to stop—that was truly fatiguing.

The riotous laughter revived their spirit of rebellion, a kind of primitive wildness that marked their flight from the oppressive, stifling canopy of the tribe and the accustomed practices of the village. They had exchanged those familiar ways for the sovereignty of these solitary places, an absolute where there were no boundaries to pen you in. Where you could stand motionless and know the utter silence around you and inside of you—for here there was nothing to divide the person other people knew from the person you were to yourself. You had to listen hard, out here, for the echoes of time and the ever-changing reverberations across space. You could see everything so clearly here in these high wide-open plateaus and the far-flung wadis.

They sat around the fire and stripped the flesh from the skeleton. They pushed the strips of meat onto skewers they made, and readied them for roasting. Abdallah bin Hamad launched into his story of the hunt: how he had come upon the young goat.

He had been climbing towards the summit, following the same path as Azzan when he had caught sight of a wad of animals in the distance. They were moving along the rim of the wadi. He'd pulled out his binoculars and adjusted them to see the animals clearly. There were three large nanny goats and a small kid. Since he had plenty of time left in which to search for honey, he changed direction, toward the wadi now, still going upward towards the four animals, having already decided to aim for the young one. The nanny goats sensed his presence and shifted direction, heading further upward toward the jabal. The little one followed, his bleating audible even at a distance. The nanny goats would move some distance and then stop to wait for their young one to catch up. Abdallah bin Hamad had to half-run to keep the animals in sight.

Near the entrance into Wadi al-Malil the larger goats stopped. They seemed to be surveying the lower reaches but apparently they found nothing amiss. Their pursuer decided to circle round from behind the smaller jabal that bisected the eastern and western rims. He knew this area very well; he knew how he could mount a sudden ambush from above, where they would be within rifle range.

The nanny goats looked round, uneasy at the sudden disappearance of the figure they had noticed. Abdallah bin Hamad was fortunate too that the wind was blowing in his direction. His scent would not reach them.

Near the summit of that small jabal he stooped over to conceal himself from them. He dropped to the ground and crawled forward until he had a good view out over the entire area. His gun was in front of him, the mouth pointed forward. He saw the animals there; they were not moving. They were still looking at the point in the wadi where they had seen him just before he vanished. He searched for the little one; he aimed at the head. He fired and the animal fell into a widening pool of blood. The nanny goats started in fright and clambered off across the rocky terrain, disappearing into Wadi al-Malil.

Now it was al-Hatati's turn to tell them about his search that evening. But all he did was to raise his eyebrows and say, I don't really have anything to tell.

Abdallah bin Hamad threw the reins to Azzan bin Said. Your turn, honey-man.

Azzan smiled and began recounting what had happened to him when he climbed to the high rim of Wadi Waala. He didn't believe there was no honey to find in the area. Surely the honey was there, but it was tucked into one of the high and remote—or completely inaccessible—spots. After all, they had not gone all the way up to the top of Wadi Waala. He thought it might be there, especially since they hadn't come across anything in any of the other stretches they had searched.

Azzan gave them his explanation for why it made sense for the beehive to be so high: the prevailing air temperature. At the very top the wind was gentler and the moving air was somewhat cooler than it was lower down in the wadis. At this time of year it wasn't possible for any bee colony to remain alive and active unless the bees had searched successfully for a home that was removed from the worst of the heat.

He was the expert on bee behavior. Yet he had learned most of what he knew from these companions who had never been stingy with their knowledge. But he was the beekeeper who had been spending most of his time with his bees; watching them for hours, studying every hive to learn what its inhabitants needed. Perhaps now he was more able than they were to read the conditions. That was why he had decided to go all that way, to make that difficult and relentless climb and to mount a search once he was in those heights. And also why he had not gotten back to their campsite by sunset.

Reaching the divide between Aqabat al-Nakhla and Wadi Waala he had stopped and sat down to rest. From there he could see the village. He was searching for something lodged in his memory, for distant lineaments, for landmarks that would lead his eyes to what he wanted to see. But the horn at the summit of Jabal al-Tayah blocked his vision; it had dropped the deep shadow of its immense shape over the entire area.

He climbed on, toward the summit. He began looking at the surroundings more closely, inspecting the various trees and rocks he found on his way, and the caves and hollows too, as few as they were. All empty. He didn't come upon anything. He still had quite a lot of time; he could get himself to the overlook where the two wadis came together, there on that high ledge. He went on inspecting every bit of his route closely, hoping he might come across the hive. Every patch of ground he covered would mean a smaller expanse left to survey later on. At some point he would get across all of it.

The wadis were bone-dry and bees had to have water. They got thirsty and so did their young. The presence of water made a location more salubrious in general, adding moisture to the air and reducing the heat so that the larvae would be more likely to survive. If the hive truly was at this height, it meant they had to fly a tremendous distance to procure water. But what could possibly stop them? These creatures who frequently flew five kilometers, day in and day out—would it really be so difficult for them to scale heights such as these? That's how Azzan was thinking as he attempted the boulder-strewn slopes of Wadi Waala.

As laborious as this kind of search was, the late afternoons always gave new hope and energy to a bee-searcher. At this elevation the wind would be picking up, cooling off the searcher's hot and sweaty skin, chasing away thirst, and even sucking the dryness from the searcher's mouth and throat. The breezes against his damp body refreshed him and lightened his fatigue. Most of all they gave him the stamina to resume the climb. Mornings were completely the opposite. The air stopped moving and the sweat began oozing from every part of one's body, the heaviness of it more oppressive than even the hard breathing, the exhausted leg muscles which only seemed more strained if one took a short rest, or the quickening heartbeat that wouldn't stop pounding. The air itself grew heavy under the fierce sun, burning hotter as the day went on, more relentless, more searing, the later it got.

Finally he found himself at the summit. He took a rest, letting himself bask in the cooler air which he felt brushing away his fatigue. If only he could sleep here. He allowed himself to relax his muscles and stretch out his legs, lying on his back, putting his empty water canteen under his head. He watched as a cloud formed overhead, half of it dark and the other half crimson. The sky was hazy as if laden with blowing dust.

On the east side of the summit he could see a cave hollow with what looked like a steep drop. Seeing it from a distance one couldn't judge how spacious the interior might be. Despite the narrow opening, it could be wide enough to shelter a mountain animal. Because he was sitting down and the sun was low enough that it didn't reach the cave, he didn't catch sight of the bees entering the narrow cleft. But when he extended his body as far as he could to the right, supporting himself on one elbow in order to take in all of Wadi al-Jarif with his eyes, he thought he saw tiny flying forms swerving and dipping there. He concentrated his sharp eyesight on the spot but the spreading shade ate up the tiny shadows made by those minute shapes.

The cave wasn't far away now. Squatting down, he could partly see it. At long last he was certain there were tiny beelike forms bobbing around the cave mouth.

Why didn't you pull the hive down? al-Hatati interrupted him. Azzan went on as if he hadn't heard his friend's query.

The beehive at the mouth of the cave was so large, he told them, that it filled the whole space and extended into the depression below. He found some sakhbar branches and brushed the bees away from the mound of honey. Now he could see it was sealed with wax and he could see how enormous it was. He had only a small jar with him. He worried that the honey would more than fill it. It would be better, he decided, to return early in the morning to remove the hive.

He had also hesitated because by then the sun had just about slipped below the summits in the distance and he was afraid it would soon be too dark to make his way back. *Mornings bring profit.* He repeated the proverb to himself.

Abdallah bin Hamad got up and went over to the fire. The wood was nearly consumed and he poked at the embers, pushing them together into a small heap. They roasted the meat in silence, but al-Hatati broke the stillness. Listen to this story…

The Final Chapter

Green sidra of the wadi, tell me
did you see the soul's companion?
the one who stole my heart
and vanished

THE CLOUDS GATHERED AND LITTLE by little they darkened across the sky. The stars vanished and the world went black. At dawn they awoke to a chill in the air that had suddenly forced itself on the summer climate. They recited their dawn prayers, drank their coffee, and decided to descend into the wadi and towards al-Nimarat. They packed and got ready to leave. Azzan bin Said was to climb to the summit at Wadi Waala to retrieve the honey he had found. He would come down along the other side of Wadi al-Nimarat to join them. He took along a large leather bag for the honey. The qurba was big enough to hold the hive he had seen yesterday. As he ascended he could still see the other two men scrambling along the slopes of the wadi. They were trying to hurry as the wail of the wind resounded louder across the plateaus.

Once he disappeared into the cleft dividing the two wadis he could no longer see them. He studied the clouds gathering in the distance. They were darker than they had been earlier and looked almost as though they were dissolving into liquid. Rain was on the way; that was certain. He hoped he had enough time to harvest the honey and get at least as far down the slopes as the spot where he would join his friends.

As he came to a halt not far from the cave sheltering the hive the rain started. It pelted down for a few moments and stopped. But he was quite sure that this was only a warning of things to come. There would be a stronger downpour. He hurried on, anxious to get to work on the hive.

He got out his knife, cut down the wild beehive and set it down to one side. He brushed away the bees with a dry, fallen sakhbar branch and as soon as he judged that most of the creatures were gone he tugged his honey sack's wide mouth directly over the heaped-up honey. He used his knife blade to scrape away the wax so that the liquid would begin to flow into his container.

Soon the bag was almost completely full of honey. All of this time and effort spent searching had not gone in vain. A hive like this deserved the strenuous search that it required and the protracted attention of several searchers. This honey would fill five or six large jars. He closed the mouth of the qurba by tightening the leather thong around it, made sure it was secure, and cleaned off his knife. He licked the honey from his fingers. The aroma that rose into his brain was the pure scent of mountain flowers mingled with the baram blossoms from the sumar trees.

He returned the empty hive to its position using a nearby rock to support it. He withdrew his head from the cave opening, ready to get to his feet. He heard the sound of thunder; it was very close. The skies were warning of an impending downpour. At the same time he thought he might be hearing a dog barking, the sharp sound pelting across the high plateaus as the thunder faded away.

He stood gazing into the distance. The rain was already coming down hard, up there on the other peaks and mountain faces, he could see. Moments later it reached this peak and soaked him through immediately.

He hoisted the leather qurba onto his shoulder and began to descend cautiously, battling the rains and the wind, trying to protect himself from the potential hazard of the lightning which was splitting the sky directly overhead. On this bare, stony jabal he could see no cave large enough to shelter him. So he walked on along the rim marking the wadi, staying away from the channels of rushing water. He was treading on stones that were beginning to slip and roll beneath his feet: the rain had loosened and softened the hard surfaces between crevices. He knew he must be very careful if he was not to slip; a fall would be dangerous. He didn't know what to do. Standing still seemed perilous, yet moving forward seemed even worse. He tried to feel hopeful about finding some kind of protected ledge or outcropping or shallow crevice where he could protect himself from the heavy rains.

He went across some soft, pebbled ground. Here his footfall seemed firmer and this gave him more confidence. He kept moving forward, though he couldn't see anything except heavy mist. A dense fog had fallen across the jabal. He kept on going and then he felt the earth give way beneath him and he was falling into a deep hole. A hidden cave, camouflaged by a layer of soil thick enough that no one would realize it was there.

His fall made a loud noise but the sound blended into the peals of thunder coming from the summit. As he fell he tried to keep his balance but he could not, perhaps because he was completely soaked. His head hit the rocks.

Below, his companions were in difficulties too. When the rain intensified they began trying to ascend the jabal, staying well away from the course of the rushing waters, because they thought this way would be safer. Al-Hatati remembered a cave on the western summit where he had slept one winter night and they headed there, but with great difficulty. Exhausted and wet through, they reached the cave, shivering violently from the cold. There they stayed, out of the wind and the rain. For three days and nights they crouched inside, the roar of the wadi beneath them blocking out every other sound. There might be a lull in the rain but then every half hour or so the storm seemed to pick up strength.

Huddled inside the cave and isolated from the world, they began to worry about their friend Azzan and then they could not think of anything else. Not hunger, not thirst. Whenever the rain let up they began scouring the slopes and summits with their eyes, hoping to see him emerge from somewhere. They shouted but their voices were swallowed up in the constant roar that seemed to fill the whole world.

On the third night the rain stopped. Completely. Abdallah bin Hamad woke up, having been so exhausted that he had finally fallen into a deep sleep—when earlier, the pleasures of sleep had deserted him as soon as he began worrying about Azzan. But this time he had slept for hours and he awoke to find that the rain had ended. He did not rouse al-Hatati. He went outside to inspect the conditions around their cave. He saw that the fog had broken up. The sky was clear and the stars shone but as he gazed down at the watercourse through the wadi he could see that the fast-moving water was still very high, running over its usual banks and moving rapidly towards the villages some distance away.

After several cups of coffee the two friends went out to search for Azzan bin Said across the nearby slopes. They called his name over and over. Abdallah bin Hamad fired repeated shots, hoping the echoes could be heard over the ongoing roar of the water. They kept at it, heading upward toward the nearby peaks, but they found no trace of him.

They agreed that al-Hatati would go back to the village and alert people to what had happened so that they could join the search. As soon as the waters subsided somewhat, al-Hatati made his way back, descending on the Wadi al-Nimarat side and stopping only at Aqabat al-Ayn. His memory took him back to the place where, much earlier on this expedition, his two anxious friends had waited for him. He reached the village and went immediately to Old Salim bin Ali's home.

Abdallah bin Hamad turned to the summit that their friend had described as he was telling them about finding the beehive. Because he knew the area so thoroughly, he could take shortcuts that got him directly there without exhausting himself on more circuitous routes. He found the little cave where the honeybee hive hung and he could tell that Azzan had harvested the honey and was gone from the site. But where? Searching all around, he came to a deep cave that he thought he was seeing for the first time. He tried to peer into the interior but he couldn't see anything there.

If he's not somewhere around here, he asked himself, where else could he be?

He descended, following the route of Wadi Waala all the way to al-Nimarat. He called out Azzan's name constantly hoping to hear an answer. He climbed upward again, searching among the crevices, thinking he might find Azzan somewhere, perhaps having fallen. But he found no trace.

The dog ran on ahead of the herd which was moving down the slope towards the place where she had seen the man, at a distance. That had been on a high plateau, looking from Wadi al-Jarif where she was trying to protect herself and her flock in a large cave. When the rain lessened for a few hours the next day, she hurried along, tugging her donkey behind her, the Saluki running ahead.

She tied a rope around a shawaa tree trunk close by. In the cave where he lay unconscious, she wrapped the rope around his chest and arms and knotted it well. She climbed out of the cave and dragged him out with the help of the donkey. With difficulty she lifted him onto the donkey's back. She managed to get him back to their cave.

His face was a mess of silt and blood. She didn't even recognize him until she had wiped most of it away.

She was taken aback by this very odd coincidence—that it was this man whom she had seen some months ago. But that had been over on the plateau up in the White Mountains. What had brought him here? She remembered the leather bag she had found with him and opened it. It was full of honey.

She cleaned his wounds and lit a fire next to him to warm him up. Sometime after the rain stopped and the sun came out, four days after the storm had begun, he opened his eyes. He had no idea where he was. It was as though he was in a dream. Or perhaps he was still in that dream where her eyes had visited him. In his half-conscious state he heard her murmuring. He didn't know, was she really whispering those words? Or was this a hallucination brought on by his fall? He tried to lift himself but the contusions on his body prevented him. She came over and stared into his face. He could see her clear soft eyes and the sweetness of her features. She gave him a smile and he felt the earth whirling around him. He closed his eyes and opened them again, thinking that maybe this would clear out the effects of his strange dream. But she was there, she was really there. Hadn't he been searching for her in all the surrounding areas? But he had not found her, anywhere.

Once he had truly woken up and was alert to his surroundings she spoke to him. This honey has defeated everyone. Are people supposed to die looking for it? Or become so lost that no one can find them again?

He smiled and a bud in his heart seemed to open as he came out of the fog in his head. Where were you? he asked her. I looked for you.

She answered with a laugh as she wiped away the perspiration on his face. Here, near you, I've been wanting that honey but it didn't come to me. Instead of you bringing me one jar of it, here I find you've brought me a whole large qurba-full.

As she said this he began to recall what had happened. The last thing he remembered was slipping and falling into the cave. He told her he thought he had just missed her, that she had been somewhere nearby, that he had looked for her but could not find her.

I don't like the area, she said. I prefer Jibal al-Hajar.

Thamna bint Ali and her herd had moved some weeks before, and had stayed for a long spell in Wadi al-Mazaari'. She had decided to head toward Jabal al-Manazil, hoping she would find sufficient pasturage there. But she had liked this spot in Wadi al-Jarif so she stayed on. In the early evening of the day on which Azzan bin Said had found the hive, she had seen the change coming in the sky, the clouds thickening. She knew that the rains would arrive in a matter of days, or likely sooner. She had looked for a safe sheltered place and had come upon this cave large enough to hold her animals and herself.

Three days he was there. She made him shair broth and fed him goat milk. He was growing very anxious about his two friends. He didn't know anything, of course; what had become of them during these days? Had the fast-moving waters swept them away? Or had they escaped? He knew that if they were alive they would be searching for him everywhere.

He told her what had happened and he told her about his friends. She said she knew exactly who they were. And she knew who he was too. And had known, ever since he was a young lad.

You're Azzan Hilliya, aren't you?

He laughed but it hurt to laugh. He felt a sharp pain going through his chest. His fall. She told him he must be quiet. She told him how it was that she had known him for a long time.

He had not changed much, she told him. His features were the same as ever. There had been a time when she passed through his village, during the period of his inebriation. He had collapsed near the Ghilala mango tree and couldn't move. She and her mother had been walking by. Seeing him in such a state her mother had shaken her head sadly, taken Thamna by the hand, and hurried her away. She was afraid he might come to and find the two of them staring at him. Something unpleasant might happen.

In fact, during those years with her mother she had encountered him numerous times in the village lanes, sometimes dragging his feet behind him because he was so drunk and other times sitting near the falaj and singing, his tongue thick. Or she might catch sight of him in the distance, children crowding around him and teasing him. The sight grieved her. He was still so young and he was destroying his youth with that dreadful alcohol.

But—I've changed.

She gazed at him, her sewing needle now still.

I know everything about you.

He was astonished. What could she know? There was a lot that he still didn't even know about himself so how could she know *everything*?

What do you know?

She laughed again and her honey-colored eyes sparkled. Her laugh made his heart flutter and so did that bewitching gleam in her eyes.

I know enough—and more.

Around midday Thamna heard a gunshot nearby and the sound of shouts. She went outside to see what was happening. She guessed they were searching for him. She must let him know.

They're looking for you.

Let me stay with you. Tell them I'm here with you and you're treating my wounds.

She shook her head. No. You have many wounds and I think something is broken.

You need to go to the hospital.

He put out his hand and seized hers and gave her a long look. He hoped she understood his question: Where will I see you?

Her smile seemed to hold tenderness and it sent warmth into his heart.

Everywhere. I'll be watching over you.

Azzan bin Said spent a full week in the hospital, recovering. Just bruises but he needed to be kept under observation for internal bleeding. When his condition improved somewhat, he went home.

The next day he headed for the plains. His beehives had been in the path of the floods, which had affected a wide area. The beehives were sitting on flat, open ground. They would have been exposed to the full force of the winds and the rainstorms that climatic conditions over the past days had caused.

Yes. His bees had been tossed helplessly in the winds and pounded by the rains. Boxes had turned on their sides, the bees had flown out and most had perished. Some boxes had rolled great distances or been swallowed by the rains. His bees had not survived.

He sat there amongst the wreckage not knowing what to do with these half-destroyed structures that were now useless. He had lost about two hundred and fifty hives; they were worth more than thirty thousand riyals. He tried to think, but he couldn't. His sense of loss was like a heavy cloud that has suddenly evacuated all the water it held, becoming a thing of no substance that floats teasingly across the surface of the sky.

He opened the boxes that were nearest and found the carcasses of dead bees inside. The hatching larvae were still on the frames and had dried out even before they could begin their life as bees. Armies of ants had attacked and occupied most of these crates, feeding on whatever honey and nectar remained there for them to find.

Hives had been scattered as far as the lower reaches of the jabal; he could see how the fast-moving flood waters had swept some of them so far away and with such force that nothing at all remained. He began trying to collect whatever wooden boxes he could find, setting them around the metal bases with the hope that he could move them back to his farm and perhaps make some use of them in the days to come.

He did not come upon a single remaining hive that was whole. They had all been destroyed in the storm that had pitched him into the cave. The storm had tossed away his beloved bee colony which he had worked so hard—for years—to maintain until finally it had begun to grow and to yield abundant honey.

What would he do now? What would his life be? He had no trade, no craft, no work that he liked to do except for the beekeeping that had come to be his entire life. The harshness of nature showed no mercy to frail creatures. It pursued its tyrannical ways without concern for the little lives it was destroying. Just as volcanoes and earthquakes wreaked their destruction, and whole cities drowned in floods, and millions of people went missing and were forgotten in nature's anger, here in its violence it had swept away everything that was his life and had left him an empty existence, wholly alone and not knowing what to do or where to turn.

He returned home broken. Crushing disappointment and a sense of failure weighed him down, no less terrible than the abyss that had faced him at the loss of his parents. He had no friend, no companion who could comfort him other than Abdallah bin Hamad and al-Hatati. He went to them and told them what he had found. He went home and shut the door and stayed inside crying for the loss of it all.

He didn't open his door. For days he stayed inside, submerged in his sorrow and his despair. His two friends came to see him and tried their best to lighten this terrible blow.

After some time he decided to go back into the mountains. But this time he went alone; he did not tell them where he was going. He packed some supplies into his bag and set out on the mountain road towards the peaks of Wadi al-Jarif. He took shortcuts, going up to

Aqabat al-Rafaas until he reached the point where she had found him. He would spend what remained of his life with her. He would never go back to the village. He would only regain his spirit if he could be with her. He was certain of that. He wanted to live the rest of his life where he could see those eyes, where he could see the warmth and dignity and tenderness and generosity and love, where he could feel contentment with whatever would happen to the two of them.

Every time he had longed to see her, she had vanished. And then, the more he had sensed that she was gone the more brilliantly she had come into view. Now she was absent again. She had left Wadi al-Jarif empty and hollow. There was not a sound, not a trace of her. He had no idea where she had gone. He sat down next to where she had built the campfire and let the ashes sift through his fingers. He guessed that she must have gone away not so long before. He tried to think where he might find her. Why had she not waited? This time, he reminded himself, he would not return home. He would go on looking for her. He would search in every one of the wadis until he found her. He would betroth her, on his own and without a guardian. They would marry, here, beneath these peaks. The eagles would keep guard and the two of them would sing one taawibeh and then another. From her he would learn how to sing these sad ballads. And maybe how to compose them too, these plaintive songs of the herders.

The one shawiya in this world—the herdswoman he loved with whatever heart he had in his chest. He listened for her voice coming from behind the rocky walls.

He listened to her calling to him: Come, come ... In this place far from all, let us live our life away from the gazes of others ... Come here, I am waiting for you in these wadis with their sweet springs, these wadis where the wind carries stories into the plains and scatters them in the void.

    He remembered what she had said to him in the cave, how she had explained that she was heading towards Jabal al-Manazil. He lifted his head and stared in the direction of those far-away summits. He set his face towards them, and he picked up his pace, and he vanished into the shadows of the next deep mountain wadi.

Translator's Note

The poem-songs [*taʿwibat*] that head each chapter were composed for the novel by Hamud al-Hajari. My translations seek to convey their spirit, though not always literally.

I have generally preferred to use local terminology for the flora that are so important to the story, though when it seems appropriate, I have used English terms.

Printed in the USA
CPSIA information can be obtained
at www.ICGtesting.com
JSHW081606131024
71572JS00002B/4